Resisting Ryan

HART'S CREEK STORIES - BOOK ONE

by

Suzie Peters

GWL
PUBLISHING

First Published in 2023
by GWL Publishing
an imprint of Great War Literature Publishing LLP

Produced in United Kingdom

Cover designs and artwork by GWL Creative.

ISBN 978-1-915109-25-5 Paperback Edition

GWL Publishing
Chichester, United Kingdom

www.gwlpublishing.co.uk

Dedication

For S.

Chapter One

Peony

"What is wrong with you?"

I stare at my reflexion in the mirror, trying to tame my hair, although I don't know why I'm bothering. It's beyond redemption. Maybe it's the damp weather, or just that I've lost the ability to control my wayward curls, but whatever the reason, they're not behaving. Talking to them isn't helping, either. Especially as there's no-one else here, so I appear to be talking to myself.

It's the first sign of madness, or so they say, but a little insanity wouldn't surprise me. I feel like I'm going crazy most of the time.

I admit defeat with my hair and put on some makeup instead. Not much, but just enough. I'm going to the Hart's Creek Hotel tonight, and while that might sound fairly grand, it isn't. That's not to say it's a dump. It's just the kind of place where you can dress up if you like, but where you'll be made equally welcome in jeans. I'm opting for the latter, because while it's March and the sun has been shining all day, it's nighttime now and it's cold outside, and my closet isn't exactly overflowing with cocktail dresses… or dresses of any variety, for that matter.

That's not because I'm not a dressing up kind of girl. It's because I can't see a reason to have lots of pretty things when I spend most of my time driving around on a tractor, tending to my family's apple orchard.

I've broken with my normal dress code, though, and rather than wearing a thick sweater, I've put on a blouse. It's got short sleeves, so I'll be wearing my leather jacket with it, but I think it's kinda pretty. It's got flowers embroidered down the front, anyway.

That's about as close as I get to pretty these days, although I suppose I could invest in a couple of dresses… if I could afford to. It's not like I don't have the space, since Luca left.

I shake my head, staring at myself again, and note the slight glistening in my eyes.

"Don't you dare cry."

There I go, talking to myself… yet again.

But I'm not going to cry. He's not worth it, and I don't miss him. Hardly at all.

Okay, so I miss having help around the farm. He was always very willing to do whatever was needed, when he wasn't working at the gym. I miss having someone to lean on, as well… someone to talk to when things got on top of me, and I guess it was nice having someone to laugh with when things were going well, too.

And, of course, I miss the sex.

God, do I miss the sex.

Luca and I had a very physical relationship, which I interpreted as love. I'm not sure Luca gave it that much thought. He just enjoyed it, while it lasted.

That's not to say I didn't enjoy it, too. What wasn't to enjoy?

Luca was incredible. I didn't ask where he'd learned his skills. I didn't want to know, and I've never been the kind of person who gets hung up on the past. All I cared about was that he was using his skills on me. He enjoyed waking me with his fingers, and believe me, there's no better feeling in this world than coming out of a blissful sleep into an even more blissful orgasm, delivered at the hands of an expert.

Stop it.

I can't think about Luca… not like that. Not about the sex.

Because the problem is, whenever I let those memories cross my mind, it's not the thought of all the things he used to do to me… all the ways he used to make me scream and beg for more. Instead, I'm plagued by thoughts of him with Stevie Pine. She's the woman he left me for… the soon-to-be ex-wife of Dawson Pine, who owns the bar in town. Stevie joined the gym over a year ago, telling Dawson she wanted to lose weight, I think. Luca kindly gave me all the details, but I wasn't listening at the time. Mostly because he'd started the conversation by telling me he was in love with someone else.

It's hard to pay attention after a bombshell like that.

I picked up the name, though… 'Stevie Pine', and I wondered if she was at the bar, telling Dawson the same story, and whether he was struggling to take it in, too.

Luca already knew Stevie before she joined the gym. She used to work with Dawson behind the bar, so almost everyone in town knew her. Me included. I'll admit, I never thought of her as a friend. She was more of an acquaintance. But she was older than me by several years, so we were never going to be very close, I guess.

Unlike her and Luca, who it seems preferred older women.

He never said so in as many words, but I think their affair had started before she joined the gym. If it hadn't, I guess they probably wanted it to, and her membership gave them an excuse to be together… or for her to be out of the house, at least. He didn't need an excuse. He worked there. And I'll be absolutely honest, I never noticed a thing. He didn't stay at work any longer than usual. Nor did he change in his behavior toward me. He still made love to me, still made me scream and beg for more… still made me feel wanted. All the time. How was I supposed to know he'd fallen for someone else?

Looking back, though, I realized afterwards that he'd stopped saying the words. He'd stopped saying, "I love you."

I guess because he'd stopped loving me when he started loving her, and even he couldn't lie to that extent.

He said that was why he was telling me about her – about their love for each other – because it felt dishonest not to. And that was when I noticed the bags by the front door.

"You're leaving?"

He saw the line of my gaze and frowned, looking sheepish.

"I'm sorry."

There was something truly insincere about the tone of his voice, and in a piece of the most immaculate timing, it was at that moment that I heard a car coming down the track. I knew, without even having to look, that it was her.

"Get out!"

He startled at the strength and volume of my voice, although I don't know why I bothered telling him to go. He was clearly leaving anyway, and he grabbed his bags without a backward glance.

"I hate you, Luca."

"I know. I'm sorry."

Did he think saying 'sorry' over and over was going to make it better? He'd lied and cheated. He'd hurt me, and he was walking out the door without a care in the world.

I watched them drive away in her sleek red saloon, tears streaming down my cheeks, and wondered if I'd ever feel anything again.

I did, of course. I felt things far worse than his deception, and even if it still leaves a sour taste in my mouth, I know I'm better off without him.

If only I wasn't so damned lonely…

I wouldn't be, of course, if Granny hadn't left me too.

She didn't leave in the same way as Luca. Hers wasn't a voluntary decision. She died in her sleep three days after New Year… just a couple of months ago now.

I thought my heart couldn't take any more after Luca left, but it seems I was wrong.

Finding her like that nearly broke me, and for the first time in the four months since he'd left me, I wished he was still here. I even wished he'd come back, if only to hold me, and tell me it would all be okay. That didn't happen, of course. There was no-one to hold me or help me, and I had to make all the arrangements by myself. Most of the village attended her funeral, but I stood by her graveside, alone in that crowd, my heart completely shattered.

"Stop this," I mumble, ignoring the dangers of insanity. I'm more worried about the dangers of dwelling for too long in the past.

Instead, I turn away from the mirror and pull on my boots. They're my high-heeled black ones, not the thick-soled ones that I've left by the front door, covered in mud… the ones I wear around the farm every day. It might be unusual for me to dress up, but even I have my limits, and I zip up my boots, trying not to think about how much Luca used to like them, and how Granny warned me about him.

She was right, of course.

"Men who look that good don't stick around," she said to me the morning after I first brought him to meet her.

"That's very cynical, Granny. And it's not true, either."

"Oh?" I remember, she was rolling out pastry on the kitchen table at the time, her hands covered in flour, and she glanced up at me, raising an eyebrow. She was a slight woman, with white hair, which she always wore in a bun at the nape of her neck, and unlike me, she bothered with dresses, rather than wearing pants or jeans all the time. And aprons... I don't recall ever seeing her without an apron tied around her waist. On this occasion, she patted down her hands on the floral one she was wearing to protect her pale blue summer dress, and reached for a pie dish from the cabinet behind her.

"Yes. My father was a handsome man, and he was faithful to Mom." I don't remember anything about my mother, except that she died when I was three months old, and that for the rest of his life, my father never looked at another woman. Such was his devotion that, even on his deathbed, over fifteen years later, her name was the last word on his lips.

She turned back slowly, tilting her head. "That's true enough," she said. "Your daddy was a good man."

"And a very attractive one."

"Yes."

"So, not all handsome men are bound to wander," I said, watching as she lifted the circle of pastry and laid it into the dish.

"Not all, no."

Her history gave her good reason for doubting, so I wasn't going to argue too hard, and in any case, I got the feeling she was only allowing me the point where it related to my father. Everyone else – including Luca – was open to speculation.

She was right about that, wasn't she? Because, let's face it, he didn't stick around.

And with everyone gone, it's up to me to keep this place going... although heaven only knows how. The work is exhausting, the stress is wearing me down, I spend most of my time wondering what on earth I'm supposed to be doing, and whether I'm doing it right, and I haven't even reached the hardest part of the year yet. I can't bear to think how I'm going to get through harvest… so I'm not going to. Especially as I'm not sure I'll be able to survive until then. The bank loan needs repaying, but I don't think I've got enough money in my account to cover it… let alone eat and keep a leaking roof over my head.

I'm well aware of all the problems. I even know the cause. It stems from last year's harvest, which was poor compared to recent ones. We had too much rain in the spring and not enough sun in the summer, so our yield was down. It's as simple as that.

What I don't know is what I'm going to do about it.

The worry keeps me awake at night, and occupies most of my time during the day, as well.

Except for this evening. This evening I'm going out, and I'm going to have fun.

I stand and grab my purse from the hook on the back of my bedroom door. I rarely use it, which is why it's in here. Normally, I just carry whatever I need in my pockets, so my hands are free for more manual labor, but tonight I want to at least give the impression of being a lady… although as I head out the front door and gaze at my fifteen-year-old truck, I wonder if I'm aiming too high. It's hard to be feminine when you're surrounded by such masculine trappings, but I don't have time to worry about it now. If I'm not careful, I'm going to be late.

Besides, I don't have much choice in transportation. I can't afford to upgrade… any more than I can afford to fix the leaking roof, or have the outside of the property repainted. There are more important things to worry about. Like surviving.

I check my watch… yep, I need to get going. I'm supposed to be meeting Laurel at the Hart's Creek Hotel in less than ten minutes, and although it's not that far, I know she won't thank me if I keep her waiting. That's not because she's impatient, but because – like me – she's not a great fan of sitting by herself in a bar. That said, the hotel bar is quite small and intimate, and nothing like Dawson's. Not that I'm saying his place is rowdy. Just that it's a lot busier.

Laurel and I used to meet up there, but since Luca and Stevie left town together, I haven't been able to face it… or Dawson. I keep wondering if he'll blame me for what happened. I don't know exactly how long they'd been married, but I'm guessing it was considerably longer than Luca and I had been together, and even if their divorce isn't quite finalized yet, I can't imagine it'll be much longer now. According to the rumor mill, Stevie filed within days of leaving him, and I don't think Dawson objected. He's not the kind of man who would have done. That doesn't mean he's a push-over. It means he was angry, and he wouldn't have wanted to forgive and forget, anymore than I would. The public humiliation alone would have been enough to put him off.

My truck starts first time. It might be old, but it's reliable, and I put it into reverse, turning it around, and wondering about my choice of heels. They make it harder to drive, although I don't have far to go, so I guess I'll manage. It's not optional now. It's too late to change. And what would I change into? My muddy boots? I don't think so.

The route into town is straightforward enough and at the top of the track, I turn right onto the main road, passing Hart's Creek Industrial Park. There's a sign outside offering units for sale or rent, which doesn't surprise me as two of the companies who used to reside here went out of business last year. There's no indication of anyone new moving in, but at least the rest of the units are occupied… for now. The redundancies hit the town hard, and even those who weren't directly affected started looking over their shoulder, feeling nervous, wondering who might be next. It hit me, too, like a lot of the other small businesses in the town. Nervous people don't spend as much, and I suddenly found I had fewer customers coming by to pick apples and buy cider. It's another thing to worry about, I guess… but not tonight.

There are several large houses, set back from the road. They're all different and are the kind of properties most of us can only dream of owning. One of them belongs to Walker Holt… Hart's Creek's resident author. I say 'author' but I think he's more of a screenwriter, or playwright, these days. He's written books, though, I know that… although I've never read any of them. They're thrillers, and not really my thing. Besides which, I don't have time for reading. I wish I did. Even the local newspaper is beyond me. That's edited by Nate Newton, who used to live next door to Walker… until his divorce forced him to sell up. Everyone thought he and Kathryn were the ideal couple, but I guess that just goes to show how wrong you can be.

I enter the town itself, driving in to Main Street, ignoring the two side turnings – Maple Street on the left and Mulberry Lane on the right. Maple Street is a quiet residential road, containing mostly single-story houses, with neat little lawns at the front, and just about enough space to park a car. The ones closest to Main Street are the smallest, and they get larger as you drive further down the road… as do the cars parked in front of them. Mulberry Lane is where you'll find the Hart's Creek's schools… both elementary and high.

The first place I come across in Main Street is Dawson's Bar. It's on the corner of Maple Street, opposite the auto repair shop, which takes up a large plot on the corner. Dawson's is a double-fronted property, with its parking lot out back, although there are a few spaces on Main Street. It has a balconied apartment above, which is where Dawson Pine lives… all by himself now.

I know that feeling, but I shake my head, determined not to dwell on it.

Beyond the bar is a row of shops, and although I'm concentrating on driving, my eye catches the bookstore, the beauty salon, the dentist's office and the French restaurant that opened a couple of years ago. I can't pronounce the name, but dining out isn't something I do, so it's not important. It's alongside the coffee shop, and the newspaper offices, and then last of all on that side, the gym. My skin prickles as I drive past it, noticing the lights are still on. That's not unusual. The place is open until eleven most nights… Tuesdays being no exception.

Opposite the gym is the sheriff's office, on the corner of Beech Road. It's next door to the public library, and beyond that is the doctor's surgery, which overlooks Hart's Green. That's where just about every event in the town takes place, from the Fall Festival to the Fourth of July picnic. I have many happy memories of times spent there with my grandmother, and my father… and even Luca.

The only other landmark is the church, which is on the other side of the green. I may not be religious myself, but I can admire the building, with its white painted wooden walls and tall steeple. The door is painted bright red, which I've always thought a little odd, but maybe that's just me, and in any case, I've reached my destination. The hotel takes up a huge corner plot next to the gym, beyond which is Cedar Street. This is another residential road, but it's very different from Maple Street. The houses here are significantly larger, and so are the bank balances of the people who live in them… unlike my own.

I try not to think about that as I turn into the parking lot, choosing a space fairly close to the hotel's main entrance.

Getting out, the wind catches my hair, and I wish more than ever that I'd been able to tame it into some semblance of order before leaving home. As I push it to one side, I glance across the street, noticing that the drugstore is still open, and that there's a light on in the florist's. I'm not sure why that is, but I guess they must be busy.

I don't bother to lock my truck. No-one's going to steal a heap of junk like this anyway, and to be honest, the crime rate in Hart's Creek is so low, our sheriff, Brady Hanson, has very little to do. He'd never agree with that, and would tell anyone who asked that he's rushed off his feet. But I've been at Laurel's house when he's called by and claimed to be 'just passing'. If he does that with just half the residents of Hart's Creek, I'd be amazed if he gets anything done in a day.

The steps up to the hotel door are spaced too widely for me, and I have to tread unevenly, leading with my right foot first, and then stepping up with my left. I take a moment before deciding which foot to move forward next, and go with the left, even though it feels odd. I'm grateful to reach the top, and pass inside, relieved that the lobby is empty, and no-one witnessed that shocking attempt at something as straightforward as walking.

I'll have to be sure to leave with Laurel, just so I have someone to hold on to. The thought of trying that in reverse, in these heels, having had a glass or two of wine, isn't inspiring.

The hotel was bought out a couple of years ago and the new owners have completely redecorated it, adding modern touches, but keeping a traditional country feel to the place. I like it, especially the bar, which is straight ahead of me. It has the feel of a gentleman's club, without the cigar smoke and stuffiness, and I glance around, my heart sinking when I realize Laurel is nowhere to be seen.

Should I have waited in the car? Maybe… although the idea of going back out there and attempting those steps again doesn't appeal. Instead, I go up to the bar, the man behind it coming straight up to me, a smile plastered on his youthful face.

"What'll it be?" he says.

Laurel and I always drink wine when we come here, and my personal favorite is the rosé from Napa Valley, so I order a glass, hand over a ten-dollar bill, and take my drink to one of the vacant tables around the edge of the room. I can see the door from here, but I don't feel too obtrusive, and to complete the effect, I take out my phone. Hopefully, it looks as though I'm happily occupied, rather than nervous about being here alone, and as I pretend to scroll, I glance up at the door, hoping Laurel won't be too long.

She's never normally late. She's one of those people who pride themselves on getting everything just right… just so.

That's not a criticism. It's how she is. And I love her for it.

She's married to Mitch, a former football player, which I guess is enough of a reason for at least half the women in town to hate her. They live in a beautiful house, too. It might not be the biggest in the area, but it's surrounded by an enormous patch of land, about mile or so away, on the opposite side of town to my farm, although they're as much residents of Hart's Creek as anyone else. They got married after what Laurel always tells strangers was a 'whirlwind romance'. That's her way of dressing up the truth, which is that she came back home from law school, with every hope of starting her career. She met Mitch not long afterwards, at the opening of his gym – the one where Luca used to work – and he swept her off of her feet… and into his bed. Mitch had something of a reputation, but being ten years older than us, he'd never featured on Laurel's radar… or mine, for that matter. He became much more significant, though, when she found out she was pregnant. That may not seem 'just right' to some people, but the fact of the matter is, fatherhood – or at least the prospect of it – was obviously exactly what Mitch needed, because he curbed his wild ways, asked Laurel to marry him, and settled down. They've been together ever since, living in wedded bliss, along with their beautiful daughter, Addison, who's three now… going on twelve.

I know Laurel will be full of stories about how wonderful life is, what a great husband and father Mitch is, and how Addison is surpassing all expectations. And I won't mind one little bit. I'm happy for her. Although I wish she'd hurry up and get here.

The clock at the top of my phone says it's coming up for seven-forty-five, which means she's nearly fifteen minutes late, and that's almost unheard of for Laurel.

My phone rings, making me jump, and Laurel's name appears on my screen, my heart sinking at the sight, because I know it can only mean one thing. I answer, holding the device to my ear, and glance around the room, a few people frowning at me for daring to take the call in here, rather than stepping outside to do so. I ignore them, and twist in my seat slightly, so I'm facing the wall.

"Laurel?"

"Hi," she says, sounding flustered. "I'm so sorry. Mitch hasn't made it home from work yet. I just called, and he says he's not gonna be able to get away for at least another hour."

"And I guess it's too late to get a babysitter." That wasn't a question. I know they're like gold dust around here.

"It is. I'm so sorry." She repeats herself, and I let out a silent sigh.

"Don't worry. We'll do it another time."

"We sure will. I need a night off."

"I'll call you later in the week, and we'll set something up."

"Okay."

I can't help feeling disappointed as we end our call. Even if our evening had been destined to be filled with tales of married bliss, it would have been better than sitting at home, worrying about paying this month's bills.

With that in mind, I guess I may as well finish my drink before I head back. It'll make the evening slightly less depressing.

I take a long gulp of chilled rosé, wishing now that I'd eaten before coming out, and I take a look around the room, my eyes settling on the most beautiful man I've ever seen in my life. I didn't notice him when I came in, but I have to say, he makes Luca look really ordinary, and for a moment, my grandmother's words spring to mind.

Men who look that good don't stick around…

Well, in this case, I'm not sure I care. If all I could do was sit and look at him, I'd be happy. He's staring at me, and I'm captivated by his dark eyes, framed in a perfect face, the stubble on his square jaw speaking of design, rather than laziness. It's too immaculately trimmed to be otherwise. His hair is equally tidy, almost black, and thick enough to run your fingers through… if you were that way inclined. He's wearing jeans – the kind of jeans that have never done a day's manual labor – with a white button-down shirt, and a casual jacket, and I can feel myself blush as he puts down his empty wineglass and, without taking his eyes from mine, walks toward me.

Chapter Two

Ryan

Dinner was a great deal better than I expected.

To be fair, even the menu was more varied than most, and I took a while deciding between the herb crusted snapper, and the miso glazed halibut. The halibut won in the end, but only because I liked the sound of the orange and chili glaze. Besides, I'm going to be here for a few days, so I can try the snapper another time.

I glance around the bar, nodding my head.

I've done okay here.

Back in the days when I traveled around more often, I got used to taking pot luck, never knowing where I'd be staying from one night to the next. But at least here in Hart's Creek, the accommodation and food have been excellent… so far.

The room I've booked is very comfortable, with a King-sized bed, a wide window seat, a couple of chairs, either side of a low coffee table, and a TV that's been perched a little awkwardly on the corner of a dresser. I imagine it would have fitted a lot more easily when televisions had smaller screens, but I don't mind. I doubt I'll be watching it.

I only arrived this afternoon, so I haven't tried the bed yet. But, despite its wrought iron frame, it didn't creak when I sat on it earlier, and it seemed fairly firm, which is a good thing in my opinion.

Of course, I haven't sampled breakfast, either, and I always say, you can't judge a place until you've eaten breakfast.

That'll come tomorrow morning... right before I get down to work.

I take a sip of wine, trying to remember why I'm here.

To buy a plot of land... obviously.

But why me? Why now?

Was it to prove a point?

This used to be my job, after all. So, did I travel all this way just to show I've still got all the negotiating skills I was once famous for?

Or should that be infamous?

Either way, I know I could have sent someone else to do this deal. I have an entire team of negotiators, all of whom would have been happy to make this trip.

And yet, here I am.

Maybe it was just that I've grown sick of going into the office, day in, day out. That's how it's been since Dad died, nearly a year ago, and I took over the company from him. Since then I haven't negotiated a thing. I've made decisions, I've run the operation, I've hired and fired and been the boss... but what I haven't done is the job I used to love.

The job I was so damn good at, I was known as the best in the business.

When Gabe Sullivan brought me this portfolio, I thought about handing it off. I even selected Adrian Marsh for the job. He's the kind of ruthless son-of-a-bitch you need to complete a deal like this, and I knew he'd get it done.

Except, right at the last moment, I changed my mind.

"You're gonna do what?" Gabe said, his eyes wide, when I told him of my plan to come up to Hart's Creek myself.

"I'm gonna handle this one." I didn't see what his problem was. So what if the CEO was absent for a few days? "You can run this place for me while I'm gone, can't you?"

We both knew he could. Gabe is my oldest friend, and he'd worked alongside my father for almost as long as I had. Having spent a lot more time in our Boston offices than me, he knows the workings of the company better than I do, and I had absolutely no qualms about leaving him in charge.

"Of course I can. I just don't understand why you'd want to go."

I didn't have an answer, and luckily his phone rang at that moment, which saved me the trouble of having to invent one. I wasn't about to tell him I'd been feeling restless for quite a while. Being stuck in an airless office is hardly my style and it's nowhere near as much fun as traveling around used to be.

That makes me wonder if maybe it's fun that's been lacking in my life… fun and female company. In my former life, I could hook up with a different woman in every town or city I visited, and as I was never around for very long, the question of commitment, or getting tied down wasn't an issue.

I smile at the irony…

I never get tied down myself, but it's been a while since I've used my rope skills on anyone else, and that always makes me a little edgy.

Dry patches happen, sure, but it's been over two months, which is a long time for me… so maybe somewhere in my subconscious, I saw this as a chance to do something about that.

Except it's not that easy.

The hotel may be comfortable, the food may be good, but so far I haven't seen a single woman under the age of forty-five, and while that's only ten years older than me, I have to draw the line somewhere.

And that's a firm line with me.

It's got nothing to do with age or appearance. I can appreciate maturity in anyone, and I get that older women come with a wealth of experience their younger counterparts often lack. The problem is they also tend to come with baggage, and I'm not up for that.

Which I guess is why I'm at the bar, by myself, enjoying my third glass of wine.

It's a particularly fine Nebbiolo, from the Lombardy region of Italy, and although I should probably have stopped at two glasses, I don't really care.

I don't care about drinking alone, either. It's something I've gotten used to over the years… but then, I do a lot of things alone. It's one advantage of being an only child. You get used to your own company. You get to appreciate the thinking time, and as there doesn't seem to be anyone worth pursuing here tonight, I guess that means I may as well…

I glance up, my breath catching in my throat, my cock hardening in an instant, as the most beautiful woman in the world walks into the room.

This is more like it.

I've always had a thing for blondes, especially when their hair is long and untamed. As far as I'm concerned, the wilder the better and although I know, in this instance, that could be down to the chilly wind that's blowing straight down Main Street, I'd like to think it hints at an inner wildness… one that might go with those flashing blue eyes and generous lips, which would look fabulous wrapped around my cock.

She stops, glances around, and then wanders up to the bar, giving me a better view of her, and I almost groan out loud. She's wearing skin-tight jeans, with a blouse tucked in at the waist, and a black leather jacket… all sexy enough in their own right. But add in the knee-high black boots with four-inch heels, and my cock starts asking me questions… like why I'm not standing beside her already.

Perhaps it's that nervous look in her eyes as she orders a glass of rosé wine, or maybe it's the fact that, as she sits down, she pulls out her phone and fake scrolls, like she's pretending to be busy. How do I know she's faking it? Because she doesn't pause… doesn't stop long enough to look at anything. Does that mean she's waiting for someone? I presume so, and looking that good, I imagine it's got to be a man.

I ignore my aching cock and its questions, because if there's one thing I've never been interested in, it's competing. Maybe that's another trait of only children. We're not great at dealing with competition, because we've never had to.

Her phone rings, which seems to take her by surprise, and she looks up and then turns away so she's facing the wall by the time she answers. She wants privacy. Is it her boyfriend, I wonder? Or her husband? A strange burning sensation knots in my chest, at the same time as I hear a low growl. I look around before I realize the sound came from me, and I cough and swallow down the rest of my wine, just in case anyone else heard me making weird, possessive bear-like noises over a woman I've never even met.

She's ended her call, and puts down her phone as she turns around again and picks up her glass, drinking at least half its contents in one gulp, which makes me smile, just as she raises her head and our eyes lock.

Husband, boyfriend, whatever… I don't care. She's worth competing for, and I put down my empty glass and walk over to her.

I've kept my eyes on hers the entire time and she's made no move. I'm not sure she's even blinked, and as I stand beside her, my cock feeling a lot happier already, she just stares up at me.

"Can I get you another drink?" Woah… does my voice always sound that deep?

She hesitates, just for a second, and then nods her head, and although I'd planned on calling it a night after that third glass, I go back to the bar, ordering another rosé for her, and a fourth Nebbiolo for myself, adding them to my tab.

Sitting opposite her, I put down the glasses and lean in a little.

"I hope I'm not treading on anyone's toes." She tilts her head, frowning, like she doesn't understand me. "You're not waiting for anyone?" *Please say 'no'.*

She gulps down yet more wine and looks right into my eyes. "I was, but my friend just called to say she can't make it." She? That's promising. "Her husband is running late and she can't get a babysitter."

I nod my head. "But you could?"

"I could what?"

"Get a babysitter."

"I didn't need one."

"Because your husband is at home, minding your three kids?" She smiles. "No. I don't have a husband."

"Okay. Your boyfriend is at home, with those same three kids… and maybe a dog."

Her smile widens. "I don't have a boyfriend, either."

"The men of Hart's Creek are clearly blind."

"Not necessarily. My ex cheated on me, and then left town with his lover, so…" She stops talking and bites on her bottom lip, my cock twitching against my zipper at the sight. "I don't know why I said that."

"The guy must've been crazy," I murmur, although my voice is loud enough for her to hear me, and she takes another large sip of wine, almost emptying her glass. I haven't touched mine, but I tilt my head toward hers as she puts it down. "Do you want another?"

She nods, and I stand, stepping over to the bar and ordering another rosé.

When I come back, she looks up at me as I sit.

"You're not from around here."

That was a statement, not a question, but I answer her, anyway. "No. I'm from Boston."

"And you're in town on business?"

"Is it that obvious?"

She shrugs. "Unless you're hiding a wife and three kids in your room."

I smile. She's fishing, and while that would normally be an instant turn-off for me, in this instance, I like it. "I don't have a wife, or any kids... or even a girlfriend, before you ask. We may as well get that out of the way, don't you think?"

She blushes, picking up her wine and taking a drink. Then she looks down at the remaining pale pink liquid before raising her head, staring right at me again. "In that case, didn't you want to know whether I've got those three kids you were talking about?"

"Are you telling me you have, and you've left them at home, with just the dog to care for them?"

She giggles, putting down her glass before she spills what's left of the contents, and my cock almost explodes at that wondrous sound.

"I don't have a dog."

"You don't have any kids, either, do you?"

"No."

I gaze into her eyes, those deep blue pools sparkling back at me, and I lean a little closer, lowering my voice.

"If you don't mind me asking, how drunk are you?"

She's had two and a half glasses of wine, but they were large ones, and she's swallowed them down real fast. I've known women to be virtually incoherent on less alcohol than that.

"Why do you ask?"

Because I want to take you to bed, but there are rules… ones that even I don't break. And besides, I want you sober enough to remember every single thing I do to you for a very long time.

"Because I need to know. Now, answer the question. How drunk are you?"

She licks her bottom lip, then bites on it, and tilts her head, staring into my eyes and driving me insane for a full ten seconds, before she whispers, "Not so drunk I wouldn't know what I was doing."

Oh… fuck…

"You have no idea how much I was hoping you'd say that."

I hold out my hand and she takes it, grabbing her purse with the other, and letting me pull her to her feet. Then without another word, I lead her from the room, into the lobby.

The elevators are over to the right, beside the reception desk, and I steer us in that direction, pressing the 'up' button. The doors open straight away and we step inside, turning around to face them as they sigh closed again. I keep a grip on her hand as I step forward, pressing the button for the third floor, and although I'm tempted to turn and face her, I don't.

I can't.

If I do, I'll have to take her. Right here, right now, in this elevator. While that wouldn't be a first for me, I want more than that…

The doors open soon enough, thank God, and we step outside, turning to the right. My room is along here, on the left, overlooking Main Street, and we stop outside it. I can feel her watching as she waits for me to open the door and I let her enter first, flicking on the lights as I close it behind me.

She turns, looking up at me, and for a split second, I expect her to say she's changed her mind. I take a half step closer and she parts her lips, her breath hitching as I grab her, one hand around her waist, the other behind her head, and I pull her hard against me. I hear her purse drop to the floor as our lips meet in a frenzied kiss, and while I normally shy from such intimacies, in this case, it feels natural… necessary. She moans as I run my tongue along the seam of her lips, and she opens to me, her breasts heaving into my chest. I lower my hand to her ass, pulling her closer and flexing my hips, my body tensing as she raises her arms, her hands roaming onto my shoulders.

Let her touch… let her touch…

She pulls off my jacket, and I hear it fall to the floor, my muscles straining as her hands rest on my biceps, just the thin cotton of my shirt between us.

It's too much. I can't take it, and I grab her wrists, pulling her arms behind her back and holding them there with one of mine, not even breaking the kiss as I yank her jacket down, leaving it just above her elbows, so she's restrained.

I feel safe now, and I break the kiss, looking down at her, unable to stop the smile from forming on my lips. Who wouldn't smile when faced with a sight like this? Her cheeks are flushed, her eyes sparkling, her wild hair even messier than before. There's a slight swelling to her lips, and just a tinge of redness, where my stubble has scraped her skin… and I've never seen anything so glorious in my life.

"Christ… you're beautiful."

She smiles and I wonder how long it's been since anyone told her that. Not since her crazy, cheating ex left her, maybe?

I reach out and run my finger from the center of her chin, down her neck, barely touching her as I let it drift lower, coming to a stop between her breasts. There's a definite stutter as she breathes in and out, and I undo the top button of her blouse, followed by the next one down, and the one below that, exposing firm rounded breasts encased in a white lace bra. I can already see how hard her nipples are, even through the gossamer fabric, but I want more, and I lower the cups, pulling them down. Her breasts are pushed upwards and I palm them, leaning down to kiss her nipples, first the left and then the right. She cries out as I gently bite on each dark pink pebble, and I feel her shaking… realizing too late that her movements have nothing to do with anything I've been doing. She's freed herself from the sleeves of her jacket, and I jump as I feel her hands on the back of my neck.

It seems she wants to hold me in place, but I can't take it, and I stand upright, grabbing her hands again, and holding them between us.

"I'm gonna have to find a way of keeping you still…"

I look around the room, my eyes settling on my tie, which I threw over the back of the chair earlier, when I was unpacking, and I smile. It's perfect.

I lead her over, letting her go long enough to pick it up, and she stares down at it, her eyes widening before she returns her gaze to me.

"Y—You're gonna tie me up?"

I nod, holding my breath. "Is that a problem?"

She tilts her head, looking at me, and then lowers her eyes to the tie again. "It's not something I've done before, but no, it's not a problem."

Thank fuck for that…

I quickly pull off her blouse, and unfasten her bra, letting them both fall to the floor, and although I'm tempted to linger… to lick those beautiful hard nipples once more, I need to know I'm safe before I do so.

"Hold out your hands."

She does as I say, staring up into my eyes while I bind her wrists, her lips parted, the bottom one quivering, just slightly.

By the time I've finished and have moved her over to the bed, she's breathing hard in anticipation, and I'm so turned on, I'm worried this will all be over way too soon. I need to slow things down… regain control.

I sit her down, and then lie her back, her head on the pillows, her body along the length of the king-sized bed, and I undo her boots, pulling them off. It would be nice to leave them on, but I need to get her out of these jeans, and I'm not gonna waste time putting her boots back on. I don't think my cock could stand the tension.

Then I unfasten her jeans, waiting a second for her to raise her ass off the bed before I pull them down. She's wearing delicate lace panties, and while I'd like to pause for a while and admire them, my cock isn't so sure, and for once I'm listening to it. I lower them, revealing a smooth, shaved pussy, her lips swollen and glistening, and I throw her panties over my shoulder, kneeling up on the bed beside her as I take her bound wrists and raise them above her head.

She watches, tilting her head back, as I tie her to the iron bedstead, and once she's securely fastened, I look down at her.

"Okay?"

She nods, and I stand, gazing down at her firm breasts, the dark pink nipples so hard and taut, I wonder if they're hurting. Her waist is narrow, and her hips slightly flared, and I think I could happily just stand here forever.

Forever? Don't be ridiculous.

She squirms, rolling her hips, and arches her back, and as I lean over and touch her, brushing my fingers from her knee to the top of her thigh, she parts her legs, exposing her glorious pussy, although I'm not ready to fuck her yet.

What am I saying?

I'm about as ready as I'm ever going to be.

I've never wanted anyone this much, but I'm scared I'm going to come within seconds of entering her, and I don't want to spoil things for her. I kneel up on the bed again, moving between her legs this time, and she parts them wider as I lean down onto my elbows and dip my head, running my tongue along her delicate folds.

She bucks off of the bed, giggling, and says, "Do you always tie your women up?"

I'm unwilling to stop what I'm doing, so I just nod my head, flicking my tongue across her clit. She gasps, grinding her hips up into me, and I smile to myself. *That silenced you.*

It also saved me having to explain why I tie women up… which is a good thing because I'm not sure I can. For someone who loves sex in all its forms, I've always found it odd that I have an aversion to intimacy… to letting people get too close. Even being hugged is uncomfortable for me. That's why I usually shy away from kissing, although I obviously made an exception tonight. I couldn't help myself. But there's something different about what's happening here… something different about her.

Apart from anything else, she tastes like nothing on earth. There's a familiar honeyed sweetness, but there's something else beyond that. It's like another depth of flavor and it's driving me crazy. I dip my tongue inside her, lapping up her juices, and then return my attentions to her clit. She's writhing, pulling her legs up higher, and moaning loudly.

"M—More," she mutters. "Please, give me more."

I insert a finger, and she sighs, like she's been waiting for me to do that, so I follow it with another, gently biting on her clit, sucking it into my mouth, and then licking it again. I reach up with my free hand, cupping her breast, and then roll her nipple between my thumb and forefinger, pinching hard on it. That's all it takes to push her over into a wild orgasm. She screams something incoherent, although I'm fairly sure I hear the word, "Yes," repeated several times, as she struggles to breathe, pleasure ripping through her trembling body.

I feel the moment it all starts to subside, and even though she's still twitching, still hauling air into her starved lungs, I pull my fingers from her, release her nipple and kneel up, licking my lips. God, she tastes good. She opens her eyes, staring up at me, a little dazed, and I shimmy to the edge of the bed, standing up as I unfasten my shirt. She stares, watching as I undress, her eyes wandering downwards as I lower my jeans and trunks, my cock springing forth, grateful to be released at last.

I have condoms in my wallet, and I pull it from my jeans pocket, take one out, and throw my wallet onto the nightstand. Then I tear into the foil packet, aware of her eyes on me the whole time as I roll it over my cock. I'm enjoying her attentions and I take my time, stroking my length, until I hear her breath hitch, and I look down at her again to find she's wide-eyed, biting on her bottom lip, her legs spread even wider than they were before.

Fuck… yeah…

She wants this. She wants me. And I've never wanted anyone more.

I kneel up one more time, moving between her legs, and without taking my eyes from hers, I enter her. Hard.

"Oh, God… yes." She grinds out the words between gritted teeth, and I pull back out… all the way out. She breathes hard, her breasts heaving. "Please…" She looks up at me. "Please, fuck me."

That's all I need to hear, and I plunge back inside, giving her what she's asked for. My hands behind her knees, I hold her bent legs in place as I hammer into her, giving her everything I've got, and taking whatever she's willing to give. She's moaning and grunting with every stroke, and never once takes her eyes from mine, even when her body quivers and I feel her tighten around me.

"Let go," I urge her. "Come on my cock."

She lets out a strangled cry as I bury myself, balls deep inside her, and as her orgasm claims her, it takes all my willpower to hold on… because I still want more.

As she calms, I pull out of her, a smile twitching at my lips, when I hear her sigh of disappointment, but then I flip her onto her front, her hands crossing above her head.

I'm faced with the most beautiful ass I've ever seen, and I kneel back, running my hands over her soft skin, squeezing and giving her a gentle slap, which makes her squeal and then giggle, before I push her knees forward, raising her hips off of the mattress and parting her legs with my own. She knows what I want, and wriggles her ass at me, making it clear she wants it too.

I slide into her easily… but then she's dripping wet, and I rest the head of my cock just inside her entrance. She edges backwards, wanting more, and I let her, holding still while she rocks back and forth, taking the first three or four inches of me… desperate for more, but unable to take it, because she's bound to the bed.

I lean over, my chest against her back, my lips beside her ear. "What do you want?"

She wiggles her hips again. "I want all of you."

"Sure?"

"Yes… please."

I straighten up, and after just a second's pause, I thrust inside her. She cries out her pleasure as I grab her hips, pulling her back onto me with every stroke, lowering my gaze and watching as my cock sinks into her… deeper and deeper.

I know I can't take much more of this, and as much as I'd love to keep going forever, my cock has other ideas. The tingling at the base of my spine is a huge giveaway, but before I reach the point of no return, I need to feel her come again.

"Now," I yell. "Come for me, now."

"Why?" Her voice is muffled, her head buried in the bedclothes, but I know I heard that right. She's asking questions? Now?

"Because I need to feel you come."

"You need it?"

"Yes… now stop talking and do as I say."

"Rub my clit."

I reach around beneath her, finding her swollen nub, and just the touch of my middle finger is all it takes. No 'rubbing' is required for her to scream and arch her back, writhing into me. She tightens around my cock, and even if I hadn't been close already, I'd have no way out now. I throw my head back, a strangled howl piercing the stillness of the room as I explode deep inside her, like never before. My whole body spasms, shockwaves running through it, and I struggle to breathe, to keep control, until I can't take it any longer and I fall forward, giving myself a minute to rest against her.

It's necessary.

It's vital.

I know I should put some distance between us, go to the bathroom – anything to avoid this intimacy – but I can't.

It's like there's something tugging at my insides, pulling me toward her. I felt it earlier, in the bar, when I came over all possessive, and before I do something really stupid, like put my arms around her, I straighten up and pull out of her.

"Won't be a minute."

She doesn't respond, but I need that distance now, and I slide off of the bed, padding over to the bathroom.

The light seems brighter in here, but I don't care. I dispose of the condom and avoid the mirror, taking my time over washing up before I open the door again, unable to stop the smile that forms on my lips when I see she's exactly where I left her... face down, her hands still tied above her head.

God, she looks good.

That magnetic tugging is back, but I saunter over to the bed, as though this feeling is perfectly normal. Which it isn't. Just like it's not usual for me to be rock hard, even though I just fucked her senseless.

I kneel up on the bed and flip her over onto her back again, her hands uncrossing in the process, and I smile when I see her rosy cheeks, bleary eyes and utterly beautiful hair, all over the place. She looks well and truly fucked, and I push her hair aside, my smile widening as she lowers her gaze to my cock, her tongue tracing a slow, lazy trail across her lower lip.

"You want more?"

She nods her head and I move closer, smiling down at her as I palm my cock and tap it against her lips. She opens, running her tongue around the head as I flex my hips, dipping inside her mouth, just by an inch or two. It seems only fair to let her dictate the rest, and she does, bobbing her head backward and forward.

"Oh, fuck..." My words are a choked-back whisper, and I place my hand on the back of her head, partly to support it, but also to hold it steady, because while I'm all about letting her call the shots, I desperately need to fuck her mouth.

As I flex my hips, she groans, her eyes fixed on mine. I nod, silently asking if this is okay, and she nods back, moaning loudly as I reach down with my free hand and part her swollen folds, stroking her drenched clit. She bucks her hips off of the bed, and I fuck her mouth, just a little deeper.

Man... she's hot.

I change from stroking to rubbing, my middle finger playing hard against her, until she squeals, and then screams, her body succumbing to pleasure, while she sucks hard on my cock. I'm not ready to come again yet, but I watch her lips surrounding me, her eyes filled with need, her body writhing, shuddering, until she calms, and then I slowly pull out of her.

She's breathing harder than ever, but I'm not done yet, and I lean over, grabbing another condom from my wallet. I have to smile as she parts her legs in anticipation, but that's not what I've got in mind… not this time, and I lean over, releasing her wrists, so she's still bound, but is no longer fastened to the bed. She looks up at me as I kneel back on my ankles, pulling her up into a sitting position, and then place my hands on her waist and lift her, so she's astride me, straddling my thighs.

"Ride my dick."

I raise her arms over my head, so they're around my neck, her wrists bound behind me. She still can't touch, but she lifts herself up, using my shoulders for leverage, and lowers herself down over my aching cock.

She takes me, inch by grateful inch, until I have nothing more to give, and then she starts to move, rising up, then slamming down onto my lap, taking me as deep as I'll go. I place one hand on her ass, supporting her, and I put the other behind her head, cradling her neck, my forehead resting against hers.

I want to kiss her, even though that's an alien thought for me, but I want to feel her lips on mine… I need to…

"Oh, to hell with it," I growl in that same possessive voice and I tilt my head, capturing her lips, pulling her close, so her breasts graze my chest, our bodies locked. Our tongues dance while she rides me, harder and harder.

She breaks the kiss before I do, staring into my eyes. "Please… take me… fuck me. Hard."

I nod, tipping her onto her back, and kneeling up, I grab her ankles, bringing her with me, so her shoulders are still on the mattress, but her ass is suspended, at just the right level. A film of sweat forms on my chest and back as I hold her there and pound into her, listening as she whispers, "Yes… Yes…" on guttural sighs.

Her hands are still bound at the wrist, but she moves them down, trying to get the angle right to touch herself. She can't, and although I've never dared do this before, I release her left ankle for a moment, balancing her leg on my shoulder, while I unfasten my tie from around her wrists. She nods her thanks, and while she grabs the bedding with her left hand, she reaches down with her right, her fingers strumming over her clit.

This isn't something I've witnessed before, having always felt the need to restrain the women I've been with, and just the sight of it is bewitching. It's also too much for me.

I part her legs again, holding her by the ankles once more, so she has better access and I have a better view, and as I feel her orgasm build, I take her even harder.

"Come… now."

I can barely speak, barely think, but she tightens around me, throwing her head back as she screams out her pleasure… like her body has no will of its own anymore… like it has to obey me.

Just that thought is enough to make me come and I slam into her, losing my mind as I let go.

Lowering her legs to the bed, I pull out of her as she turns over and curls up, completely spent, although there's a satisfied smile on her face, which makes me feel about ten feet tall.

I go to the bathroom, disposing of the second condom, and wash up before returning to find she's fallen asleep, just where I left her. I stand, gazing at her, smiling. She looks perfect… not only just fucked, disheveled and beautiful, but in my bed.

There's no way I can get the covers out from under her. Not without waking her, and that would be a shame. Still, there's a throw at the end of the bed, and I unfold it, lying down beside her, as I pull it up over us. Then, in an unheard-of act, one I've avoided all my adult life, I pull her into my arms.

She feels soft and warm, and I hold her close against me, smiling as she snuffles and then nestles against my chest, like she belongs.

That thought ought to scare me. Holding her ought to feel wrong. But it doesn't. Nothing has ever felt so right, or so good.

I'm not going to ask myself why that is, or why I've never tried this before. I already know the answer. It's because I've never wanted to. With every other woman I've had in the past, I've been quick to leave, or to make it clear to them they need to leave, unwilling and unable to give them anything more than sex.

I've never had any complaints, either.

Because this is the one thing I do better than negotiating.

I'm good at this, and the smile on her lips tells me that, despite my recent dry patch, I haven't lost my touch.

I just wish I'd taken the time to ask her name.

That's not a first for me. I've had sex with more than enough nameless women in the past.

This time, though, I really want to know, and I'll admit, I even feel a little guilty for not asking.

Still… that's something I can fix in the morning.

In the morning?

Since when?

I don't do the morning after. That's the whole point of leaving… so you don't have to face the cold light of day and the questions that inevitably come with it.

"Was it okay?"

"Can I see you again?"

"Do you want my number?"

Or the one I dread most of all…

"Why are you like this?"

I shudder at the thought. Those kinds of intimacies aren't something I've ever wanted... ever needed.

Is this time any different?

She snuffles again, and I gaze down at her perfect face, her lips a little pouted.

Of course it's different. I don't care about the cold light of day, or the questions. I want to know what her name is, and I want to say it all the time... when I call her, when we're having dinner, and breakfast, and most of all, when I'm coming inside her.

She sighs and snuggles against me, and I pull her closer. It's an instinct, like breathing... like this overwhelming desire I have to protect her. From what, though? What am I trying to protect her from?

Me?

God, I hope not.

Because for the first time in my life, I don't just want more.

I want it all.

Chapter Three

Peony

He's gripping his cock, his hand close to the base, and I stare, mesmerized, knowing already what he can do with it, but wanting more... wanting to taste him. He taps it against my lips and I open my mouth, licking the tip. With a smile, he flexes his hips, giving me an inch or two, and I raise my head off of the bed, taking the rest... or as much of it as I can.

"Oh... fuck." He chokes out the words, which would make me smile if I didn't have my mouth so very full, and then I feel his hand come around behind my head, holding me steady. There's something in his eyes. I'm not sure what it is. Need? I'd like to think so, but either way, he starts to move... to take my mouth, and although I've never done this before, I love it, and let out a slight groan.

He nods his head, like he's checking I'm okay, and I manage a slight nod back, because I'm more than okay. I'm on cloud nine, and he takes me even higher, when he reaches down between my legs, his fingers finding my clit with ease and stroking it.

I part my legs, hitting something hard...

What's that?

I crack my eyes open, the images fading in the dim dawn light as I realize the something hard is a man's leg. *His* leg.

It wasn't a dream...

The fact that his arms are around me, our naked bodies still bound, is enough to tell me that, as is the aching in my muscles.

I raise my head, seeing that I'm covered with a throw, and that I'm in a hotel room. I can't make out the furniture properly, but it's definitely a hotel room. It has that feeling about it… that impersonal feeling of not being lived in.

I lower my head again, looking at the man beside me, the memories flooding back.

The bar… the wine… flirting… fishing.

Coming up to his room in the elevator and wishing he'd kiss me, and that moment when he did, when I lost all sense of reality.

Clearly.

I wasn't drunk, though. I was light-headed, but like I told him, I knew what I was doing.

I knew I wanted him to bind my wrists, to tie me to the bed and make me come.

And he did.

God, did he make me come.

I've never felt anything like it… not that first time, or the second, or the third.

I don't know how many times he made me come in the end, I just know that when I drifted off to sleep, unable to take any more, I'd never felt more satisfied, or more happy.

Does that justify what I did?

Of course it doesn't.

I mean, I don't even know his name. I didn't when he was fucking me to the point of losing my mind. And I don't now.

So, the question is, how could I have let him do all those things to me?

I shake my head.

No. It wasn't about 'letting'. I wasn't just a willing participant. I was an advocate, begging him to take me, pleading with him to fuck me.

And he did so… perfectly.

Does that mean I want to face him? To admit my shame?

Hell, no.

He persuaded me into his bed without even having to try… without even having to ask. There's no way I want to deal with the repercussions, the fall-out… the guilt.

I gently take his arm, raising it enough to roll out of his grasp, and although he stirs, he doesn't wake. I sit up, gazing down at him, and even in the dim light, I can see how perfect he is, his masculine form lying close beside me. Memories come flooding back, of his rippling muscles, his toned and tanned body, controlling mine. It's strange… I felt so safe, even though I was powerless. I didn't know him – I still don't – and yet I've never trusted anyone more than I did him, as he tied me to his bed, ensuring I had no escape. Not that I wanted one. I wanted him… all of him. And that thought makes me feel even more ashamed.

I've slept with a man I don't know, and that's not who I am.

Except it seems it is.

I slide out of bed, the covers edging downwards, exposing him, and as I stand, I suck in a breath.

Dear God.

He's aroused… enormous, just like in my dream. Except it wasn't a dream, and I gaze down at him, my eyes fixed on his perfect cock, with its huge bulbous head and thick, veined shaft.

How on earth did that fit inside me?

I know it did, because I can still remember how glorious it felt, and how hard I came, so many times. It makes me shudder, just thinking about it.

I'd always thought Luca was big… that nothing and no-one could satisfy me like he could. He might have been my first, but I genuinely thought I'd struck gold with him. I even envied Stevie, when they left together, knowing what Luca could do, hating that he'd be doing it with her, and not me.

But this man… this perfect man… he's in a whole other league. Not just with how he looks, but what I know he can do, and how he made me feel, and…

I sigh, shaking my head.

How could I?

It's bad enough that it happened, but to be sitting here daydreaming about it is too shameful for words.

I grab my clothes, searching them out in the gloom. My blouse and bra are over by the chair, where he dropped them, right before he bound my wrists. My jeans are at the corner of the bed, alongside my boots. What I can't find are my panties. I clutch my clothes in my arm, hunting around, making as little noise as I can, lifting his shirt, which is lying on the floor beside the bed… but there's no sign of them anywhere.

He stirs again, turning over, and out of fear that he'll wake with more questions than I want to hear, I pull on my jeans and boots, foregoing my panties, then slip into my bra and blouse. My jacket is over by the door, where it fell, once I'd squirmed out of it, and my purse is directly beneath it. Picking them both up, I creep from the room, glancing back as I open the door to check he's still sleeping. He is, thank God, and I duck outside into the brightly lit hall, pulling the door closed behind me.

There's no-one out here. No-one to witness my humiliation, and I rush along the hall to the stairs, rather than taking the elevator. I feel like I'll attract less attention that way, and once I'm on the ground floor, I poke my head around to check if the coast is clear.

There's a man sitting at the reception desk. I don't recognize him, and he's staring at his phone, earbuds plugged in, so hopefully he's too distracted to notice me. It seems better to focus on the door than on him, and I hurry across the lobby and out to the parking lot, cold air hitting me straight in the lungs.

I pull on my jacket, somehow managing the steps with ease, despite my heels, and I run to my truck, jumping in. I wish I owned a quieter vehicle now, the growl of the engine more like that of a jet in the otherwise silent morning, but I slam it into reverse and slide out of the space before starting my journey home.

The roads are deserted, and it only takes a matter of minutes to get back to the farm, where I let myself in, flopping down onto one of the chairs by the table in the kitchen, my head falling into my hands.

I'm torn between shame and pleasure, because no matter what I've done and how out of character it was, I can't believe how good it felt.

The thing is… who was he?

And why did I let him do all those things to me, no questions asked?

Was I so desperate for sex – for affection – that I was willing to do anything?

It seems so.

I had been willing, too. I knew what I was doing when I let him lead me from the bar. It wasn't as though I couldn't have stopped him. One word would have done it. But I wanted him… not just sex, not just affection… him.

My pussy was dripping when I watched him wrap his silken tie around my wrists. My body was on fire at the way his eyes darkened as he led me over to the bed. I didn't know exactly what was to follow, but I didn't care. I just knew it would be good…

I wake with a start, my head slipping from my hands. The time on the microwave reads six-fifteen and I realize I must have fallen asleep. It's only forty-five minutes since I got back here, but it's time to get up now, anyway. There are things to do, and life goes on, regardless of the heart-stopping night I spent with him.

Him.

The man with no name.

I want to find that concept amusing, but I'm too enveloped in guilt, so I get up and wander through to the bathroom, stripping out of my clothes, and doing my best to ignore the fact that my panties are missing. Because I don't need any more reminders of what I've done…

The water is warm and welcoming, and I grab the soap, washing myself from head to toe, trying to be mechanical about it, rather than thinking of his hands, and how it would feel to have them wander over me, his strokes so masterful.

That's a good word for him.

Masterful.

A man who can make a woman come like that, so many times, and in such quick succession, can only be described as a master at what he does. But there was also something commanding about him. He told me to come, and I did… like my body wanted nothing more than to obey him.

I put the soap down, letting my hands wander, cupping my breasts and tweaking at my nipples before I move my right hand down over my stomach, parting my legs and leaning back against the tiled wall, my fingers strumming over my clit.

"Oh… yes."

I remember his tongue, his teeth, his fingers. I remember him watching me touch myself, while he took me so hard, holding my legs wide apart. His body shone with sweat, glistening off of his muscles, and his words echo through my head. "Come… now," and I tip into a shattering orgasm, pulling on my nipple until it almost hurts, my body convulsing, yielding to him, even though he's not here.

I'm breathless and even more overwhelmed with remorse than I was before, and I shut off the water, getting out of the shower and wrapping a towel around myself.

What's the matter with me?

Isn't it bad enough that I slept with a stranger, without reliving it at the first opportunity?

I dry off quickly, brush my teeth and pick up my clothes from the floor, taking them with me into my bedroom, where I dump them into the laundry hamper. My hair takes a while to blow-dry, but once it's there, I pull on some fresh underwear, a pair of jeans, and a sweater, refusing to think about what I've just done, and I go back out to the kitchen.

More than anything, I need a cup of coffee, and am waiting for the machine to filter it through when my phone rings. It's in my purse, which I left on the table, and I pull it out, seeing Laurel's name on the screen. She'll want to talk. I know she will. But how am I going to do that without telling her about last night? We tell each other everything… always have.

I could ignore her, but she'd only worry, so I connect the call, saying, "Good morning," in a bright and breezy voice that's so false it's bound to arouse her suspicions.

"What's wrong?" she asks, proving me right.

"Everything."

I sit at the table, my body deflating.

"Everything as in the farm, or life, or what?"

"Just everything. I can't believe what I've done."

"Why? What have you done?"

"Had sex with a stranger."

There's a very slight pause before she says, "Who was he?"

"I don't know. If I did, he wouldn't be a stranger."

"You mean you don't even know his name?"

"I don't know anything about him, except he's from Boston and he's here on business, although for all I know, he could have left already." That thought makes me a little sad. I don't know why. I think I'd die of embarrassment if I ever saw him again, so wanting him to stick around makes little sense.

"When did this happen?"

"Last night, at the hotel. When my best friend didn't show for our date."

"Are you saying it's my fault?"

"No." I sigh. "I'm saying I obviously have the morals of an alley cat."

"Did he make you purr?" I can hear the smile in her voice, and my lips twitch upwards, even though I don't mean them to.

"Oh, be quiet."

"That means he did."

"Yes, he did. Spectacularly."

"In that case, I need details. What was he like?"

"Tall, dark, handsome… a little brooding, maybe. Built like a god."

"Our age? Older?" She hesitates. "Or younger?"

"I'm not a twenty-six-year-old cougar."

"Is there such a thing?"

"Probably not."

"So that means he was older?"

"Yes. Mid-thirties, I'd have said."

"And he knew his way around?"

"Oh, God… yes."

"But you didn't think to ask his name?"

"I wasn't capable of thinking." *Clearly.*

"Maybe not before, or during, but what about after?"

"I fell asleep."

"And this morning?"

"I snuck out before he woke up."

"Why?"

"You've never woken up in bed with a stranger. You wouldn't understand."

"I understand better than you think. Remember me? The woman who lost her virginity in a one night stand?"

"Yes. But that was different. Mitch wasn't a stranger."

"He was to me. He might have lived in Hart's Creek, but he'd been away for years, and so had I. We didn't know each other, and even if he introduced himself and told me he used to play football, that was about the limit of my knowledge when I went back to his place with him."

"We have more in common than I thought," I murmur and she chuckles.

"Maybe, but unless the sex was disastrously bad last night, I don't see why you didn't wait for this guy to wake up and at least have a conversation with him."

"The sex definitely wasn't bad. It was incredible."

"In which case…"

"I felt ashamed, okay?" I raise my voice, just slightly, but then lower it immediately. "If you must know, I still do."

"Why? You had a night of amazing sex. Even if you didn't know his name, that's no reason to beat yourself up. He almost certainly isn't. And besides, it's not like he lives here. You're not going to bump into him in Main Street. You're never gonna see the guy again, so what does it matter?"

She has a point, I guess. I doubt he's woken up this morning feeling like I do. He's probably notched me up as another of his many conquests and gone on his way. Why should I feel differently, just because I'm a woman… just because society has a set of expectations for me, that it doesn't have for him?

"You're right."

"I know I am. Just promise me one thing."

"What's that?"

"Promise me he used a condom?"

"He did."

I can understand why she'd be worried about that, after what happened between her and Mitch. For her, it worked out okay. Mitch stood by her. But if the man from last night had been less cautious, I might be in real trouble now. As it is, there are no consequences to what I've done... to what we've done. Or at least none that are going to come back and bite me.

"So, what did we learn?" she says, sucking in a breath.

"To drink less, or at least eat something before swallowing the better part of half a bottle of wine."

"And?"

"To make sure and get the guy's name, if anyone ever invites me to their hotel room again."

"Or at least check their driver's license, so you know what to call them."

"Good plan."

"And maybe accept that no-one's perfect?" she says.

"Oh... I don't know. He was pretty damn close."

She giggles and I join in.

"Okay," she says, eventually. "Now we've dealt with your problems, I'll get around to the reason for my call."

"Oh, yes?"

"I was gonna ask if you wanted to come out with me and Addy today. I was gonna take her down to the creek, and we wondered if you'd like to come too."

"I can't. I've gotta cut the grass. All forty acres of it."

I love Laurel like a sister, but sometimes I wish she'd remember that my time isn't my own. I can't just take off when I feel like it, and I don't have a husband to support me, or my business. There's no point in saying any of that, though. She knows it already. Only sometimes she forgets.

"Don't worry. I just thought I'd ask, to make up for last night. We can do something soon, though, can't we?"

"Of course."

Addison calls out for something in the background. "I'd better go," Laurel says. "I'll call you."

She hangs up, and I put down my phone, getting up to pour myself a coffee and fix some toast. I ought to eat a little more than that, but I don't have time now... although heaven knows when I'll get to eat anything else today.

I always leave the tractor around the side of the house, and once I've finished breakfast, I make my way outside, shivering against the cold, and climb up onto it, starting the engine. The mower attachment is around the other side, by the barn, and it's easier to drive the tractor around there, than drag the mower here. I hate having to hook it up. It's so fiddly, and was one of the things Luca used to help with, usually doing it in the morning before heading off to work at the gym.

I shake my head, reversing the tractor into position. I refuse to think about Luca today.

That man from last night may still be a stranger, but he did things to me that Luca never even got close to.

I shudder, although that's nothing to do with the chilly breeze, as I think about how it felt to be the center of his world, even if only for a few hours. That's how he made me feel... like there was nothing and no-one on this earth that mattered as much as I did. And while I know that was only temporary, it's a feeling I'm going to struggle to forget.

I check behind me to make sure I'm in the right place and then cut the engine, climbing down, and walking around back, pulling the mower attachment forward just by a foot or so. It's heavy, but I manage, and am just studying the coupling, trying to remember how it goes together, when I hear a car coming down the track. I stand, moving to one side so I can see beyond the tractor, my eyes settling on the sleek, black Mercedes that's moving ever closer. It's an unusual car to see in these parts, and I wonder who it might be. Someone who's lost, probably, and I stretch my back, arching it slightly, as I recall how I felt when I woke this morning. My body ached then, and still does now, if I'm being honest. I've always thought of myself as being fairly fit, my life on the farm keeping me active enough, but that man stretched me in ways I'd never thought possible, and even though my muscles are arguing with me, it's a feeling I could get used to.

The car pulls over to one side of the track, slowing to a halt right by the fence, and I wait while the door opens, my breath catching in my throat as a man wearing a dark gray suit steps out, and raises his head, looking right at me.

It can't be, can't it?

He smiles and I feel my stomach tighten, a pool of heat gathering at my core. My eyes drop to his tie… that same navy blue tie he used to bind my wrists last night. I can still remember its silky softness against my skin, and I know I'm blushing, just at the thought of it.

Oh, God… how can this be happening?

Chapter Four

Ryan

I wake to an empty bed.

There's nothing unusual about that. It happens every day, whether I'm at home, or in a hotel room, like this one. There's never anyone beside me, and over the years, I've grown used to it.

I've grown used to making up excuses, too…

"I'm leaving town tomorrow."

"I've booked a 5am alarm call."

"I have a breakfast meeting."

They all work equally well, and have become a necessary part of my arsenal, because sleeping with someone is too intimate for me. It's even more intimate than sex, and therefore, it's not something I've ever wanted.

Until now.

I wanted it with her.

I wanted to wake up beside her, to hold her, to talk to her, to find out her name, and hopefully laugh about the fact that we did so much together without even knowing what to call each other. After that, I wanted to kiss her and make love with her, all over again.

I never said she had to go; never mentioned leaving town, or having an early meeting, or even talked about this morning… and yet she's gone, and the loneliness is surprisingly intense. It's so intense, it actually hurts.

I regret even more now that I didn't find out her name. How am I going to track her down, if I don't know who I'm looking for?

Track her down?

I shake my head, rubbing my hands down my face. What's wrong with me? Since when did Ryan Andrews pursue a woman like that? I might pursue them into bed, if I think it's worth it, but beyond that? Hell, no. I'm not that kind of guy.

At least, I wasn't before last night.

Turning over, I notice the indentation in the pillow, where she obviously laid her head for at least a part of the night, and I let my hand rest against it.

God… she was good.

She was more than good. She was the best. And even though I know I'll never have her again, I know I won't forget her, either. How can I? She did something to me that no woman has ever done before.

She made me want it all.

"Stop it."

I mutter the words out loud as I turn over again and sit up on the edge of the bed. Guys like me don't get to have it all. I'm just contemplating what having it all might mean… the sacrifices, the compromises, and the joy of waking up beside her every day, when I notice something white under the chair.

Unsure what it is, I get to my feet and step over, bending to pick it up, a smile forming on my lips, when I see it's a pair of lace panties. I remember taking them off of her last night and throwing them over my shoulder. This must be where they landed, and I guess in her haste to leave, she couldn't find them without turning on the lights.

I'm torn between feelings of disappointment and arousal. Disappointment that she must have wanted out of here so much, she didn't care about abandoning her underwear, and arousal that she drove home – wherever that might be – with no panties on. Arousal wins, my cock hardening as I recall her perfect shaved pussy, and I raise my hand, holding the lace garment to my nose to inhale her sweet scent. It reminds me of what it felt like when she came on my tongue, and I know I'd sacrifice anything, make any compromise she needed, for just one more taste of her.

I put her panties on the end of the bed, wandering through to the bathroom, and straight into the shower.

Regardless of my fantasies, I'm in Hart's Creek for a purpose, and I can't afford to lose sight of it, or of getting the day started, although it's impossible not to think about the fact that, if she'd stayed, I'd have wanted to shower with her.

That would have been a first for me, too.

One of the things about avoiding intimacy and not spending the night with anyone, is that you don't get to do things like take a shower together, or a bath. Or even just brush your teeth at the same time, while staring into a mirror… into each other's eyes.

I wish I could have done all of that with her, though.

I wish I could have washed her body, let my hands wander all over her, from the very tips of her toes, to that crazy wild hair of hers. I'd have liked to let her wash me, too. And I'm surprised that the thought doesn't scare me. Normally it would.

The idea of being touched has terrified me ever since that first time when Alexa Jones got too familiar and it was all I could do not to freak out. It wasn't her fault. She wasn't to know what would happen. Hell… *I* didn't know it was going to happen. Not until it did. But the memory of that episode was what made me decide to restrain the women I went with… so I'd never have to feel like that again.

It was different last night, though. I didn't feel the same inhibitions or fears. Okay, so there were a few nagging doubts when we first got up here. That's why I tied her up to start with.

But I released her. I've never done that before, although I'd do it again… with her. If only I knew who she was.

Dammit.

I'd give anything to have her here with me now, her hands around my cock. The thought makes me shudder, but this isn't fear. This is anticipation. It's a deep-seated need, and I stroke along the length of my hard-on, closing my eyes as I let my imagination take over…

"Is this okay?" she says, her hands gliding over me, back and forth.

"It's perfect."

I feel her move, sense a slight change of angle, and then her mouth comes around me. She's kneeling, her lips surrounding the tip of my cock as she pumps harder.

"You want my come?"

My voice is a throaty groan, and she moans back her approval…

Within seconds, I climax, not into her mouth, but up the wall opposite, unable to control the howl that fills the room. It's a howl of despair, not pleasure, because I've never had an orgasm that felt less satisfying in my life.

I know why, too. It's because I want her. Just her. No-one else will do.

Not now.

I turn, resting my forehead against the cool tiled wall.

I'm so screwed… metaphorically, at least.

Don't get me wrong. It's not the thought of monogamy that's worrying me.

What's worrying me is how to go about finding the woman I want to be monogamous with.

I can hardly ask around town, can I? Where would I begin?

I don't know anything about her, except she's the one woman in the world for me.

I groan out loud, washing my come off of the wall, and shaking my head as I shampoo my hair.

I could have saved myself all this trouble if I'd just asked her name

Or maybe kept her tied to the bed, so she couldn't get away…

I'm wearing a suit today, because I'm here to do business, and once I'm dressed, I wander around the bedroom, gathering up my clothes from last night, which are scattered across the floor… like hers must have been, I guess. I fold them and dump them on the chair, turning to see her panties still lying on the end of the bed. Leaving them there for someone in housekeeping to find isn't an option, although if I put them with my things, and someone sees them, they might get the wrong idea about me. So I pick them up and shove them in my pants pocket, my cock hardening, and a warmth filling my body. It's a strange sensation, but I like it, and I pat my pocket, a smile twitching at my lips. I might not be happy about the fact that she left in such a hurry, or that she left at all, but at least I can feel a little closer to her, and if that sounds pitiful, I really don't care.

I'm one of the first down for breakfast, but that suits me fine, and I sit in the dining room at the rear of the hotel. It has a view across the terrace to the hills beyond, and I study the menu, ordering scrambled eggs, Canadian bacon and home fries, with a pot of coffee. The guy serving me is in his mid-forties and doesn't write anything down. He just smiles and asks if I'd like a newspaper to read while I'm waiting. I accept and he brings me back something called the Hart's Creek Courier, along with my coffee.

"A local paper?" I say, looking up as I take it from him.

"Yeah. It's been going since before I was born."

I smile as he walks away again, flipping through a few pages, my smile widening as I read headlines, such as 'Spring Comes Earlier This Year', and 'Librarian to Retire After Half a Century'. I wonder if the librarian concerned will thank whoever wrote that, but I don't bother reading the article to find out. These things are probably of vital importance to the people who live here, but this is hardly the Boston Globe, and I put down the newspaper, and resort to my phone, checking on things of more national significance, which keep me occupied until my breakfast arrives.

The eggs are cooked to perfection, as is the bacon, and I don't think I've ever tasted home fries quite this good.

It doesn't take me long to clear my plate and as the guy comes to remove it, in between serving a few other people who've arrived in the meantime, I ask him to pass on my thanks to the chef.

"I'll do that," he says with a smile, and I finish my coffee before getting up and returning to my room.

I check my watch, seeing that it's still only eight-thirty, which makes it a little early for house calls, so I sit in one of the chairs and open my briefcase, pulling out the file I put in here yesterday morning before I left the office. It's plain blue, and anonymous, but I flip it open and sit back, reading the details of the place I'm going to be visiting.

It's an apple orchard on the outskirts of the town, run by a single woman called Peony Hart. I can't help thinking what a pretty name that is, although I know it won't help my negotiations if I think of this woman in personal terms. This is business… nothing more, nothing less.

My researchers have done their homework, discovering that she's twenty-six years old, and has just inherited the farm from her grandmother, who died in January.

I lower the file, unable to stop myself from imagining how that felt. I've got first-hand experience of it, having inherited my company from my father last spring. Of course, that was a much bigger affair than an apple orchard. I was older, too, and had been Dad's understudy for years. But that didn't make the transition any easier.

Business or not, I'm going to have to tread carefully with Peony Hart. Although studying the farm's accounts, I can't imagine she'll find my offer unwelcome. It'll solve a lot of problems for her, and doubtless remove a great deal of stress from her life, at a time when I imagine she's feeling the pressure.

I've managed to kill half an hour, and feel like at least I've got a better idea of what I'm up against, although I can't help feeling a little sad that the deal will probably do itself. I've always been so good at talking people round, and the idea that Peony Hart is probably going to bite my hand off to sign on the dotted is a little disappointing. Even so, I put away the file, close up my briefcase and grab my car keys, heading for the door.

Outside, it's chilly but sunny, and I make my way around the side of the hotel to my car, climbing in and starting the engine. I open the briefcase again, finding the address, and tapping it into the Sat/Nav, which says it'll take seven minutes to reach my destination, and that I need to turn right onto the highway. I do as I'm told, passing along Main Street, as the navigation device instructs me, and driving out of the town itself. There are some industrial units on my right, and then the Sat/Nav warns me I'm going to need to turn left in two hundred yards. I can already see the turning, and slow down to take it, noting a sign which reads 'Hart's Creek Apple Orchard' with the words 'Home-made Cider for sale' underneath. At least I know I'm in the right place and I enter onto a narrow track with fencing on either side. Beyond the fence, I can see apple trees, their leaves just coming out, and although my knowledge of such things is fairly limited, I have to smile. This is nothing like the commercial scale of orchard I'd been expecting. Rather than being planted in rows, the trees seem to be much more haphazard, like you'd find in someone's backyard… although there are a lot of them, stretching for as far as I can see.

The track is dusty and dead straight, and ahead of me, there's a large house, surrounded by smaller barns and buildings. The house itself is formed in an L-shape, with steps up to a porch at the front, a door in the center, and windows on either side. In front of the one on the left is a rocking chair that looks a little forlorn… kinda like the house. It's clad with wooden panels, which have been painted in a pale blue, although it's badly chipped and I can see, even from here, that the roof tiles could use some work.

The accounts weren't lying. This place is on its way out, and I shake my head, wishing again that I'd found a better deal on which to re-invigorate my negotiating skills. Peony Hart would be mad to say 'no' to an offer like mine.

I pull up alongside the fence, noticing a compact tractor, parked inside the 'L' of the house. It isn't in much better condition than the buildings surrounding it… or the truck that's parked over by one of the barns. The entire place has seen better days… not that I care. I'll be demolishing the buildings in no time at all. Although I think a strong gust of wind could easily do the job for me.

I grab my briefcase, stepping out of the car, and that's when I see her.

She's standing, staring at me, her hair blowing wildly in the wind, her porcelain clear skin pinking, reminding me of last night.

My heart does a weird stop-start in my chest, and my cock hardens in an instant, even though all I'm doing is looking at her… and thinking about the fact that this woman's panties are burning a hole in my pocket.

I smile, unable to help myself, but rather than smiling back, her eyes drop to my tie… the one I bound her with last night, and as I watch the blush creep up her cheeks, I realize she's embarrassed. That's not my fault, though. Not really. I'm here on business, so it's natural for me to wear a tie, and although I brought a second one, I spilled coffee over it when I stopped on my drive up here. It was stained, so I asked someone at the hotel to launder it yesterday, on my arrival. That left me with just this one, and while I could take it off, she might think I'm embarrassed, too… and I'm not.

Not that I'd seriously expected to see her again, but I guess I hoped that, if I managed to track her down, or our paths should cross, she might at least be pleased to see me.

Except it seems she isn't, judging by the look on her face.

I'd say confusion was competing with her embarrassment, and neither was coming out on top right now.

That leaves me with two options.

I can either be completely open about what we did last night, or I can pretend it didn't happen. To be honest, hell is going to have to freeze over before I can do that, and while I don't think I'm capable of being totally up front with her about what she did to me, and how she made me feel, I think it's best if we face up to it, like adults.

I step away from my car, and walk over to her, letting my eyes roam downward over her body, my cock reminding me of what a dumb idea that is as it hardens to painful proportions the moment I take in the sight of her skin-tight jeans. They're similar to the ones she was wearing last night, although these are a shade lighter, with a tear slashed right across the left knee. Her feet are encased in thick-soled boots, caked in mud, and I recall her sexy black heels from last night… the contrast making me smile. She's also got on a chunky pale gray sweater, which does absolutely nothing to hide her perfect figure, and I switch my briefcase from my right hand to my left, so I can fasten my jacket, in the hope it'll hide my erection. No matter how turned on I am, there are things that need to be said, and I don't want to distract her, even if she's distracting the fuck out of me, just standing there.

I'm right in front of her, gazing down into her upturned face, longing to run my fingers through that wild hair, and I know I need to say something. 'Hello' feels inadequate, but even I'm not prepared for the words that spring out of my mouth.

"Why did you leave?"

I guess it's a fair question, considering I woke up to an empty bed this morning, but is that really how I want to start this conversation?

She stares up at me, her blush deepening, and ignoring my question, she tilts her head and says, "How did you find me?"

"I didn't. I was coming here anyway. You're the reason I'm in Hart's Creek."

"I am?"

I pull out my card from my inside pocket, handing it over. She takes it, studying it closely, and then looks up at me. "Ryan Andrews?"

"Yes."

I wonder if she's been thinking about my name as much as I've been thinking about hers.

"Andrews and Son Properties?"

"Yes."

The logo is right above my name, and although I'm a little put out that she didn't say anything about that, or about last night, I'm even more disappointed when she holds out the card to me, wanting to give it back. There's no way I'm taking it, and after a few seconds, she puts it in her back pocket and says, "Whatever you're selling, I'm not buying."

Did last night mean nothing to you?

"I'm not here to sell, I'm here to buy."

She stares at me, frowning. "Apples?"

I smile. "No. Real estate." I look around, waving my arm. "You seem to have quite a lot of it."

"I do. Forty acres, all told."

I already know that. It's in the report in my briefcase, but I nod my head, like it's news to me. "Forty acres?"

"Yes. And it's not for sale."

I move a little closer, her eyes widening. "Don't be so hasty."

"I'm not. I'm just telling you, my farm isn't for sale… not at any price."

Man, she's stubborn.

I think I can wave goodbye to any hope I might have had that she'd be pleased to see me. She's glaring at me now, her eyes on fire, and although that's probably bad for business, it makes me want her… more than ever.

Chapter Five

Peony

This has got to be the most humiliating experience of my life.

I've barely stopped blushing since he got out of his car, although it seems my embarrassment is the least of my problems…

How am I supposed to concentrate when my body's still humming from everything he did to me last night… and from the orgasm I gave myself in the shower this morning, when all I could think about was how a perfect stranger had made me come so hard? How am I supposed to think straight when that same perfect stranger is standing right in front of me, looking even sexier than I remember, in his designer suit, wearing the tie he used to bind my wrists to his bed, while he fucked me senseless?

It's impossible.

Although I guess I ought to look on the bright side. He obviously hasn't found my panties yet. If he had, I imagine he'd have handed them over and completed my humiliation, while he asked me why I left him.

Is it so hard to work that out? Can't he see I'm not the kind of girl who sleeps around? Is it beyond his imagination to understand that I couldn't face him after everything we'd done?

I guess it must be.

Ryan – as I now know him to be called – steps a little closer. He's close enough that I can smell his body wash, and I struggle to breathe, overwhelmed by him and that divine, intense scent, not to mention the way he's staring at me with those dark brown eyes. The same eyes that have seen me naked, and watched me come…

"Any price?"

"Yes. I mean, no." I can't remember what I mean now, he's got me so flustered. "My farm's not for sale," I repeat, just to be sure he understands.

"Are you saying that because of what happened last night?"

His voice is low, husky, and too sexy for words, but I'm damned if I'm going to let him get to me. I step back, putting some necessary space between us, and I stare up at him. He's not playing fair, coming here, looking this good.

"No. We had sex. So what?" I raise my voice a little as I put my hands on my hips. "That doesn't mean I'm gonna sell you my farm, no matter how great it was." I look him up and down, wondering what possessed me to say that, although my mouth runs away with me again before my brain can catch up. "Your cock might be amazing, Ryan, but believe me, it's not *that* amazing."

I think that was supposed to make me sound sassy, but it would have been far better left unsaid… especially as the latter part isn't even true. His cock is amazing. Period. It's a thing of beauty, the stuff of dreams… of fantasies. But why did I have to say that to his face?

I can feel my cheeks heating, and if running were an option, I'd do it. But I can't. I have to face this out, and I glare up at him, surprised by his frown. I'd have expected a smirk from him, at the very least. He shakes his head, moving closer again.

"Thanks for the compliment… I think. But I'm a little confused."

"You are?"

"Yes."

"Why?"

"Because you said we had sex."

Now I'm the one who's confused. "I know. Don't you remember it?"

"Of course I do. But is that all you thought it was?"

"Why? What else did you think we were doing?"

He shrugs his shoulders. "It doesn't matter."

The breeze catches my hair and I pull it back from my face. "It matters to me."

"It really doesn't. If that's what you wanna call it, go ahead."

I'm not sure what else it can be called. We had sex. Wild, crazy, breathtaking, life-changing, spectacular sex. Fortunately, I keep my mouth closed this time, rather than saying any of that aloud, and instead, I let out a sigh of frustration. "Okay, so having had sex with me, and arrived at my farm unannounced, aren't you at least gonna ask my name?"

He smiles now, which makes my stomach flutter, damn him.

"I already know your name."

"How? I didn't tell you." I remember every second of what we did last night and I know my name never crossed my lips. Not once. I also know how embarrassed I felt this morning when I woke up and realized what we'd done, without even knowing each other's initials.

"I told you. You're the reason I'm in town. I was coming here anyway this morning, so I know you're Peony Hart." He smiles again, his eyes sparkling this time, in a way that drowns my treacherous pussy. "It's a pretty name, by the way."

Damp panties or not, I can see his game, and I shake my head. "Oh, please…" I turn away, but he grabs my arm, pulling me back, his body hard against mine. I can feel his arousal and I look up, seeing a flash of something in his eyes. It looks like anger, but how can that be, when he's so hard... so turned on?

"What does that mean?" he growls.

I don't feel intimidated or scared. I know he won't hurt me, like I know I'll take my next breath... like I knew last night would be incredible, even before he closed his bedroom door, even before he led me from the bar, I think. It would be incredible now, too, if I let my guard down... if I leaned in to him just a little further, or reached up and touched his cheek... showed any sign of intimacy, or longing.

I can't, though, no matter how much I crave him. Because he wants to take my home... my livelihood... my life.

"It means you want something from me. You want my farm. I don't know why, but you do, and you think that saying something nice is gonna get it for you."

"No," he says, letting go of my arm, although he doesn't move away and neither do I. I can't. I'm too breathless with need to do anything. "That's not how I operate."

"Oh? Really?"

He narrows his eyes. "Yes. Really. How was I supposed to know that the beautiful woman I noticed the moment she walked into the bar last night was Peony Hart? All I knew was that I couldn't take my eyes off of you... that I had to have you... that I wouldn't rest until I had. But I didn't know your name, or that you were my reason for driving up here, any more than you knew who I was. Please don't assume I'm the kind of guy who'd use sex to close a deal, or that I had any ulterior motive in doing what I did, because I didn't. Last night was entirely about pleasure, not business... and the only reason I'm saying I like your name, is because I do."

I don't know how to reply to that. I hadn't been expecting such sincerity from him, and rather than say anything that might give him the opportunity for further candor, I turn away and simply mumble, "I'm busy," moving back to the tractor, and bending over to raise the mower attachment to the coupling.

As usual, it's a struggle. The damn thing is so heavy and cumbersome, and as I'm about to attach it, I drop it, cursing under my breath as it clatters to the ground.

"Let me."

I feel the heat of his body again, right behind me this time, his hand reaching between me and the tractor as he lifts the mower attachment with ease. I could argue with him that I can manage… except I clearly can't, and I'm relieved to have his help. Stepping back to give him space, I trip over his briefcase, and as I stumble, he lets go of the mower, catching me before I fall.

"Are you okay?"

"I'm fine."

"Sorry. I should have warned you I'd put my case down."

"It was my fault for not looking where I was going."

He stares down at me, and for a moment, the air between us crackles with tension. It's entirely sexual, our bodies drawn together, just like they were last night. It doesn't help that he's still got his arm around me, or that his lips are only inches away, and that I can remember how it felt when he crushed them to mine.

"I—I should probably get on with connecting your mower to your tractor," he says, surprising me with his stammer. "As long as you're sure you're okay?"

I nod my head, and as he steps away, I murmur, "Thank you."

He turns back, smiling, and then concentrates on the job in hand, although he doesn't get a lot further than I did.

"The mower isn't aligned with the tractor," he says.

"Shall I move it? The tractor, I mean. I can line it up better."

"No, it's fine. I'll just move the mower attachment instead." He pushes it back, his muscles flexing through the fabric of his suit.

"You'll get dirty."

"No, I won't."

With very little effort, he maneuvers the machine into place and, just as easily, couples it to the rear of the tractor.

Once he's done, he turns around, facing me again.

"If what I said about your name just now sounded insincere, then I apologize."

"It's okay."

"I realize that last night complicates things, but…"

I hold up my hand, and he stops talking. "I think the less we say about last night, the better, don't you?" *Especially in the context of you coming here to buy my farm from under me.* Because that's what he's here for, regardless of everything else.

"Really? That's how you feel about it? Even though the sex was great and my cock was amazing?"

The smirk I'd been expecting earlier is there now, and I wish I'd kept my mouth shut.

"Yes." I can't deny a word he's just said. What would be the point? "You might be in the habit of having one-night stands, but I'm not."

He flinches, and I wish I hadn't said that, either. It was hurtful and ungracious. It hit home, too. His brow furrows before he tips his head to the right, frowning down at me.

"You could've fooled me."

Wow… I hadn't expected that. For someone who was so concerned for my safety only a few minutes ago, and who just held me in his arms looking like he could happily devour me for the second time in twelve hours, that seems a bit below the belt.

"What do you mean by that?"

"Simply that, even if you're not in the habit of sleeping with strangers, I didn't have to force you into it. I didn't have to drag you to my bed, Peony. You came willingly… several times, if I remember rightly." He moves closer, breathing hard, and lowers his voice, whispering, "You wanted me, so don't deny it… to me, or yourself. You wanted my cock, just as much as I wanted to bury it inside you. Like I told you, there was no ulterior motive. I didn't lose myself in you in the hope it would sway your decision to sell your farm to me."

Lose himself? Did he really just say that?

"Then why did you?"

"I would have thought that was obvious."

Not to me. I stare at him, hoping for more of an explanation. He's not about to offer it, though and, after just a second or two, he turns, walking away, and picks up his briefcase without breaking his stride.

That was annoyingly smooth of him.

My body is on fire, partly with anger, but mostly with need, because I know what he can do to me. I know he's right, too. I knew exactly what I was doing last night, and hearing what it meant to him, and how much he wanted me, is breathtaking. It wasn't just hearing it, either. I could see it, too. There was something in his eyes when he said those words, about burying himself inside me… about losing himself. It made me want to ask for more, to beg for more… just like I did last night.

It's too late now, though. He's already in his car, the tires kicking up dirt as he turns it around and drives away.

I push my hair back from my face again, and lean against the tractor, recalling how he coupled the mower so easily, how his muscles flexed and rippled as he moved, reminding me of how good he looked last night.

"Oh, stop it."

I'm being superficial.

So what if he looks good both with and without clothes? So what if he has an amazing cock, and a smile that can melt my panties? It's of no significance to me.

None of that matters.

What matters is that he's here to buy my farm.

And I'm not selling.

I push myself off of the tractor and wander into the house. The mowing can wait for a while. I need coffee first… and I need to calm down.

I pour myself a cup and sit at the table, shaking my head and leaning my chin on my upturned hand. I'm not sure that could have gone any worse. Obviously, I wasn't expecting him to come here. I wasn't expecting the man who made all my sexual fantasies into a reality, to arrive at my farm and tell me he wanted to buy it. But is that any excuse for the way I reacted? Is that a valid reason for being so rude?

Embarrassment got the better of my manners; there's no doubting that. I was angry with him. Not just for who he is and what he does, but for bringing up our one-night stand in his first sentence. He could have been more subtle, couldn't he?

Of course he could. Although based on last night, I guess subtlety isn't his strong suit.

What's getting to me more now, though, is the fact that, having dealt with that so badly, I know our one-night stand is all we're ever going to have.

I won't deny I'm attracted to him. Who wouldn't be? Except there's no point in thinking like that, or in wondering what it might be like for him to lose himself inside me all over again, because it's never going to happen.

It'll be a cold day in hell before I sell my farm to him, which means we're on opposite sides now. We want different things, and I can't see either of us giving up without a fight.

In which case, bring it on.

Because the sooner he realizes he's lost, the quicker he'll leave, and then I can put this whole sorry episode behind me.

At least I can, once I've stopped my body from throbbing with need for him…

Chapter Six

Ryan

I pace my bedroom floor for the fiftieth time since I got back here, moving toward the window, sighing and turning to pace in the other direction, as I push my fingers back through my hair.

Could that have gone any worse?

Why did I have to open my conversation with Peony by asking why she'd left me this morning? It wasn't the most sensitive thing to say, was it? Although it didn't escape my notice that she didn't answer me. I guess that was probably because she was embarrassed. How do I know that? The cute blush on her cheeks gave it away, and I could have kicked myself for not just introducing myself, and avoiding the topic.

Except I didn't want to avoid it.

I wanted to talk about it. I wanted to re-live it, to hold her, to kiss her, to understand why I'd woken to an empty bed, after the most magical night of my life.

Only she didn't.

She didn't want to talk about it at all. Not because it hadn't been magical for her, too. Because it had. And that's not me being big-headed. She told me so herself. Her precise words were that the sex was 'great', and that my cock had been 'amazing', although she qualified that last comment by saying it hadn't been *that* amazing. At the time, she was trying to prove to me I couldn't use sex to persuade her to sell me her farm, no matter how good it was. It was a kind of negative compliment… I think. I was confused by it all. I still am. Hence the pacing.

I guess my confusion wasn't helped by the way she was talking. She kept referring to what we'd done as 'sex', when to me, it had been so much more. Couldn't she see that? Couldn't she see it was something special… something different?

Obviously not. At least, it wasn't for her, no matter what it meant to me.

That became even clearer when she accused me of paying her a compliment, just to sweeten the deal. All I'd said was that I liked her name, but she practically accused me of sleeping with her just to get her to sign on the dotted line.

Okay, so with hindsight, she didn't actually say that, but I felt the implication. I was angry. I grabbed her, even though I knew I shouldn't have done… especially as the net result of my actions was that I pulled her body hard against mine, making it impossible to concentrate on anything other than my burning need to take her. Her breasts were crushed against my chest, her hips and thighs pressed to mine, and I knew she had to be able to feel my erection. She didn't say a word, but she didn't pull back, either… not even when I let go of her arm, although she seemed surprised by my answers. I don't think she'd expected me to reveal how much I'd wanted her. I hadn't expected that myself, but the words just poured out of me in a rush, and although I thought she might come back at me with some kind of snarky remark, all she did was to say that she was busy.

Had I gotten under her skin?

I hoped so, but only in a good way… only in a way that might make her realize how much last night had meant to me.

She made a complete mess of trying to attach the mower to the back of the tractor then, and it was impossible for me to stand by and watch her struggle, which was why I stepped in and did it for her. That was when she nearly fell over my briefcase, which I'd stupidly left directly behind her, not thinking she'd have to step back out of my way. I caught her before she fell, and for a few brief moments, it was as though all our differences were forgotten, like she wanted me as much as I wanted her. I wondered for a second or two about kissing her, just to dispel the sexual tension that was sucking all the air out from between us. She was staring at my lips, breathing hard, and I was so tempted to taste her again… except I kept wondering if she'd push me away. I didn't think I could handle the rejection. So I said I ought to get on with connecting the mower to the tractor, in the vain hope she might tell me not to… and beg me to kiss her instead.

She didn't… obviously. She just said 'thank you', which was better than the accusations she'd been hurling, but not at all what I needed to hear from her. What I needed to hear was a plea of, 'fuck me', in that same urgent voice she'd used last night… except I think hell might have to freeze over before that happens again.

Especially after I tried to apologize… not for leaving my briefcase in the way, but for any insincerity she might have felt was in my compliment, and for the awkwardness of having slept together. I wasn't saying I regretted any of it, just that it made things difficult. Her response to that was the last thing I wanted to hear, and I think her words are going to haunt me for a very long time… 'I think the less we say about last night, the better, don't you?'

Was she serious?

It seemed so, and while she didn't deny that the sex had been great, or my cock amazing, she threw out an insult about me being more accustomed to one-night stands than her.

I imagine that's perfectly true, but why did she have to say it? Why did she have to remind me of my past, when all I wanted to think about was a future… with her? I think it was the realization that it had meant so little to her – that it was just sex, just a one-night stand – that made me react so badly, and I'm ashamed now of what I said.

Not only did I remind her she'd been a very willing participant in everything we'd done together, but I let slip how much it had meant to me. I'd done that earlier, in a way, when I'd explained how I'd felt when I saw her walk into the bar… how I'd felt like I had to have her. But this was different. Saying that I'd lost myself in her was something else, and I don't know what possessed me to put that out there.

I shake my head, recalling how I drove away at that point, unwilling to continue our conversation, just in case I said something even more personal… like 'I love you'.

I stop pacing, my body chilling.

Love?

Who the fuck said anything about love?

I was thinking about sex, wasn't I? Admittedly, the best sex I've ever had in my life – or am ever likely to have, for that matter – but sex, nonetheless.

Not love.

Definitely not love.

I rub my hands down my face.

Except it wasn't just sex, was it?

That was the crux of the entire problem. It was what riled me so much. Peony had called it sex. 'We had sex.' Those were her words, and although I knew that was what we'd done, it wasn't enough of a word to describe what it had meant. Not to me. I'd thought of it as making love… a concept I'd never experienced before, but which I knew I wanted again, and even if that concept involves that same four letter word, I can't deny it.

What we had wasn't just sex, or fucking, it was making love.

The problem is, she also said 'So what?', so no matter how much it meant to me, it obviously didn't mean as much to her. Which is why she called it 'sex', I guess.

I sit down, sick of pacing, and try to forget about sex, and making love, and instead I focus on what I'm going to do with the rest of my day.

I'd planned to spend it negotiating with Peony, but that's clearly not going to happen, and there's no way I'm going back to Boston yet. Gabe would never let me live it down. He was convinced I'd lost my touch. That was why he was so dubious about me coming up here to clinch this deal, and maybe he was right. Maybe I should have left it to Adrian.

I shudder at the thought of him negotiating with Peony, though. He has a ruthless way of going about things, and I know she'd have felt intimidated by him.

No… I did the right thing in coming myself. Even if I am screwing it up royally.

Let's face it, I haven't even made her an offer yet.

Although how I'm going to do that when I'll be struggling to persuade Peony to give me the time of day now, I don't know.

If only we hadn't slept together…

"Don't be ridiculous," I say aloud to the empty room.

I can't regret what we did, no matter what it costs me in terms of this deal, or how confused she's got me.

I get up again, finding it hard to settle, and make myself a coffee. It's not as nice as the coffee they serve in the dining room downstairs, but I'm not in the mood for people… other than Peony.

As I sit on one of the chairs, my cup in hand, I wonder about ordering lunch in my room… until I remember I don't eat lunch.

"What's wrong with me?"

I haven't eaten lunch for years. That's why I've always placed so much emphasis on breakfast. So, why would I be thinking about food? And why am I talking to myself?

Because I'm feeling out of sorts, I guess.

In all my life, I don't think I've ever handled a situation so badly as I did this morning's. I'm renowned for being cool and calm in just about any set of circumstances, and this morning, I blew it. I was the polar opposite of cool and calm, although, in my defense, I've never let anyone get to me like Peony has.

I've strayed into unknown territory.

But was that a good enough reason for walking away?

I put down my cup and sit forward.

Of course it wasn't. Aside from the fact that I never walk away from a deal, I can't walk away from Peony.

And that means I need to go back and face her again...

Only this time, I need to get it right.

Because it's about more than her farm. It's about more than the deal.

I can shy away from the word as much as I like, but I know I'm in love with her, just like I know my own name – and hers now – and that means I've got to negotiate the deal of a lifetime.

It's the deal for our future.

Mine and Peony's.

We were good together. We were the best. And deep down, she knows that too. I'm not being arrogant about this. I'm really not. If I wasn't here to buy her farm, I think we could have found a way to overcome her embarrassment about last night... maybe even to laugh about it. Because she wanted me just as much as I wanted her. I could feel it just now, even while she was fighting it... and she was fighting it. I was all too aware of the battle raging inside her.

All I need to do is drive out there, stay calm and work things out with her... because this time it matters. More than ever.

I've waited until just after three before setting off for Peony's farm again. I'd like to say I've used the time wisely, but in reality, all I've done is clock-watch, drink bad coffee, and pretend to work. Actual work is impossible when I'm this distracted, but I've made a good show of reading reports on my laptop… although nothing much has sunk in, and if anyone were to ask about the content, I'd struggle to explain any of it.

Still, that's not the point.

The point is, I'm on my way back to Peony's farm, hoping I've given her enough time to finish mowing the grass, and that we can talk.

I park in the same place as I did this morning and, although there's no sign of her, the tractor is parked around the side of the house, so I guess that means she must be here somewhere.

I get out, bringing my briefcase with me, and walk up the steps to the front door, knocking on it twice, and waiting. The paintwork is in really poor condition, the old wood exposed to the elements, and I wonder how this place survived the winter… and how Peony did, for that matter.

She pulls open the door, making me jump, and I stare down at her, noting that she's still wearing those sexy torn jeans and her gray sweater, although she's removed her boots, revealing thick, cream-colored socks. There's a blush on her cheeks already, which doesn't augur well, and she leans against the door frame, making it clear she's got no intention of inviting me in.

I put down my briefcase, accepting that unspoken fact, and she folds her arms across her chest. That action has the unfortunate effect of pushing up her breasts, which is very distracting, and my cock hardens instantly. I wish I'd fastened my jacket, although I can't do it now. It would be too obvious.

Instead, I keep my eyes fixed on hers, taking a breath to speak, just as she opens her mouth.

"Why are you here?"

That's not the most friendly of greetings, but I expected it, or something like it.

"Because I want to talk to you. I feel like we got off on the wrong foot."

"When? Last night, or this morning?"

"This morning." It's tempting to add 'of course', but I don't. I'm staying calm… or trying to. I'm also trying to persuade her I'm not the bad guy here, and to get her to understand what she means to me, and that this isn't just about her farm, even though that's ostensibly why I'm here. "There was nothing 'wrong' about last night. Not as far as I'm concerned."

Her blush deepens, and she lowers her eyes, although I'm not sure that helps because they fasten straight on to my tie, and all the memories that clearly evokes. Her embarrassment is almost overwhelming and I long to step forward, to hold her, and tell her it's okay… that she's got no need to feel like this. I can't understand why she's so obviously beating herself up over what happened… especially not now we've found each other again, and can talk it through. Or we could, if she'd just admit how much she enjoyed being with me. But I can't say any of that, can I? I can't tell her that being with her is the best thing that's ever happened to me, that finding her is the answer to my prayers… that standing here before her is like a dream come true.

All I can do is to put her at ease… just a little.

"Can we talk?" I ask, softening my voice, and she raises her head again, looking into my eyes.

"What about?"

I smile, relieved that she hasn't dismissed me out of hand. "Well… talking about last night seems to make me say things that embarrass you – even though they shouldn't – so why don't we discuss my offer?"

"If you're talking about your offer for my farm, I'd like to point out that you haven't made me one yet."

"No, I haven't. But I'd like to."

She shakes her head, sighing heavily. "There's no point, Ryan. I've already told you, my farm isn't for sale, and while I don't mean to be rude, I…"

"Really?" I interrupt her before she says something offensive that I think we might both regret. "I know what you're like when you're being accommodating…" I pause, noting the blush on her cheeks again.

"I thought we agreed to forget about that."

"When?" I frown down at her. "When did we agree that?"

"This morning."

"You didn't say forget about it. You said you thought it was best if we didn't talk about it. They're two entirely different things. One of them is no fun at all, although as I just said, I'll do it to avoid you unnecessary embarrassment."

"And the other?" she says, looking up at me, with what I'd be prepared to swear is a twinkle in her eyes.

"Oh… that's impossible. There's no way I can forget what we did." She sucks in a sharp breath, and it takes all my willpower not to reach out and pull her into my arms… to capture her face, tip it back and kiss her. Hard. "That's not what you want, though, is it?"

"W—What?" She's struggling to speak and to breathe.

I move just a little closer, leaning in. "You don't want to forget about it either, do you?"

She stares up at me, neither of us blinking, and then she swallows hard. "Y—You said you wouldn't talk about it."

"I know." I step back again. "So, about my offer…"

She holds up a hand, although I notice it's shaking.

"I've already said, there's no point."

"You're telling me you don't even want to listen to what I'm offering? You're not interested in hearing how much I'm willing to pay for your land?"

"No. Like I said – repeatedly – it's not for sale."

I step back and turn slightly, looking around for emphasis. "But you're on your own here. It must be hard work."

She comes outside, joining me on the porch, although rather than looking around at her farm, she gazes up at me, her eyes narrowing. "How do you know I'm on my own?"

"Because I do my research… and besides, you told me last night, you don't have a husband, or a boyfriend."

"I might employ someone…" Her voice fades as I shake my head, moving around in front of her.

"Not according to my researchers. So, unless the orchard fairies have decided to step up and help with spraying, and mowing, and harvesting, not to mention all the administration that goes with running a place like this, I'm gonna hazard a guess you're doing it all by yourself. I'm also gonna guess you don't get a lot of time to just kick back and enjoy yourself."

"I manage." She raises her chin defiantly, and I lower my head, so our lips are almost touching. I can feel her breath on my cheek, and I hold her gaze.

"I noticed."

She blushes again. "Let's get one thing straight… like I said earlier, I don't make a habit of… of doing… of doing what we did last night."

"I'm glad to hear it. Not that I'm judging, you understand."

"Good."

I'm so tempted to ask if she'd consider doing it again, but I'm not sure how she'd react… and besides, over the last few minutes, while we've been stood here, so close I could reach out and touch, I've realized that I like flirting with her. It's more fun than having sex with anyone else I've ever met, and if that's what it's going to take to convince her I'm not the man she thinks I am, then I'll do it… and I'll enjoy it, too.

"Now, getting back to my offer…" I say with my most wicked of smiles.

She shakes her head, although I notice her eyes are drawn to my lips. "Which part of 'my farm isn't for sale' do you not understand?"

I tilt my head, like I'm giving that some thought. "Any of it, really. It doesn't make sense."

"It does to me."

"Care to explain why?"

"No. I don't have to explain myself to you."

She squares her shoulders, and I sense we're veering into difficult territory again. If I'm going to win her over in the long term, I think it's best to quit while I'm vaguely ahead in the short term.

I step back, putting some space between us. "Fair enough."

She frowns, as though she doesn't understand my move, or know how to make hers. "I—I'm sorry you've wasted your time coming out here."

I bend, picking up my briefcase and walk down the steps, taking them sideways, so I can keep my eyes fixed on hers. At the bottom, I turn, facing her, and walk backwards towards my car, hoping to God I don't trip and fall on my ass.

"My time wasn't wasted, Peony."

"Oh?"

"I got to see you, and that's always time well spent."

She blushes, yet again, and as I reach my car and get inside, I can't help noticing that she's still staring, even though the tinted windows mean she won't be able to see me. I'm staring back, wondering if she's thinking that I only said all that so she'll come around to my way of thinking and speak to me about my offer... and ultimately sell me her farm. I know it's a possibility she'll assume I'm that cynical, even though I'm not.

She doesn't realize this is about her. Even my offer for her farm is about her now.

It's about protecting her and doing what's right, because I love her, and I'll do whatever it takes to keep her safe.

Chapter Seven

Peony

It's been two days since Ryan drove away, in a much more calm way than he did the time before that, and I'll admit, I watched his car until the moment it disappeared from sight.

I even stood on the porch for a while afterwards, wondering if he'd change his mind and come back.

He didn't.

Why would he?

Just because I wanted him to?

Of course not. And besides, how would he have known that? I never gave him a hint that I wanted him, or how much… although, looking back, I wonder if he knew. He seemed to sometimes, with the way he looked at me, the way his eyes sparkled and his lips twitched upwards as he spoke. He reminded me that afternoon of the man who'd flirted with me about children, and husbands, and dogs, and then whisked me away to his bedroom.

Still… that was Wednesday. Today is Friday, and I haven't seen or heard from him since. I'm feeling torn between relief that he's given up in his pursuit of my farm and has left town for good… and disappointment that he didn't mean what he said. Because he said a lot, and while some of it was about the farm, quite a lot of it was about us.

Us?

What am I thinking? There is no 'us'.

No matter how turned on I was by seeing him again… which I was.

It wasn't just about seeing him, either. It was about flirting with him. That's what we were doing, and I think we both knew it, although I'm not sure that him flirting with me made much sense.

He'd already taken me to bed, and I'd made that easy enough for him, so why would he flirt with me?

I wasn't about to ask, and before I could work out if it meant anything, he left.

I was surprised he gave in so easily, and even if I was confused, wondering about the flirting, and the farm, and whether I wanted him to go, or stay, his parting shot still took my breath away. When I apologized for his time having been wasted, he said that it hadn't been… because he'd been able to see me again.

I wished then that he'd come back, take me in his arms and kiss me, but he didn't. He drove away, and although it took me a while, that was when I realized it had just been a line.

He can't have meant it. Or, if he did, he'd only have said it, so I'd listen to his offer.

I don't like to think of him playing me like that, or that he'd flirt with me for the sake of his business, but it makes more sense than anything else. That thought has been plaguing me over the last two days. I liked the idea of him flirting with me for pleasure, but I keep coming back to the fact that he was here to do a deal, and that he's probably used to employing whatever means are necessary to get what he wants…

I shake my head

What's the matter with me?

Why am I still thinking about him? Even if I'm not someone who has sex with strangers, there's no need for me to make such a drama about what happened. I'm sure he's forgotten all about me already.

Besides, I've got other things to think about.

Ryan was right. It's hard running a farm by yourself, and I keep being reminded that I am by myself… not just because I'm so tired, but also because my accounts need doing.

Desperately.

It was something that Granny always used to take care of. Even when she couldn't manage much of the physical work anymore, she still handled the book work. I think that was mostly because she knew I don't have a head for figures, and she knew that to let me loose on them would be dangerous. As it stands, with invoices backing up behind me, and the bank breathing down my neck, I need to decide what I'm going to do. Should I look at them myself, or employ someone else to do it for me?

I know I don't have very much money, but getting someone professional to do the job seems like the best idea. I'll only make things worse if I try to do something I'm really not good at… especially when that 'something' is as important as the accounts.

With that in mind, I've made an appointment this afternoon to see James Greenwood. He's one half of Hart's Creek's only firm of accountants, the other half being Owen Clayton… and while I'd have rather seen Owen, James was the only one with an appointment this week. Don't get me wrong, I've got nothing against James Greenwood. It's just that Owen is closer in age to me, and I feel we'll probably speak the same language. I'm less certain what to expect with James, and I'm a little nervous about our meeting, although I'm grateful he's agreed to let me have a half hour of his time, free of charge.

Speaking of which, I'd better be leaving, because I imagine he's the kind of man who appreciates punctuality, if nothing else, and I'm due to see him in ten minutes.

My journey into town is uneventful and I park up outside the drugstore, the offices of 'Greenwood and Clayton' being on the two floors above. As I get out, closing the door, I can't help glancing over toward the hotel, my heart sinking when I see there's no sign of Ryan's black Mercedes. I don't know why I'm surprised by that. I knew he'd gone home already, no doubt to move on to the next deal… and the next woman.

That thought hurts more than I would have expected, but I square my shoulders and give myself a mental telling off. Like I said to him… we had sex. So what?

The fact that I still ache for him means nothing… and even if it does, it'll pass.

I've got more important things to worry about.

I turn, crossing the sidewalk, and push the button on the intercom at the side of the door to the right of the drugstore. While I wait for someone to reply, I glance down at myself, wondering if I should have dressed up a little more. Okay, so I've put my hair up, taming it for once, but that's about it. My jeans are still the torn pair I've been wearing for the last three days, and my sweater is the navy blue one Granny gave me a couple of years ago. It's comfortable, but I'm not sure it's suitable for a meeting with an accountant.

Still… it's too late now.

"Hello?" I hear a disjointed voice over the intercom and lean in.

"Hi. It's Peony Hart. I've got an appointment with James Greenwood."

"Oh, yes. Come on up."

I hear the door click and push on it, going inside and climbing up the narrow staircase ahead of me. At the top, I turn to my left, because there's nowhere else to go, and enter a hallway that leads to the back of the building. The first door I come to is marked with a sign that says 'Reception', and I open it, poking my head around.

Inside, behind a desk near the window, is Sylvia McQueen. She's worked here as a secretary for as long as I can remember, and she looks up at me over the top of her half-moon glasses, with a smile on her face.

"Why, Peony… come on in."

I open the door more fully and enter the small room, which houses her desk, three filing cabinets, and four chairs, all placed along the wall behind the door. The computer on her desk looks ancient, even by my standards, and I wonder for a moment whether that's because her bosses see upgrading computer hardware as a waste of money.

She stands now, stepping out from behind her desk, and I feel even more under-dressed, noting her smart skirt and blouse, and her tidy steel-gray hair.

"How are you?" she asks.

"I'm fine."

I know that what she really means is, 'how have you been getting along since your grandmother died?' and if I were being honest, the answer wouldn't be 'fine' at all. But what can I say? People don't always want to hear the truth.

"I'll let Mr. Greenwood know you're here," she says, nodding toward the chairs, and I sit down on the second one in, while she leaves the room.

I'm suddenly nervous, although I don't know why. I've known James Greenwood all my life, like most people in Hart's Creek, and although my family have never had any dealings with him, I've got nothing to feel scared about.

I'm not sure it's fear that's coursing through me, though, as much as a sense of inadequacy. I ought to be able to do this by myself, rather than needing someone else to do for me. It's only math, after all.

"Come this way," Sylvia says, walking back in, and I get to my feet again following her out into the hall, and going along it, right to the end, where she opens a door without knocking, and steps through it, waiting for me to enter.

I smile at her, and she smiles back, nodding to the right, and I turn to find James Greenwood, standing behind a rather grand, oak desk.

There are two windows behind him, and a quick glance to the left reveals a large black leather couch with a low coffee table set in front of it. This is a much more ostentatious space than the one provided for his secretary. The computer on his desk is considerably more up-to-date as well, and I revise my earlier opinion. Maybe Sylvia just likes her old hardware and doesn't want to change it.

"Miss Hart," James says, offering his hand as he comes around the table, the door closing softly behind me.

"Mr. Greenwood."

He's a tall man, in his mid-fifties, with light brown hair that's only graying at the temples, and has steel-rimmed glasses, which sit atop his long, narrow nose. His suit is navy blue, his shirt a paler version of the same color and his tie is a deep red… all very conservative, which I think is probably a good sign in an accountant, and I take his hand. We shake, which gives him the opportunity to lead me toward the two chairs which have been placed in front of his desk.

"How are you?"

In his case, I get the feeling he's asking about me, and my business, rather than his question having anything to do with my grandmother, but I give him the same answer as I gave Sylvia, and he smiles.

"Please take a seat."

I do as he says, watching, while he goes back around the desk and sits in his large leather chair, pulling it closer to the desk as he smiles across at me.

"Now… what can I do for you?"

It seems the small-talk is over, but I guess time is money, and he's all about the money, so I sit forward slightly, and take a deep breath. "It's my accounts." I don't know why I said that. Why else would I be here? But he doesn't comment, he just nods his head and smiles. "My grandmother used to take care of them, but since her… since her death, I have to admit, I've been at a bit of a loss."

"I see. Well, it's only been a couple of months."

"Yes, but the last time she looked at them was probably October or November of last year."

He nods. "So, you're six months behind?"

"Yes."

"Are you paying your bills?"

"Yes. But I don't feel like I'm on top of things, and with the harvest still a while away yet, I need to be."

"You do, indeed," he says, frowning.

"The problem is that figure work has never been my strong point."

"It's not for everyone. But luckily that's why there are people like me in the world."

"So, you think you can help?"

"I'm sure we can. The thing you're going to need to decide is what level of service you require from us."

"There are levels?"

He smiles. "Yes. It all depends on how much work you require of us, and if you're willing to do any of it yourself."

I'd rather just hand everything over, given the choice. The thought of balancing books makes my blood freeze, but as we've already established, time is money, and I don't think any of this is going to be cheap.

"Before I decide on that, can I ask how much this is going to cost?"

My bank balance is already dwindling, and I've grown quite fond of eating. The last thing I need is to blow it all on accountancy fees and end up starving myself out of business.

"We have a range of packages," he says, getting up and going to a cabinet in the corner of the room. He opens it, pulling out a brochure, which he brings back to me, with a smile on his face. I take it from him and glance down at the glossy cover, my stomach churning. Knowing how much I paid for the little cards I leave in the local shops to promote the farm during the late summer and fall, I dread to think how much this brochure cost. I imagine it was more than I make in a month, though.

I flip through it, just briefly, and hold in a gasp when I see that for their most basic package, they charge one hundred and fifty dollars per hour. *Per hour?*

That's a joke, right?

The last time I looked at my accounts, I figured it would take me days to work my way through them… and these guys want a hundred and fifty an hour? I don't have that kind of money.

"Would it be okay if I took this with me?" I say, closing the brochure and holding it up.

"Sure. Read it through, take some time, and if you've got any questions, get back to me."

I wonder if he realizes I'm fobbing him off, trying to get out of here before I cry.

"I will. And thank you for your time."

I suppose I should be grateful that this appointment came free.

At least I'm no worse off than I was when I walked through the door, even if I am feeling a little humiliated.

There's nothing like being reminded of your place on the ladder of society… and that mine is right at the bottom.

He stands, shaking my hand again, and I make my way to the door, sighing out my relief when I close it, and then rushing along the hall and down the stairs.

I feel thankful to have escaped, and even though I'm clutching the brochure to my chest, I know I won't be studying it… closely, or otherwise.

I lean against the door of my truck, wondering what possessed me to think I could afford a professional accountant. I'm barely scraping a living, so who was I kidding that I could pay anyone who charges fees like that?

"Peony?" I look up, hearing my name, and I shudder when I see Ryan crossing the street toward me. He's smiling, which makes my insides melt. My heart flips over in my chest and my skin tingles with need for him, none of which is helped by the fact that he's wearing his suit, and that tie… again.

I can't smile back, though.

He's not supposed to be here.

He's not supposed to keep doing this to me.

Chapter Eight

Ryan

I saw Peony from my hotel room. I'd been drinking a cup of coffee, staring out the window and wondering how late I dared leave it before driving over to her place… and there she was.

She climbed out of her beaten-up truck and glanced toward the hotel. That made me smile, wondering if she might be looking for me, contemplating why I hadn't been back to see her since Wednesday afternoon…. two whole days ago now. She turned away again, though, and walked straight across the sidewalk, pressing a button beside the door next to the drugstore.

That had me intrigued, and I put down my cup, leaning against the window frame and watching.

After just a few moments, she pushed on the door and went inside, and I grabbed my jacket from the back of the chair, shrugging it on as I went out of the room, and straightening my tie as I walked down the hall to the elevator.

This seemed like too good an opportunity to pass up, and once I was outside, I ran across the road, checking out the name on the door Peony had just gone through. It said 'Greenwood and Clayton', which was singularly unhelpful, so I pulled out my phone and searched for them. They had a website… a fairly slick one, which revealed they were accountants.

Accountants?

Their offices might be small and inconspicuous, but judging from their website, their charges would be on the more expensive side. They seemed to aim at corporate customers, not people like Peony, and I wondered what she could be doing here. I didn't want to insult her, but they seemed a little out of her league.

Could she have come to consult them about my offer?

Hardly.

I haven't made her one yet.

And there's a reason for that.

It's the same reason I haven't been to see her for two days.

I spent yesterday re-working the figures and re-typing the proposal, knowing that if I'm going to get her to take me seriously, and free her from the yoke of running the farm, and worrying about money all the time, I'll have to make it worth her while. Gabe would tell me I'm crazy, but I don't care. It's my company, and I'll do what I like with it.

Of course, having re-written everything yesterday, I had to get the hotel to print it out for me this morning, and once that was done, I returned to my room to get ready to drive out to Peony's farm.

I would have done, too… except Gabe called.

He needed to tell me about a deal Adrian had just done for a plot of land in Vermont.

"Vermont? I thought he was looking at the development in East Lyme."

"He was. He still is, as far as I know, but he heard about this vacant plot in Vermont, and went after it."

"Without checking with me first?" There was a brief silence. "Where is this plot of land?"

"Close to Rochester."

"How close is 'close'?"

"About ten miles."

Alarm bells were ringing in my head. "Can I just ask… is this plot in the middle of nowhere?"

"Pretty much. There's a small village about three miles away, but that's only got about three hundred inhabitants."

"For fuck's sake…"

"I know, I know. I've already explained to him that the land we buy needs to be close to small towns, and that those towns ideally need to have between two and four thousand people living in them… that there's rural, and then there's rural."

"Why the fuck did you need to explain that to him? He's worked for us for nearly a year. He ought to know how we operate by now."

"What do you want me to do?"

"I take it we're committed to this deal?"

"I'm afraid we are. He attended the auction late yesterday afternoon, and called me early this morning to get me to wire the funds."

"How much are we talking about?"

"Half a million."

"For how much land?"

"A little shy of fifty acres."

"You're telling me he got it for ten thousand an acre?"

"Yes."

"What's wrong with it? Aside from the fact that it's in the middle of nowhere?"

"As far as I can tell, absolutely nothing. He emailed me the details, and I can't find anything wrong at all. Obviously, I don't know how hard it's going to be to get building permissions."

"No." That alarm bell rang a little louder, but there was no point in paying it too much attention. The deal was already done. "Okay. Wire him the money, but tell him to call me, will you?"

"Sure, boss."

We ended our call quite quickly after that… partly because I didn't want Gabe to question me about how things were going with Peony's farm, and partly because I was too angry to carry on the conversation.

Adrian's gamble might not have completely backfired… if we're lucky. The land was certainly a bargain, but I had yet to find out whether we'd be able to build anything on it. My father's way of working had always been to stick with commercial construction, and we'd made a name for ourselves in that field, either working on behalf of clients, or in our own right. There was no knowing what the authorities were going to permit with the plot of land Adrian had purchased in the company's name. It was possible they'd limit us to building residential properties, and although that wouldn't be the end of the world, I wasn't sure it was a direction in which I wanted to be dragged by one of my employees.

I didn't enjoy having my hand forced. That was what I wanted to talk to Adrian about. I was angry with him for making a decision like that without talking to me. He hadn't even tried… not a call, not a text message, not an email. Nothing. And that made me mad.

It made me too mad to consider going to Peony's place.

I knew I had to be calm when I spoke to her… and besides, it occurred to me, I could take advantage of the delay and suggest we discuss my offer over dinner.

As I paced the floor, still clutching my phone after my conversation with Gabe, I wondered about calling her. I wanted to see her, obviously, but I could ask her to have dinner with me, couldn't I? Here at the hotel.

Of course, I quickly dismissed that idea. What if Peony assumed I had an ulterior motive in doing so? She'd have been quite right. I didn't just want to sit opposite her at dinner; I wanted to take her to bed again… to make her scream my name, now that she knows what it is.

Before we could hope to do any of that, though, we needed to overcome her embarrassment… and we needed to discuss my offer for her farm, so everything was out in the open. Calling her suddenly didn't seem like such a good idea. I wanted her to be able to look me in the eye, so there could be no room for doubt between us. I reasoned to myself that, if I drove to her place, we could talk, and then I could ask her to dine with me at the French restaurant on Main Street. What I didn't expect was that I'd see her from my hotel room, going into the offices of a firm of accountants.

Could it be that her financial situation is even worse than I expected? Ordinarily, that might work to my advantage, but I'm not even thinking about my offer, and how I might normally lower it in similar circumstances. In fact, standing outside their offices, my stomach has just turned to lead at the prospect that she might be so worried about her position, she's decided she needs professional advice.

I wish she'd come to me first… given me the chance to help her.

But it's not too late.

At least, I hope it's not.

I wander over the road, leaning on the wall between the restaurant and the coffee shop, waiting for her to come out.

She takes a while, and I use that time to study the menu that's displayed by the door of the French restaurant. It makes my stomach rumble with hunger, and I smile, hoping I can persuade Peony to come back here with me later, so we can try this place out together.

I've only just turned around again when the door opens, and she comes out. I can see her better now than I could from my hotel window, noticing that she's wearing those torn jeans again, along with a blue sweater that looks about four sizes too big. Maybe it's a man's sweater, and the thought crosses my mind that perhaps it belonged to her ex-boyfriend. My body shudders at that idea, my skin prickling, and I shake my head, trying to erase the thought of another man touching her, as I wander back along the store fronts until I reach the gym, and then turn, crossing the road. This way, I'll appear to be coming from the hotel, and although that might seem a little devious, I don't want her to think I've been spying on her. I don't think she'd like that.

And besides… I haven't been spying. I've been watching. Closely.

She's leaning back against the door of her truck, clutching a folder or brochure to her chest, and I call out her name. She looks up, frowning, which isn't very promising, although I'm not deterred and I keep a smile etched on my face as I close the gap between us, until I'm standing right before her.

"Are you okay?" I ask, and her frown deepens, her head tipping to the right.

"I thought you'd left town."

My smile widens. "Why? Did you miss me?"

God… I love flirting with her.

She shrugs her shoulders. "I just assumed you'd given up."

"Me? Give up? You don't know me very well, do you?"

"I think we've already established, I don't know you at all."

"That's not strictly true. You know parts of me very well indeed." She blushes, which doesn't surprise me in the slightest. "Do you want to have a coffee with me?" It's too early in the day to suggest dinner, and I can't see her inviting me back to the farm. But that's no reason not to spend some time with her. Everything else can wait… for now.

She pushes herself off of her truck, standing upright, and looks up into my eyes. "I don't have time."

"Then make time."

"I—I can't." I sense the hesitation in her voice, and without another word, I take her by the elbow and, checking for traffic, guide her across the street.

"Yes, you can." She's not putting up a fight, or trying to pull away, and I lead her toward the coffee shop. "I promise, I won't talk about the farm, or my offer for it. How's that?"

We've reached the door, and as I open it, she looks up at me. "What are we gonna talk about, then?"

"Whatever you like."

She goes inside, with no further cajoling from me, which feels like a victory in itself, and after looking around for a second or two, selects a table near the window.

She takes the seat facing the door and I sit opposite, waiting while she puts the brochure she's been holding on the wide window ledge beside us, and I take the time to glance around. This place is small, but stylish… more stylish than I might have expected, with dark wood tables, soft cream-colored chairs, a white counter, with a few stools set in front of it, and blackboards behind, showing the range of drinks available. There are cakes and cookies on display, but I've suddenly lost my appetite… for food, anyway.

"What can I get you?" I ask, turning back to find Peony staring at me… or at my tie, to be more precise. I try not to smile and focus on her face as she looks up at me.

"Just a flat white, thanks."

"Anything to eat?"

She shakes her head and although I wonder if that's because she's trying to minimize the amount of time we have to spend together, I'd rather not think about that.

The point is, she's here now.

There are a few other people in here too, but I ignore them and once I'm at the counter, I place my order for a flat white and an Americano, and while the young woman prepares them, I turn around, my eyes fixed on Peony. Is that because I'm scared she'll leave? Of course it is… but it's also because I enjoy looking at her.

I pay by card, then carry the cups back to the table, sitting opposite her again, and leaning in a little closer, so I can lower my voice when I say, "You still didn't answer my question."

"Which one?"

She looks concerned. Does that mean she's worried I'm going to ask her why she left me the other morning, after we'd made love? I'd still like an answer to that, but not here… not now.

"Are you okay?" I ask, noting the relief on her face and the slight sigh that reaches me across the table. "You seemed a little troubled when you came out of that door just now." I glance across the street toward the accountant's office. "Is everything all right?"

"Not really." I'm surprised she's opened up enough to say that, and I tip my head slightly to one side, hoping to encourage her to go on. "I was just visiting an accountant."

I know that already, but manage to look surprised, raising my eyebrows and sitting back slightly.

"Ahh… I see. And I guess, because of who I am, you probably don't want to talk to me about what you discussed?"

She shrugs. "It wasn't anything confidential. I went to see if they could help with keeping my accounts up to date. I've never been great with figures, and I'm falling behind, but even I'm enough of a mathematical genius to work out that I can't afford their fees." She shakes her head. "They're astronomical. There's no way I can use them."

I sit forward again, resting my hands on the table, close enough that she could reach out and touch them, if she wanted to, although she doesn't.

"It's not something you could tackle yourself? Most accounts work isn't that difficult."

"Maybe not, but whenever I look at it, I just glaze over... mostly with boredom." I chuckle and after a moment, so does she. "Besides, I'm so busy on the farm, I don't have time, and I know if I tried, I'd make a mess of it, either through tiredness or incompetence."

"I can't believe your accounts are that complicated." She opens her mouth, but I hold up my hand and she closes it again. "I'm not saying that to insult you, or to make you feel inadequate. I'm just wondering if you're using a hammer to crack a nut."

"What do you mean?"

"I get that you don't feel comfortable doing them yourself, but do you really need a firm of accountants when a bookkeeper will probably be able to do the job just as well, for a fraction of the cost?"

"A bookkeeper?"

"Yes. I'm sure there must be someone around here who'd fit the bill."

She frowns, like she's thinking. "I can't think of anyone, but I can ask around, and maybe check on the Internet."

"It would be worth a try."

She nods, and then her brow furrows, and she narrows her eyes at me. "I don't get it..."

"Get what?"

"If you're not giving up on buying my farm – which I'm guessing you're not – then why are you helping me?"

I pull my hands back, clasping them on my lap beneath the table, and I wonder for a second or two whether I can lie to her. I'm not sure what I'd say if I did. Nothing is springing to mind, and in any case, I don't like the idea of lying to Peony. It feels wrong.

"I didn't like the worried expression you had on your face when you came out of that office. If there's something I can do about it, then I'd like to do it."

She stares at me, bemused, and then says, "So, if I told you I was worried about your offer, would you withdraw it?"

I smile. "I haven't made an offer yet... remember?"

She sighs, a little louder than before, and I know I scored a point. Not that I'm looking to score points over her, and I get no pleasure from the victory. She turns her head, staring out the window, and I take a moment to study her. Without a doubt, she's the most beautiful woman I've ever seen, and although I prefer it when she wears her hair long and untamed, I like it this way, too. With it up, in this loose arrangement behind her head, I can see her long neck and clear skin, although my eyes are drawn to her lips. I can still feel them around my cock, and I sit forward slightly, in the hope she won't notice how hard I am... yet again.

The movement seems to startle her, and she turns back, although she doesn't say a word. I can't help thinking that maybe what's turning me on the most is that I know how easy it would be to un-tame her hair... to loosen it with just a touch of my hand. I'm so tempted to reach out, but I can't. We may be talking – occasionally – but we're nowhere near the touching stage... yet.

"I like your sweater." The words leave my lips before I have the chance to stop them, and although I'm reminded of my thoughts from earlier, I have to smile as she looks down at it, tugging slightly on the sleeve.

"Thanks. It's one of my favorites."

"Is there a reason for that?"

I'm fishing, and I know it... although whether she'll have worked that out is another matter. She has no idea I'm jealous of who might have owned the sweater before her, and the fact that it's her favorite just makes things worse.

"No... just that it's comfortable, and I guess I have fond memories of it."

"Oh?" *Tell me more, please?*

"Yeah. My grandmother gave it to me for Christmas a few years ago, and we laughed so much, because she'd bought the wrong size."

"But you kept it, anyway?"

"Yes. It's warm, and it reminds me of her."

I'm relieved. Of course I am. But more than that, I'm sad. I'm sad for her. She so clearly misses her grandmother, and I want to hold her and tell her that grief doesn't last forever. It fades. Time heals.

I sip my coffee, because I can't hold her, or say any of that, and she copies me, looking at me over the rim of her cup, before she puts it down, resting her hands on the table and studying me for a moment longer before she says, "Why me? Why are you picking on me and my farm?"

"I'm not picking on you, Peony. You're not a victim here." *If you'd just hear me out and listen to my offer, you'd realize that.*

"Really? It feels like I am. It feels like you're taking advantage of the fact that I'm doing such a lousy job of running the place."

"Is that what you think?" I can't deny that what she's saying is partially true. It's not that I think she's doing a bad job, just that she's been given a lot to do, in difficult circumstances, and she can't afford to get help. But that's not why I'm interested in her farm. "So, you don't think it could be because your orchard is on a great plot of land, near a popular tourist destination?"

"Not entirely, no. Hart's Creek isn't that popular. There are plenty of other tourist destinations you could choose from, and my land isn't that great. The drainage is pretty poor... certainly in the lower field. But I'm guessing you're aware of that, if you've done your research."

"I am."

"Then why my farm in particular? You're surely not gonna tell me you buy successful businesses?"

"Sometimes. But you're forgetting. I'm not buying your business. It's your land I'm interested in." I lean closer. "Not exclusively, you understand."

"You mean you're looking to buy somewhere else in Hart's Creek?"

"No."

She stares at me for a moment, her brow furrowed in confusion, and then I see the moment of realization, and I hear her sharp intake of breath, the blush spreading up her cheeks. That's when I know she's understood.

This is about her... and us.

Chapter Nine

Peony

I know I said I'd ask around about bookkeepers, but for the life of me, I can't think who to ask.

I've spent the morning thinking it through, while I've been clearing the barn. I've even had a search on the Internet over lunch, which got me nowhere, and I feel no further forward than I did yesterday when I left the coffee shop with Ryan.

I'll admit, that's partly because I'm still feeling so confused by him.

I hadn't expected him to be here. Just seeing him was bewildering enough, my mind torn between relief that there might still be a chance for that non-existent 'us' I can't stop thinking about, and resentment that he clearly wasn't giving up on buying my farm.

It probably didn't help that my meeting with James Greenwood hadn't gone as well as I'd hoped, and seeing Ryan only made me feel more inadequate… reminding me he's a success, and I'm on the verge of losing it all.

Still… I can't think about that now. Just like I can't think about us.

There I go again… with that fantasy 'us'.

I finish my sandwich, pushing my laptop aside. I'm all out of ideas for where to search online in my efforts to find a bookkeeper. There are plenty of small businesses in the town, but I imagine they're all a great deal more successful than mine, and probably use Greenwood and Clayton… or have the intelligence to do their accounts themselves.

My phone rings, making me jump, and for a moment, I wonder if it might be Ryan. I've never given him my number, but I imagine he knows it. He seems to know everything else about me.

I pick it up, turning it over and sigh out my relief – at least I think it's relief – when I see Laurel's name on the screen. I connect the call, putting it on to speaker, so I can clear away my lunch while we speak.

"Hi," she says, as I take my plate over to the sink.

"Hello. How are you?"

"I'm fine. I haven't heard from you for a few days, so I thought we ought to catch up."

"Yeah. Sorry about that. I've been busy."

"When aren't you busy?"

"Never."

She chuckles as I run some water into the sink. "So, what's been keeping you occupied? You haven't had any more liaisons with strangers, have you?"

"No, but…"

"But what?"

I shut off the water and go back to the table, sitting down. There's something intimate about this conversation, and yelling it across the kitchen, over the sound of running water, while I wash the dishes, feels inappropriate.

"He came to see me."

"Who? The guy from the other night?"

"Yes."

"You mean he's still here?"

"Yes, he's still here."

"But how did he find you? I thought you didn't know each other's names."

"We didn't. But it turns out he came to Hart's Creek to see me."

"And he just happened to sleep with you?"

"I guess." I'm not sure I like the sound of that, or how it makes me feel about myself, but that doesn't make it any less true.

"So, on a scale of one to ten, how embarrassing was it when you both realized who you were?"

"Oh… easily an eleven. It didn't help that the first thing he said was, 'Why did you leave?'. I mean… what was I supposed to say to that?"

"The truth, maybe? You could have told him you felt embarrassed about sleeping with a man you didn't know."

"I wouldn't have thought it needed saying."

"Okay," she says, like she doesn't agree with me, but she's not going to argue. "So, what happened?"

"Nothing happened. Not in the way you mean."

"So there wasn't a repeat performance?"

"Of course there wasn't."

"Why not? I thought he was perfect, or pretty damn close to it. I thought the sex was incredible."

"It was." I don't need reminding of how incredible it was. "But it's not that simple."

"Yes, it is. You liked him… and don't pretend you didn't. I imagine he liked you too, because he's not insane. Sleeping together without knowing who you are might be an unusual way to start a relationship, but why can't you just go with it and see what happens?"

"Because he's here to buy my farm."

"Excuse me?" I can hear the surprise in her voice, and saying the words myself makes me shiver… makes it all too real.

"That's why he's here in Hart's Creek. He wants to buy my farm. Or, at least, the land it's built on."

"But it's not for sale, is it?"

"No. I've explained that to him several times now, but he doesn't seem to be listening."

"Don't take this the wrong way, but he didn't… he didn't sleep with you intentionally, did he? As a way of trying to seal the deal, I mean?"

"No. That was one of the many things we argued about when he made his intentions clear on Wednesday morning."

"You mean he came to see you the morning after you slept together?"

"Yes… not long after you and I spoke on the phone."

"And it's taken you until now to tell me?"

She sounds appalled, and I can't help smiling. "I'm sorry. Like I say, I've been busy." And preoccupied.

"Okay, so you asked him if he'd used sex as part of the deal, did you?"

"Not exactly. If I remember rightly, he'd said he liked my name, and I assumed he was just saying that to sweeten me up. He took offense and told me he really did just like my name… and that when we'd met in the bar the night before, he had no idea who I was, or that I was the woman he'd come to meet. He said he couldn't take his eyes off of me… that he had to have me."

"God… and you didn't drag the guy straight to your bedroom?"

"No. I won't say I wasn't tempted, but I was distracted at the time."

"What by?"

By him, his body… the tie he was wearing, by memories of what he'd done with it the night before, and what he'd done to me. "By the fact that he wanted to buy my farm."

"But surely, once you'd told him it's not for sale…"

"Like I said, he wasn't listening, Laurel. He's still not."

"You mean you've talked since?"

"We talked yesterday. He took me for coffee."

"To talk about the deal?"

"No, although we talked about the farm. I'd just come from seeing James Greenwood, and it hadn't gone well."

"Why not?"

"Because I need someone to help with my accounts, but I can't bankrupt myself in the process. It would be self-defeating. Ryan suggested I should find a bookkeeper instead."

"Ryan being the guy from the other night?"

"Yeah. Sorry, I didn't make that very clear, did I?"

"It doesn't matter." She pauses for a second. "I don't understand why he'd do that."

"Do what?"

"Make suggestions to help you out when he's trying to buy your business."

"I know. I thought the same thing, which is why I asked him."

"And what did he say?"

I can feel myself blush and wonder about lying. But why should I? "He said he didn't like the look on my face when I came out of James Greenwood's office, and that if he could do something to help, then he would."

There's a moment's pause and then she says, "You're sure this guy is only here for your farm?"

"I don't know." I really don't. He's got me too confused to think straight. "I asked why he was picking on me, and he said he wasn't."

"Does it feel like he is, then?"

"In a way, yes. I'm scared I'm gonna lose everything, Laurel."

"Have you explained that to him?"

"I've tried." At least, I think I have. I may not have put it into those words exactly, but I've made it clear I'm not interested in selling to him. "He said the reason he wants my farm is that it's on a great plot of land and it's near a tourist destination."

"Which kinda makes sense when you think about it."

"I don't care how much sense it makes. I can't sell to him. This place means too much to me."

"Did he mention what happened between you the other night, or was it all about land and contracts?"

"No. He hasn't said a word about it since Wednesday afternoon."

"I thought you said he came in the morning."

"He did… and then he came back again in the afternoon. Things hadn't ended well in the morning, and he came back later to… to…"

"Apologize?"

"I don't remember the word 'sorry' leaving his lips, but he said we'd gotten off on the wrong foot. He seemed to want to make amends."

"Which is nice."

"I guess."

"And that was when he talked about what had happened the night before?"

"A little. I found it embarrassing, and said we should forget it, but… he said that was impossible." I remember what it felt like when he said he knew I didn't want to forget about it either… the burning need that threatened to overwhelm me.

"And that was all he said?"

"There were a few other things." None of which I feel like discussing with Laurel. "What was odd, though, was that he didn't mention my panties."

"I'm sorry? Your panties?"

"Yes. I left them in his room."

"As a memento?"

"No, silly. When I woke up beside him that morning, it was still dark, and I couldn't find them. I didn't want to wake him by turning on the lights, so I left them behind. I thought he might have mentioned finding them… maybe said that he was getting the hotel to launder them, or something. But I've seen him three times now, and he hasn't said a word."

"Has it occurred to you that he didn't find them… that maybe housekeeping found them instead?"

"Don't say that."

"Why not? No-one's gonna know they belong to you. You don't put your name in your underwear, do you?"

"Of course not. But surely, they'd return them to him, wouldn't they?"

"Who knows? It depends who found them, I guess, and whether they felt like keeping them."

"To wear, you mean?"

"Don't be naïve, Peony."

"Oh… God." I feel a little sick at the thought of what someone might do with my underwear. "That's the last thing I need right now."

"Because your mind is filled with thoughts of Ryan?" she says, teasing.

"Maybe… although I'm more concerned with my accounts at the moment."

"Do you want me to come over and take a look? I'm no expert, but I do everything Mitch needs on a monthly basis, and he just gets Owen Clayton to cast an eye over it all at the end of the year."

"Do you think you could?"

"Sure. I'm not saying I'll have time to do them regularly, but I can show you the ropes." It might not have been what I had in mind, but she's made it sound simple enough, and I'll save a fortune if I can do it myself. "It'll have to be in the evening, though," she says. "There's no way I can concentrate with Addy running around, and I don't know exactly when I'll be over, because Mitch seems to be working late just about every night since…"

"Since Luca left?"

"Yeah. Sorry to bring him up."

"That's okay. I haven't thought about him for ages."

"No… because you've got someone better on your mind."

"I—I don't know about 'better'."

"Oh, come on. I never heard you get so breathless over Luca. Not once."

"Maybe, but Luca wasn't trying to kick me out of my home."

"No. He was more interested in getting into Stevie Pine's panties. And Ryan isn't trying to kick you out. He's made you an offer, hasn't he?"

"Not yet. I think he might have done yesterday at the coffee shop, but we were interrupted. He had to take a call."

"From his wife?"

"No. He's not married."

"You checked?"

"Yes. Before we slept together."

"I see." I can hear her smiling and I shake my head, even though she can't see me.

"He checked if I was married, too."

"Right… and this was just casual for both of you." She chuckles, even though it's not funny. "Who was the call from if it wasn't his wife?"

"Someone who works for him. A guy called Adrian, I think. Ryan apologized and said he had to leave." And when I heard the tone of his voice as he was speaking into his phone, I was relieved about that. He sounded angry, and I didn't want to witness his conversation.

"Okay, so the guy hasn't made you an offer yet, but I'm sure he will. He's not taking the farm, Peony. He's buying it."

"No, he's not. Because it's not for sale... which is why I need help with my accounts."

"Yes, you do. Sorry. I'll talk to Mitch and see if he can get home a little earlier one evening next week, and I'll get back to you... okay?"

"Thanks. And I'm sorry if I'm being a little abrupt."

"That's okay. You've got a lot on your mind."

I have. There's no denying that. We end our call, and I close my laptop, relieved that I can abandon my fruitless search for a bookkeeper and get on with something more productive.

"Peony?" I glance up to see Ryan coming across the street again. At least he's not wearing that damned tie today, although I'm not sure that helps, because he's wearing jeans and a button-down shirt... just like he wore on the night we met in the hotel bar. In a moment of panic, while trying not to picture him undoing his shirt, and lowering his jeans to reveal that perfect cock, I set my bag down on the seat of my truck, rearranging it so the sanitary pads I've just purchased in the drugstore aren't on top anymore. Then I close the door and turn as he comes up to me.

"Are you spying on me?"

He smiles. "No."

I glance over his shoulder toward the hotel. "Can I ask... where are you parking your car?"

"It's down the side of the hotel. Why? Have you been looking for it?"

I wish I hadn't asked now. In fact, I wish I hadn't needed to come into town at all. I'm only here because I remembered I needed to pick up some bread for tomorrow, and grab a few things at the drugstore. The sanitary pads weren't completely necessary. My period isn't due for another ten days, but as I was here…

"No," I say, remembering to answer at last. I may have glanced at the hotel, but 'looking'? Never.

"Have you found a bookkeeper yet?" he asks, clearly sensing my discomfort.

"I haven't, but my friend is gonna come over and help me."

"Friend?" He frowns, tilting his head.

"Yes. Laurel. I was supposed to be meeting her at the hotel the other night, when…" I let my voice fade, wishing I'd found some other way of describing her. One that didn't involve a reference to the night Ryan and I spent together.

"I see. And she's a bookkeeper, is she?" he says, and I wonder if he's as keen to avoid the subject as I am. He can't have forgotten about it. He said that was impossible.

"No. She trained as a lawyer, but her husband owns the gym, and she does his accounts. She's far more intelligent than I am."

He steps closer. "Hey… don't put yourself down. If all you need is someone to show you how it's done, I could do that. Only I thought you were dead set against doing it yourself."

"I was, but Laurel's convinced me to give it a try. I just need to wait for her to have a free evening."

"You're sure you don't want me to help? I'm available anytime."

"No, it's fine, thank you."

He leans in, close enough that I can feel his breath on my cheek. "You're not scared of being alone with me, are you?"

"Of course I'm not."

He stands up straight again, smiling. "Good. In that case, have dinner with me."

I feel like he did that on purpose… cornered me into saying I feel comfortable with him, to give me no way out.

"I can't. I'm too busy."

It's a standard excuse, but that doesn't make it any less true.

"You've got to eat."

I shake my head, backing away as far as the side of my truck will allow. He's right… I do have to eat, and I'm also scared of being alone with him. I'm scared that I want him so much, I won't be able to hide it, or to resist him.

"Sorry. I really can't."

You make me want far more than I should.

I turn and pull open the door of my truck, shoving my bags to the other side and climbing in. I go to close the door, but Ryan's holding it.

"It's just dinner, Peony."

"Is it?" He tilts his head. "It's not dinner and my farm?"

He pushes his fingers back through his hair. "Forget the damn farm."

"How can I?"

I yank the door away from him, slamming it closed, and start the truck, reversing out of the parking bay before he has the chance to say anything else.

As I drive away, I look in my mirror and see he's still standing there, looking a little lost, and I'm tempted to turn around and go back to him… except I know I can't. Because, for all his words, I know we can't forget the farm, or that he wants to take it from me.

I've been home for an hour already, and I know I ought to think about cooking something. The problem is, I feel restless.

And I know why.

It's because of Ryan, and what he does to me.

He makes me lose my mind. I don't even know him, but he makes my body hum with need, and just sitting here on the couch, thinking about him, I'm wet… so wet I'm tempted to touch myself, just for some relief. I ache for him, but it's a purely physical response…

Isn't it?

There's nothing more to it than that.

It's not love. It can't be. Even thinking that feels like a betrayal of my ancestors. It feels as though everything they fought so hard to achieve will have counted for nothing… because I let a man come between me and doing what was right.

And yet, I want him… so much.

"Why?" I mutter, trying to blink away my tears. Why couldn't I have met him under different circumstances?

I wipe my eyes with the back of my hand, letting out a sigh, and get up, going over to the refrigerator, just as I hear a car coming down the track. It's late for visitors, and I'm not expecting anyone. Laurel wouldn't give up a Saturday evening with Mitch to come help with my accounts… and she'd have called first. I scurry over to the front window, like it's going to make a difference if I scamper about, rather than just walking, and I peek outside. For a moment or two, I'm blinded by headlights, but they're quickly extinguished once the car has parked up alongside the fence, and I let out a gasp as I recognize the outline of Ryan's Mercedes.

I step away from the window and lean against the wall beside it, my heart pounding in my chest. I've got seconds before he knocks on the door… seconds to decide what to do. In which case, it would help if I knew why he was here.

I can hardly look out again. He'd see me. But why would he be here?

The knocking at the door makes me jump, even though I'm expecting it, and with the lights on I can hardly pretend to be out, can I?

"Who's there?" I call. It seems sensible, considering it's dark outside, even if I know exactly who's standing on the other side of the door. He doesn't know I've been looking, does he?

"It's me… Ryan."

There's nothing for it. I'm going to have to face him. I push myself off of the wall and step over, pulling the door open. He holds up a bag with the name of the French restaurant printed on the side.

"You wouldn't agree to come out to dinner with me," he says, smiling. "So I brought dinner to you."

I can't believe he's done this. Didn't he get the message? Clearly not… because I didn't pass it on. I didn't tell him I'm scared of being alone with him, did I? In fact, I denied it. I could kick myself for that, because this is where being truthful would have paid off. If I'd just said 'yes', when he asked, this wouldn't be happening, would it? Okay, so I'd have been embarrassed, having to explain why I'm scared. But so what? What's a little embarrassment between former lovers? And sure, he might still have found a way of asking me to dinner. But to be honest, both of those things seem like minor inconveniences, compared to the alternative of actually having dinner with him… here in my home.

I'm not sure I'm strong enough…

"You didn't need to do that."

He frowns, lowering the bag. "Are you always so ungracious?"

I can feel myself blush, and deservedly so. That wasn't a very nice thing to say. "I'm sorry. I'm just tired."

It's true.

I am tired. I'm also confused, and humiliated, and I wish he'd make the decision for me.

I'm beyond deciding what to do, or what's right, or for the best. But he could take away all the strain and worry, and just pull me into his arms and kiss me. He could make everything better with one touch. I know he could…

"I can leave this here and go, if you'd prefer?" He holds up the bag again, but I shake my head.

"No, it's fine."

I step back and, after just a second's hesitation, he comes inside.

Chapter Ten

Ryan

This isn't going anything like as well as I'd hoped.

To be honest, I'd never expected Peony to turn me down when I asked her to dine with me in the first place, and I guess I should have paid more attention. I should have taken her more seriously, instead of just viewing her refusal as a setback in my plans.

The problem was, I wasn't listening.

I was also frustrated, because I'd put my plan on hold once already, and wasn't expecting to do so again.

I'd intended asking Peony to have dinner with me yesterday, but the timing felt wrong when she was so despondent after her visit to the accountants. And in any case, Adrian called just as we were finishing our coffee, and that ruined the moment.

Having asked him to get in touch, I couldn't decline his call, but that meant leaving Peony at the coffee shop. I knew there was a strong possibility I'd lose my temper with him… or at the very least, have to come across as the boss, and I didn't want her to witness that. I didn't want her to see me as that man, when she was already feeling like a victim to my big business methods. It seemed better to walk away than to tarnish my already stained reputation.

As it was, the call with Adrian didn't last very long. It was just long enough for me to listen to him telling me that the plot of land he'd bought on the company's behalf in Vermont was 'too good a deal to turn down', and for me to tell him that, in future, I'd prefer it if he didn't pull a stunt like that again. He was surprised. That much was obvious. He thought he'd been doing me a favor.

"I'd assumed we could use it for housing," he said. "There's a profit to be made in it, and that's what was going through my mind when I was bidding."

"Was it? So it didn't occur to you we've never been in the residential market before now?"

"Is that a reason to turn down such a good offer?"

"Not necessarily, but if it's all the same to you, can I make the decisions about my company and where it's going?"

He coughed. "Oh... yeah. Sorry."

I shook my head. Was 'sorry' enough, considering how much money he'd potentially blown? "In future, I want you to run your deals past me."

"All of them?"

"Yes."

"But..."

"There are no 'buts', Adrian. I've always given you and the other negotiators a fairly free hand. That stops now."

"For all of us?"

"Yes."

"So you're not picking on me?"

I was reminded of Peony, but I focused on my conversation with Adrian.

"I'm not picking on anyone. But this is my family's company, Adrian. It's my name over the door."

He accepted what I was saying then, but I could tell he was doing so grudgingly, and after I'd finished the call, I emailed Gabe, letting him know what I'd said, and that I wanted it passed on to all the negotiators that no deals were to be done without being authorized by either me, or him, first.

I trust Gabe to act in the company's best interests, and he knows it. So does everyone else… and if there's any doubt, they'll understand it when they get his message.

Having wandered across the street to take my call, I wasn't sure if Peony would have waited for me, and was disappointed when I turned around to find her truck had gone. We'd said 'goodbye' before I'd answered the phone, though, so I don't know why I was surprised, and I strolled back to the hotel, telling myself that waiting another day might be beneficial.

Like I say, she was a little despondent after her meeting with the accountants, and I hoped that twenty-four hours might give her time to recover from that. I was going to drive over to her place this afternoon, but I saw her arrive in town and waited until she came out of the drugstore before running across the street to ask her… although I took my time going about it.

Call it nerves, call it inexperience. Whatever it was, asking her to dinner didn't come naturally to me… any more than being rejected.

That's not because women fall over themselves to accept my dinner invitations. It's because I'm not used to asking.

I'm not used to dating.

I'm not great at taking 'no' for an answer, either.

And that being the case, I decided against making an exception.

I remembered that the French restaurant here offered a takeout service, and in a flash of inspiration, thought, why not?

If Peony wouldn't agree to come out to dinner with me, why not take dinner to her?

It seemed like the perfect solution… at least it did in my love-addled head, and I said as much to her when I arrived at her place, although I didn't mention the word 'love'. Obviously.

What I hadn't expected was that she would practically slam the door in my face. She didn't. I'm being metaphorical. But she might as well have done. The look in her eyes did the slamming for her, which was why I offered to leave the food and go, because no matter how much I want her, or how much I love her, even I can tell when my feelings aren't reciprocated.

She invited me in, her manners getting the better of her in the end, but I'm starting to wish she hadn't. The atmosphere between us is so frosty, I'm scared the food won't stay warm long enough for us to eat it in these icy surroundings.

"Shall we put the main courses in the oven?" I suggest, before they freeze.

"Okay."

She wanders from the living area into the kitchen and I follow her, smiling at the decor, which is just what I would have expected. It's old-fashioned, but not dated, which suits the place… and her, I think.

"I like your home."

She turns, taking the bag from me and setting it down on the wooden countertop beside a wide five-ring stove. "I presume that's your way of saying it looks a lot better on the inside than it does on the outside."

Man, she's sensitive.

"No. I'm saying I like your home. I'm not trying to insult you, or the place where you live."

She stares at me for a moment and then turns away, opening the bag. I want to suggest I'll help, but I'm scared she'll bite my head off, so I just stand, feeling out of place, and look around. We're in the shorter part of the 'L' of her house, and I guess the bedrooms occupy the longer wing. This section is completely open plan, with the kitchen here in the back corner. Like I said, it suits the place, its wooden cabinets working better in here than more modern ones would. The kitchen table is made of oak, its surface pitted and gnarled from years of use, and I smile at the mis-matched chairs that surround it.

While Peony takes cartons from the bag, studying the labels and putting some in the refrigerator, and others into the oven, I turn and cast my eye over the rest of the living space. It's enormous, although all the furniture is gathered around the roaring fire in the center of the far wall. My cock twitches at the thought of making love to Peony on the rug in front of it, although she's way too frosty to contemplate that right now.

On either side of the fire are two huge couches, both covered with throws and blankets, all in neutral colors, with end tables that have lamps set upon them, giving a soft glow to the room. It's beautiful. I'd go so far as to say it's romantic, and if it wasn't for the fact that I can't think what to say without causing offense, I'd be happy to spend a lot of time here.

I bought a bottle of wine from the restaurant, selecting a light red, and I jump at the sound of the cork popping from the bottle, turning back around to see Peony pouring it into two large glasses.

She turns, holding one out to me and I step closer, taking it from her, watching as she sucks in a breath and swallows hard.

"Thank you for this." I'm not sure she means that, but I clink my glass against hers, and we both take a sip of wine. It's as light as I expected, with a hint of cherry in the background, but she doesn't stop to savor it, putting her glass down on the table. "I'll… I'll get some plates, and, um…" She seems flustered, and darts to a cabinet beneath the microwave, taking out some dishes and bringing them back to the table, together with a jug of silverware, which she puts in the middle, alongside the wine.

"Shall I get the appetizers?" I say and she nods her head, her hands shaking as she sets the table.

God, this feels uncomfortable. What happened to the woman who I tied to my bed the other night... who sucked my cock so expertly, and begged me to fuck her? Where is the woman whose panties have made a home in my pocket, and who's made a home in my heart?

For fuck's sake... it's not supposed to be like this.

I've never let anyone get close to me before, and I know why now. It's got nothing to do with my intimacy issues. It's because relationships are complicated, and love hurts.

Had I expected her to fall at my feet? No. Throwing herself into my arms might have been nice, though. I'd have caught her if she had.

And I wouldn't have let her go.

I grab the two cartons from the countertop, along with the small container of dressing, and bring them back to the table. Peony has finished laying it, and we both sit down opposite each other, feeling awkward. At least, I feel awkward. She looks like she'd rather be anywhere than here.

"I—I wasn't sure what you'd like, so I got a choice." She looks up, nodding her head just slightly, and I open the cartons. "There's a beet salad with candied walnuts and goat's cheese, which comes with the vinaigrette." I hold up the container of dressing. "Or there's a smoked salmon platter, which is accompanied by a hard-boiled quail egg, caviar, and a dill and lemon oil."

"Caviar?" she says, the corners of her lips twisting upward, in the evening's first show of a smile.

"Yes." I smile back.

"Is that what you normally have for dinner on a Saturday night?"

"All the time."

"In that case, I'd hate to deprive you. I'll take the beet salad."

"I don't mind. You can have the salmon. I'm sure I'll survive without my weekly quota of caviar."

She shakes her head, reaching for the box that contains the beet salad. "I've never had it, and I'm not sure I'd like it."

"Caviar?"

"Yes."

She's serving out the beet salad onto her plate, adding the vinaigrette, and I do the same with the salmon. Once it's done, I put a little caviar onto my fork and hold it out to her. "Try it."

She studies it for a moment and then leans forward, opening her mouth and letting me pop the fork inside. My cock hardens as she closes her lips. I retract the fork, and I watch while she swallows, tilting her head to one side.

"It's not as oily as I thought it might be."

"Do you like it?"

"It's a little salty for my tastes, but it's okay."

I smile. "At least you tried it. I always think you should experiment with new things, don't you?"

She looks up, breathing hard, her eyes locked on mine, and then she licks her lips, running her tongue along the lower one in a slow, teasing motion. My cock presses hard against my zipper and I ache to be inside her again, the moment only broken when she lifts her fork and takes a bite of goat's cheese, her eyes closing in rapture.

"God, that's good."

I chuckle and start eating my salmon. "You like goat's cheese?"

"Yes. I like the sharpness of it." She stares at me for a moment, like she's intrigued, and I put down my fork.

"What's wrong?"

forget about the deal I came here to negotia...
changed since I met her. I've changed since I m...

She'd rather just change the subject.

"Do you live in a house or an apartment?" she as...
making conversation with a stranger… which is what I...
am to her, even though I've tasted her honeyed sweetne...
seen the longing in her eyes when I joined my body with...
her soft skin against mine and listened to her beggin...
more.

"An apartment."

"A modern one?"

"Yes. But that doesn't mean I'm all about mode...
just happens to be convenient for the office."
defending myself? I guess because it feels like she'...

We've both finished our appetizers, and she t...
putting it on top of hers and stands, carrying th...
sink, before she returns with clean dishes.

"Do you want some help with getting things...
I ask, going to get up.

"No, I'm fine, thanks."

I do my best to disguise my sigh and watch...
containers from the oven, bringing them to the table and se...
them before us.

"I hope I've chosen something you'll like," I say as she takes
her seat again and I open the boxes.

"This is the pan seared sea bass. It comes with gratin
Dauphinois, roasted asparagus and a hazelnut butter. The
alternative is roasted duck breast, with Brussels sprouts, carrots,
fingerling potatoes and a berry jus."

She leans forward, looking inside the cartons. "Now, that is a
hard choice. Which would you prefer?"

I shake my head. "It's up to you."

"You don't really eat caviar every week, do you?"

"No. I think I've eaten it maybe twice in my life..."
returning her attention to her beet salad, and a silence...
between us. It feels like that frost is coming back with...
determined to keep it at bay, I reach for my wine, take a sip, a...
say, "I hope red is okay."

"Red?"

She looks up, confused.

"Yes. Red wine. You drank rosé the other night, but I thought
red would go better with what I ordered."

She's blushing, presumably because I mentioned the other
night, and I wish I'd found a way around it now… although I also
wish she could just accept that we slept together. Or better still,
admit that she enjoyed it… because she did. I know she did. I can
still hear her screams of pleasure, even now.

"Red's fine," she says.

"Has your friend said when she'll be able to come and help
with your accounts?"

That feels like safer territory, although she frowns at me,
which makes me wonder…

"Not yet."

"My offer still stands."

She shakes her head. "I don't think that would be appropriate,
do you?"

"Why not?"

"Isn't it obvious? You want to buy my farm. Why on earth
would I let you see all my figures?"

"I've already seen them. At least, I've seen the returns you filed
for the last five years."

She opens her mouth, then snaps it shut again, pausing for a
second before she says, "You have?"

"Of course. I told you, I've done my research."

I’m a little surprised by that, but I push the box closer to her, and help myself to the sea bass, the aromas driving me insane.

Peony is arranging the sliced duck breast and vegetables on her plate, and pours over the jus, catching a drip with her finger, and licking it off. My cock responds to the sight, and I stare at her as she closes her eyes.

“That’s incredible,” she murmurs, opening them again, and without thinking about it, she dips her finger into the pot and holds it out to me. “Have a taste.”

She could have tipped some into a spoon, or handed me the pot, but I’m not going to complain about licking it from her finger. I take her hand in mine, just so she can’t change her mind, and dip my head, lapping the sauce from her fingertip. As my tongue touches her skin, she sucks in a breath, our eyes locking, and although I half expect her to pull back, she doesn’t. It’s like the moment has captured her, and me with it.

I don’t know how long we sit like that, but eventually, she clears her throat, and I release her.

“W—What did you think?” she asks, stammering over her words.

“Of the sauce, or holding your hand?” She stares at me, but doesn’t answer. “The sauce was sublime. I imagine it’ll go really well with the duck. As for holding your hand…” She’s staring into my eyes, waiting for me to finish. “That was magical.” Her eyes widen, her lips parting slightly, and although I’m tempted to ask if we can hold hands again, I know I need to tread carefully. If I push too hard, she’s likely to shut down on me again… and that’s the last thing I need. “Shall we eat before it gets cold?”

She nods her head, lowering her gaze to her plate. The sea bass is perfectly cooked, and the potatoes are the best I’ve ever eaten.

“Cle—” “rather, what I’m ... worth?”

“Not that it matters.”

“...matters to me.”

“Why?”

“Because it feels like you’ve been spying on me.”

“It’s business, Peony.”

“Not to me.”

We dip into silence once more, but I can’t stand it, and I put down my fork. “Can’t you just forget about the farm for one night?”

“Have you?”

“Yes.”

“You mean you’ve given up? You’re not interested in buying it anymore?”

“I didn’t say that. I said I’d forgotten about it for tonight. It would be nice if you could, too.”

“Why?”

“Because then we might be able to enjoy ourselves.”

Part of me expects her to suggest I can leave, if I’m finding it so horrible being here, and to be honest, I’m tempted… not because I don’t want to be with her, but because it’s so obvious she doesn’t want me around. She doesn’t say that, though.

Instead, she studies her plate for a moment, and then looks up. There’s a sadness in her eyes, bordering on despair, and they’re glistening slightly, making me wonder if she’s going to cry. I want to take back everything I’ve just said, but I don’t get the chance.

“I’ll do my best,” she says quietly. “Just for tonight.”

“I’m sorry.”

She shakes her head, and although I’d like to explain my apology, I realize she doesn’t want to hear it. She doesn’t want to know that I didn’t mean to be so abrupt, or that while I can’t

"How's the fish?" she asks, after a few minutes. It seems we're sticking to the safe subject of food, and if that means we can have a conversation, I'm okay with it.

"It's perfect. How's the duck?"

"Fantastic." She cuts up one of her potatoes. "But it's nowhere near as good as these potatoes." I watch as she places it in her mouth, closing her eyes in evident ecstasy.

"Mine are good, too."

She opens her eyes again, and for a second it feels like neither of us is thinking about potatoes. I'm not imagining her desire. I remember what it looks like from our night at the hotel. It's there for anyone to see and hear and feel. Except Peony, it seems. She's determined to remain oblivious to her own needs.

She coughs and looks away. I offer her more wine, but she declines and I wonder if that's because she recalls what happened the last time we both had a little too much to drink. I don't mention it, though, and we finish our main courses in no time at all.

The desserts are in the refrigerator, and while Peony fetches them, I clear away our plates.

"You didn't have to do that," she says when she turns around, coming back to the table.

"I don't expect you to wait on me."

She sets down the two cartons she's carrying and then fetches two small plates from the cabinet beneath the microwave before she sits opposite me again. As she rifles through the jug of silverware, finding a couple of spoons, I open the cartons, and push them closer to her, so she can see what's on offer, and once she's inspected the contents, she looks up at me.

"That's not a hard decision at all."

"Because you get sick of the sight of apples?"

She smiles. "No, because the alternative is chocolate."

I smile back and she nudges the apple tart in my direction, keeping the chocolate mousse for herself. I serve the tart onto my plate, cutting through the light pastry, and watching as Peony takes a spoonful of mousse from the glass container in which it's been provided. She lets out a slight moan of satisfaction as she swallows it down, and I can't help but smile at her reaction.

"I take it that's good?"

"It's better than good."

I smile, watching her eat, between mouthfuls of delicious apple tart.

"Can I assume you like chocolate?" I ask as she scrapes around the bottom of the dish with her spoon.

"Of course."

I nod my head, finishing my dessert, and push my plate aside.

"Shall I help with the dishes?"

She frowns. "I'm sure I can manage."

"I'm not going to leave you to do it all by yourself." *And I want to spend some more time with you.*

She nods, giving in, and we both get to our feet, Peony making straight for the sink. I notice the dishwasher beneath it, and am surprised when she starts running hot water, and adding a good squirt of dish soap.

"You're not using the dishwasher?" I say, coming up behind her as she turns and hands me a dishtowel.

"No. It suffered from a terminal illness about a month ago, and I can't afford to replace it… yet."

I notice the pause before she says the word 'yet', and knowing how bad things are for her financially, I realize it's going to be some time before she can rectify the situation. I open my mouth to offer to buy one for her, but close it again, the offer unspoken. She'd almost certainly reject it, and probably lecture me on how she can manage perfectly well without me or my money. Either that, or she'd look upon it as a bribe, and considering how fragile things are between us, I think it's best left… for now.

Besides, there isn't actually very much to do. It's not like we had to cook anything, so there are only a few plates and knives and forks, and once they're done, and I've stacked the dry dishes on the table ready for her to put away, I fold up the cloth, leaving it over the back of one of the dining chairs.

Peony is wiping down the countertop, although it doesn't really need doing, and when she's finished, she turns to me, leaning back on it, and taking a deep breath. "Thank you for dinner," she says, which feels like I'm being dismissed.

"You're welcome, although if you're being honest, you'd have to admit, you didn't want me here, did you? The food may have been good, but you could have done without the company."

I can't see the point in pretending it's been a comfortable evening for either of us, and it feels like the time has come to be up front about that… or at least to get her to be up front.

She steps forward, shaking her head and looking pained. "It wasn't that, Ryan."

"What was it, then? The atmosphere has been horrible, all evening."

"I know. I know it has, and I'm sorry about that, but you have to admit, things are difficult."

"Because we slept together?"

She blushes, yet again. "Because we slept together, and because you want to buy my farm. I don't want to sell it, and you know that. We're on different sides here. We're enemies."

That's a strong word. It's one that pierces my heart and makes me pause for a moment to catch my breath before I reply, "We're not. Not really."

"Yes, we are. We want completely different things."

No, we don't. I want you, and I think, deep down, you want me too. You're just too scared, too confused, and too embarrassed to admit it.

"So? That's business."

"Except it's not business for me, is it? It's personal. I—It's my life." Her voice cracks and I stare at her, seeing the emotion bubbling beneath the surface. It wouldn't take much for her to cry, and I don't want that.

I step closer, lowering my voice. "I get that, Peony. Really, I do."

"Does it change your mind?"

"No, but you haven't heard my offer yet."

She pushes her fingers back through her hair. "Fine. Tell me what you're offering… but remember, I know for a fact that the average cost of land around here is twenty thousand dollars an acre, so don't for one second think you can short-change me."

I smile down at her, noting her steely eyed expression. "I thought you said you weren't any good with figures."

"I'm not. But I'm not stupid, either."

"I never thought you were."

"Good. So, what's your offer?"

"I don't have the paperwork with me. Believe it or not, I came here to see you tonight, not to talk business. I think I said that earlier, and although I know you didn't believe me, it's the truth."

She stares at me for a moment, her eyes softening, as she licks her lips and heaves in a deep breath. "Okay. Why don't we talk it over tomorrow?"

"Sure. I can come by at ten in the morning, if that works for you?"

"You don't mind? What with it being a Sunday and everything?"

"I don't mind in the slightest… not if I'll get to see you again."

"Y—You want to see me again?"

"Yes. I thought I'd made that clear already."

"Did you?" She looks bewildered and I smile.

"I thought so, but I guess maybe I wasn't clear enough." She gazes up at me, and I step closer still and deliberately lower my voice. "It seems I'll have to try harder to get my message across."

She doesn't say a word, but just continues to stare at me, dumbfounded, and I step away and walk backwards toward the door, my hands buried in my pockets, the right one finding her panties and clutching them.

Should I give them back, I wonder?

Hell, no.

Aside from the fact that she'd be mad at me for keeping them and carrying them around for the last few days, I like having this little piece of her with me all the time, and I run the soft lace between my fingers.

"See you tomorrow," I say as I reach the door and open it.

"Y—Yes. See you tomorrow."

She still sounds confused, but I'm hoping that's a good thing… that maybe I got to her, like she's got to me.

I guess only time will tell…

Chapter Eleven

Peony

I can't sleep…

I know why, too. I feel guilty over the way I behaved tonight.

Ryan was right when he called me ungracious, and even though I let him into the house, I still wasn't as polite, or as kind, as I might have been.

In my defense, I'd like to say that's because he's my enemy… just like I said to him. He wants my farm, and I'm not giving it up. We're opponents in a battle of wills. Why would I want to sit down and have dinner with my rival?

Because that wasn't why he was here?

Because every time I look at him, I want him just a little more?

Because he says things that make me think he wants me too… maybe just as much, if not more than I want him?

He said he wanted to see me again, and he wasn't talking about the farm. He was talking about me… about us. The 'us' that doesn't exist anywhere other than in my head, where it's starting to make a home.

Except I can't let it… because he wants to take my family's farm and turn it into God knows what. A housing complex, or a shopping mall, probably.

I turn over, pushing down the covers. My skin feels too sensitive. I need air.

I need to breathe.

No. I need him.

Why does it have to be like this?

Why do I have to want him so much?

My need for him is clouding my judgement... making me do things I wouldn't normally do. That should be obvious, I guess, from the fact that I slept with him without knowing his name, but since when have I offered a man a taste of something on the tip of my finger? I knew when I did it he'd have to lick it off. I wanted him to.

What must he have thought, though?

That it was magical.... evidently.

Or was that just a line?

How am I supposed to know? Was he just saying that, and telling me he wanted to see me again because he wants to buy my farm? Does it have anything to do with me at all?

And why, oh why, does my body ache like this? My nipples are so hard, they hurt. My pussy is yearning to be touched, and licked, and...

"Oh, to hell with it."

I throw back the covers, turning onto my back, parting my legs as my hand moves down, my fingers finding my swollen clit with ease.

"Oh... oh..." I let out a sigh, circling over it, and I close my eyes, recalling his touch, his tongue... his cock.

I tweak my nipple, rolling it between my thumb and forefinger, rubbing myself harder and harder, and spreading my legs wider still, craving more. I dip two fingers inside my entrance, gathering up my dripping juices and smearing them over my hardened nub.

"Please, Ryan... please fuck me."

The memory of his cock, deep inside me, pounding into me, is enough to push me over the edge, into a spiraling orgasm, my body clenching, submitting, as wild screams leave my lips, filling the room.

I calm slowly, turning to my side, and wrap my arms around myself, missing his tender embrace, wishing he was here to hold me.

I haven't done that since the morning after I slept with him, and I know why now.

I feel empty without him, and it hurts.

I'm a little late getting up, but in a way, that's a good thing. It means I don't have time to think about last night. I can't spend too long dwelling over what it felt like to sit across the table from Ryan, admiring his lips, remembering his kisses, longing for it all to happen again. I can't waste ages in the shower, reliving that moment last night when I made myself come, letting my imagination go as wild as my orgasm.

I don't particularly want to, either, because no matter how much I crave him, I can still remember how I felt afterwards. That feeling of longing and loneliness that kept me awake until the small hours, wishing he could have been beside me, urging me to greater and greater heights.

I've got things to do around the farm today, but for the purposes of this morning, I feel the need to dress more for business than work, distinguishing between the two, in as much as my choice of clothes will allow. I find some jeans that don't have holes in, and put them on over my underwear, followed by a white vest top. It's a little tight across the chest, but that's okay because I'm wearing a pale blue and gray check shirt over the top. I'm leaving it unfastened, but I roll up the sleeves, because they're slightly too long for me. I dry my hair, surprised that it's behaving itself for once. That saves me from putting it up, which is just as well, because I'm running out of time. I could put on my black boots, but aside from the fact that they remind me of the other night, when I met Ryan at the hotel, I guess there's an outside chance he might want to look around the farm. In that case, I'll need my work boots on. They're by the door, caked in mud, as usual, and I've got no intention of wearing them now. So, I pull on some thick socks, which may not be exactly business-like, but they're better than bare feet… especially when it's as cold as it is today.

Ryan's due here in less than fifteen minutes, and I use that time to tidy the kitchen and living room, and put the coffee on, remembering that I need to be hospitable, even if he is the enemy.

The enemy who, even when he's not here, can make you come so hard, you're in danger of losing your mind.

The coffee's just finished brewing when I hear his car coming down the track, and I shake out the nerves from my hands, rolling my shoulders and tipping my head from side to side to relieve the tension, before opening the door to greet him.

He's parked already, and is reaching into his car for something, so I wait, letting out a sigh, when he stands and I see he's wearing he's wearing his suit. Is that better than the jeans and button-down shirt? I'm not sure. His tie is still so distracting. Doesn't he own another one? Or is he teasing me with it? Reminding me of that night… and how good it was to be tied to his bed?

Is this a ploy to put me off?

If so, it's not working… *much.*

He strides up, climbing the steps and stands before me, his briefcase in his hand. The ends of his hair are still damp, and I can smell his body wash, which makes me wonder if he overslept a little, too. Might it have been for the same reason? Could he have been thinking of me…? Could he have been…?

Stop it.

He's here on business.

"Would you like to come in?" I step aside, remembering my manners at last.

"Thank you."

He comes inside and I close the door, leading him across to the kitchen table. He follows, putting down his briefcase and staring directly at me.

Is he trying to intimidate me?

I'm not sure. There's something in his gaze that's far too reassuring to be threatening, and I feel that familiar heat at my core, my body tingling with need... yet again. How can he do this to me, with just a look?

"C—Can I get you a coffee?"

"Yes, please."

"You take it black, don't you?"

"Yes. How did you know?" He seems surprised, and he's smiling, too.

"I noticed at the coffee shop."

He nods his head, his smile widening. "You mean, like I noticed you don't take sugar?"

"Probably."

I feel myself blush and duck past him, going around the table to fetch some cups from the cabinet. I've got my back to him, so he can't see my hands shaking as I prepare our drinks, and I take a deep breath before I pick them up and carry them to the table, setting them down.

He waits for me to sit in the same chair I used last night, and he takes his seat opposite, his eyes fixed on mine. "How are you?" The intensity of his gaze makes it hard for me to think of him as my enemy. I'm struggling to think at all...

"I'm fine, thanks." *I didn't sleep very well, because I wanted you... beside me, inside me... just here, with me.* "How are you?"

"Not too bad."

I'm not sure what that means. It's not the same as 'good', or even 'fine'. Should I ask?

No!

He might feel obliged to tell me, and his answer might not be something I want to hear. I mean, what if he's been up all night 'losing himself' in someone else? I shudder at that thought, my heart clenching in my chest, and the words, "Did you sleep okay?" fall out of my mouth before I can stop them.

"Not really."

"Oh?"

What am I doing? Not only is his personal life none of my business, but I really, really don't want to hear about it... especially not if he's spending it with another woman.

"Yeah. I was... um... preoccupied."

"With anyone I know?"

I could kick myself, but before I can retract my question, his face darkens, his eyes narrowing, and I'm reminded of his visit last Wednesday, when I made him angry... right before he stormed off in his car.

I still don't feel threatened, but I wish I could learn to keep my mouth shut and my nose out of his private affairs.

"Is that what you think of me?" he says in a low whisper.

"I apologize. It's none of my business. I shouldn't have..."

"Answer the question, Peony. Do you seriously think I'd sleep with someone else?"

"I—I don't know. I..."

"Seriously? You think I could make love with you, make it clear I want to see you again, and then fuck another woman?"

"No, I don't." Not when he puts it like that. I hold up my hands in surrender. "I'm sorry. That was unfair. I didn't mean anything. I just... I just..."

His face clears in an instant. "You wanted to know what had kept me awake?"

"What you do with your evenings – or your nights, for that matter – has nothing to do with me."

"Hasn't it? I think it has." He leans forward, clasping his hands together on the table in front of him. "I think you have a right to know what I'm doing."

A right? "You do?"

"Yes. I don't like the idea of you thinking so badly of me, but I guess there's no difference between you wanting to know what kept me awake last night, and me needing to know whether that sweater you had on the other day used to belong to your boyfriend... and whether you'd kept it for sentimental reasons."

"My sweater?"

"Yes."

What's that got to do with anything? "Is that why you were asking about it? Because you thought it had belonged to my ex?"

"Yes. I didn't like the idea that you couldn't bear to be parted from it. And just so you know, the reason I couldn't sleep last night was because I was thinking about you."

"Me? Don't you mean the farm? The deal?"

"No. I mean you, Peony."

I struggle to breathe. Should I tell him I had the same problem? That I made myself come, but missed him so much afterwards it didn't seem worth it?

"I'm sorry."

"What for? Keeping me awake? Trust me, you don't need to apologize for that."

"I wasn't. I was apologizing for doubting you."

"It's okay." He snaps open his briefcase and pulls out some papers, although he doesn't refer to them. He keeps his eyes fixed on me. "Now... before you forget that I'm your enemy and actually start to like me just a little, shall we get down to business?"

He's teasing. I'd almost go so far as to say he's flirting. I know he is… and what's more, I like it.

Damn him.

I suck in a breath, take a sip of coffee, and push my cup to one side, leaning in a little. "Sure."

Without even glancing at the papers in front of him, and keeping his eyes locked on mine, he says, "You're quite right, the going rate for an acre of land around here is twenty thousand dollars. I'm willing to offer you thirty thousand, which equates to one point two million dollars for your land."

He smiles as he stops speaking and I swallow hard, trying to take that in, and to act normally, even though my palms are sweating, my heart beating way too fast in my chest.

One point two million dollars?

I never expected anything like that. I thought he'd offer me the going rate. Even that would have been more money than I could hope to make in my lifetime… but this? This is beyond anything I could have dreamed of.

That doesn't mean I'm going to accept him, though.

"What about the property?" I say, noting how his smile fades, his brow furrowing.

"The property?"

"Yes. The house, the barns and outbuildings? They're worth something too."

I'm not being greedy. I've got no intention of accepting, regardless of how much he offers. All I'm doing is trying to put him off.

He shakes his head. "Not to me, they're not."

"You mean you'd demolish them?"

"Of course I would. I can hardly build around them, can I?"

"But I thought you liked my house."

"I do." He sighs, shaking his head once more. "Okay. Let's call it one point five million, all in… if it makes you feel better."

I sit back in my seat and gaze at him for a moment or two. He's staring at me, and although I don't know what he's thinking, my mind is filled with memories of his lips on mine, his fingers, his touch, his tongue…

It's a struggle to draw breath, but I manage it and I clasp my hands on my lap so he won't see them shaking.

"I'm sorry, but I still can't sell." He opens his mouth, but before he can say anything, or maybe increase his offer to ludicrous proportions, I get in first. "It's not the money, Ryan. Your offer is very generous."

"Then why?"

"I know you expect me to say it's because of what happened between us the other night, but that's got nothing to do with it."

"Really?" I can hear the doubt in his voice, and although it's disappointing, I'm not surprised.

"Really. This is about history. It's about doing the right thing." I sigh, wondering if he's got the imagination to understand. "Hart's Creek gets its name from my ancestors, going back generations, and since the first property was built in the town, there's always been a Hart here."

"How? You inherited the farm from your grandmother. Unless she broke with tradition and didn't change her name when she married, how could she have still been a Hart?"

"Your research might be thorough, but it's not that thorough. Granny's husband left her when she was pregnant with my father. He had an affair and ran off with the other woman. After that, she reverted to her maiden name and developed an inbuilt distrust of men."

"That rubbed off on her granddaughter?" he says, resting his hands on the table.

"No. If it had, I might have been better prepared for when my ex did exactly the same thing. I might have listened when Granny warned me it wouldn't last."

"She warned you? Why?"

"She told me that men who look that good don't stick around."

He pulls his hands back slightly. "Your ex was a handsome man, was he?"

"Yes, although he wasn't anywhere near as handsome as…" I stop talking, wishing I could learn – once and for all – to engage my brain before opening my mouth.

"Wasn't anywhere near as handsome as who?" he asks, his lips twisting up into a heart-stopping smile.

"No-one. It doesn't matter."

"Yes, it does. Finish your sentence."

My body heats under his gaze, and I know there's no going back. "As you. He wasn't anywhere near as handsome as you. Okay?"

He tips his head from one side to the other, like he's trying to decide if that's okay or not. "Does that mean you think I won't stick around, either?"

"I don't know, and I'm not sure it matters, does it?"

"Doesn't it?"

I feel like we're losing our way here. Or I am, and I clear my throat, sitting upright to try to regain some control. "We've gone off topic."

"Have we?"

"Yes. I was telling you about my ancestors… about the reason I won't sell my farm to you, or anyone else, for that matter. There had been a Hart in Hart's Creek for years, but the farm itself was started by my great-great-grandfather. There's no way I can walk away from what he and his children built up. I can't let you take it from me."

He holds up his hands. "I'm not *taking* anything from you. I'm offering you a considerable sum of money."

"I know, but I still can't."

"So, you'd rather let the bank have it, would you?" I shake my head, but he doesn't stop. "That's where you're going, Peony. I've seen your figures. I know where you're headed, and unless you do something, and do it quickly, you've got no way out of the situation you're in."

Tears prick behind my eyes. I know things are bad, but hearing it put into words like that is hard to hear. The sense of failure is almost overwhelming… except I've got no intention of letting him see that.

"I—I'll find a way… somehow." My defiance is ludicrous. I know how little money I have in the bank. It's obvious to me how dependent I am on the next harvest to see me through, and that it's still only the spring, and I've got to get through to the fall before I can hope to see a return. I'm not an idiot. I'm just being made to feel like one.

He sighs, shaking his head, and picks up the papers, returning them to his briefcase, although I'm unsure why he took them out. It's not like he's even glanced at them.

"Are you giving up?" I ask as he snaps the briefcase closed.

"Hell, no." He looks up at me. "Even if I didn't want your land for a specific reason, I know this is the right thing for you to do."

"It doesn't matter how much you offer me…"

He stands, the movement interrupting me. "I'm not gonna increase the offer. I've got budgets to work to, and I'd be insane to pay you any more."

"Then I don't understand."

He leans over, and I struggle to breathe again, just having him this close to me. "I'm gonna try to persuade you to accept, if I can."

"Y—You won't. There's nothing you can say or do to make me change my mind."

He bends even closer… so close he could kiss me, especially as I'm looking up at him, our lips maybe an inch or two apart. "Nothing?" he says, his voice a low growl.

I lean back, putting some necessary space between us. "No."

He stands upright, although he's still gazing into my eyes. "We'll see."

He picks up his briefcase, moving toward the door and after a second's pause, I get up and follow. Part of me wants to ask if he has to leave… if he can't stay for another coffee. But I'm too confused… too humiliated. He's made it clear this meeting was about business, even if he has spent a lot of it flirting with me. Not only that, he's also reminded me I'm not very good at running the farm I'm so desperate to protect. I didn't need that, especially not from him… not when he turns me on so much. I want him to feel as mortified as I do, and having admitted I find him handsome, I don't feel like I have anything left to lose.

"Can I ask you something?" I say as he opens the door, and he turns on the threshold, looking back at me.

"Sure."

"Did you find anything in your hotel room the morning after I stayed with you?"

He turns around fully, so he's facing me. "You didn't stay, Peony. You ran away… and in case it's escaped your attention, you still haven't told me why."

I've got no intention of explaining myself, and I step forward, going on the offensive. "Okay, I ran, but that's not the point. The point is, did you find anything of mine in your room?"

"Why? Have you lost something?"

That's not the answer I was expecting. I thought he'd have to confess to having found my panties. Instead of which, it seems he hasn't… and this conversation is backfiring on me, rapidly.

"Y—Yes." I can hardly say 'no', can I? Not having asked in the first place.

"Is it valuable?"

"No." I can feel myself blushing.

"Well… I haven't found anything, but I can check with housekeeping, if you like."

"No, it's fine. Honestly."

"You're sure? It's no trouble."

"No, really."

Why did I bother to say anything? Why did I think I could score points over him?

All I've done is embarrass myself even further, while he's the one who's nodding his head and walking away, like the cat who got the cream.

Damn him.

Chapter Twelve

Ryan

Every time I walk away from Peony, I feel more and more dissatisfied… bewildered… frustrated.

Is that because I want to stay with her, to take her in my arms and tell her I'm in love with her and that I never want to let her go?

Probably.

Except I can't do that. It's not what she wants to hear.

On this occasion, though, my frustration and bewilderment aren't just because I want to stay with her. They're because I don't understand her. I've been back at my hotel for over an hour now, sitting on the chair by the window, with my head in my hands, and I still don't get it.

I suppose I was being optimistic, hoping that if I offered her enough, she'd accept. But to turn me down out of hand? No… I didn't see that coming.

Don't get me wrong, I know she's not doing this on a whim, or to be difficult. I heard every word she said about her family belonging in Hart's Creek. I even heard what she said about the farm, and I understood it, too, because I feel exactly the same way about my company. My father started it and worked all his life to build it up. I know that better than anyone, and there's a heavy sense of responsibility on my shoulders to carry it on, and to make it even bigger and better. But that doesn't mean I'd commit financial suicide over it, which is what Peony seems hell-bent on doing.

All for forty acres of land.

That's all it is at the end of the day. It's just land. There are more important things in life. She must realize that.

And surely to God, she has to see that she can't go on as she is now.

I let out a sigh, pushing my fingers back through my hair, and I pick up my briefcase, putting it on the table in front of me, and popping it open. Moving aside the document I prepared for my meeting today, I pull out the one I brought up here with me… the one I amended to reflect the higher offer. I open it, glancing down at the figures Gabe and I prepared while I was still in Boston, unaware I was going to come up here and fall in love with Peony Hart.

The figure of eighteen thousand dollars per acre jumps off the page at me, and I shake my head, reading on a little further to the justification for the low offer, which was entirely because of the poor drainage that Peony already mentioned to me.

I dread to think what my father would have said if I'd gone to him and said I'd offered more than double the value for a property… which is what I've just done, having allowed Peony to talk me up by an extra three hundred thousand for a house and outbuildings that I know I'll only demolish at the earliest opportunity.

I can see him now, getting up from behind his desk, and asking me in a quiet, but firm voice, who on earth ever talked me up on a valuation?

No-one.

That's who.

No-one has ever talked me up in price.

Until now.

And even then, she still said 'no'.

Is that why I'm feeling so disgruntled? Because for the first time in my life, I've lost out in a negotiation? I've always thought of myself as being one of the best in the business, but I've just been handed my hat by someone who needs this deal even more than I do.

Is that it?

Or is it because that 'someone' was Peony?

Of course it is.

Not only am I frustrated that she won't take the best offer she's ever likely to get for her land, but I'm scared for her. I've seen her figures, and they don't add up. She has a loan with the bank, but she doesn't even have enough money to get through to this year's harvest. Unless she can renegotiate that loan, she's going to become insolvent in the next couple of months. And if something goes wrong in the meantime…

I shudder, shaking my head.

It doesn't bear thinking about.

Why can't she see that selling up is her best option? This has nothing to do with me wanting the land anymore. It's about her, and doing what's right.

Somehow, I have to get her to understand that there's no room for sentiment in business.

Trying to preserve her family's farm for the sake of her ancestors won't help, if the bank are going to repossess it, anyway.

It's common sense. Although I saw the look on her face when I said that. There were tears in her eyes, and while she still spoke with defiance, it was ill-placed. Everything – and I mean everything – is stacked against her. Last year's harvest didn't yield as much income as the previous four years. I don't know why that was. Her figures don't give me enough information, so it could have been the weather… it could have been market forces.

Whatever the reason, her income last year was down twenty percent on the year before. On top of that, she's on her own now. She doesn't have her grandmother, or her ex-boyfriend to help around the place, and while even she acknowledges it's a struggle, there's nothing she can do about it, because she doesn't have the funds to employ anyone.

She's caught between a rock and a hard place, and she's refusing to take the offer of a way out.

Because she's stubborn.

And she's frustrating.

But she's also beautiful, and vulnerable, and funny. She's got a smile that could light up a room, and she's so damn sexy, even when she's trying not to be.

I put the report back, closing up my briefcase, and get to my feet, shrugging off my jacket. I won't be doing any more business today, and it's Sunday, so I may as well get changed and relax… if such a thing is possible, considering how frustrated I'm feeling.

I take off my tie, laying it over the back of the chair, alongside my jacket, and I can't help smiling, as I look down at my other tie… the one the hotel returned to me a couple of days ago, duly laundered and stain free.

I could have worn it today, but I like wearing the blue one. Aside from the fact that it's become my favorite tie since the night I used it to bind Peony's wrists, I like the way she blushes whenever she looks at it. Sure, I wish she wasn't so embarrassed by what we did together, but the way her cheeks pink up whenever she sees me wearing this tie… it's enough to make any man smile. Why? Because I don't think her response is entirely about embarrassment. Her eyes always widen. She either parts her lips or licks them, and she breathes a little heavier, too. I swear to God, if I were to touch her pussy, it would be dripping. She relishes the memory, just as much as I do, and while that thought doesn't help very much, I still like it.

I liked that moment of sexual tension there was between us this morning. There was no getting away from that. I could feel it, and I know she could, too. I could read it in her eyes, in the way she kept looking at my lips, like she wanted me to kiss her… like she was having to fight her instincts to ask me… to beg me, like she did the other night.

Is that why she said 'no' to my offer? Because she's struggling so hard with her feelings over having slept with me?

I hope not. It wouldn't augur well for the future… the future I'm so desperate to realize with her. Okay, so she might have said her decision had nothing to do with what we'd done together, but I'm not so sure.

Just like I can't be sure why she's still so embarrassed. She has no reason to be. It would be different if we'd made love with each other, and felt it was a mistake never to be repeated… if we'd regretted it, or hated it, and yet were still being forced to meet up. That would be something else.

As it is, it's obvious neither of us feels like that. I want her so much I can't think about anything else, and while she may not feel exactly the same, she's clearly not repulsed by me. She said as much herself. She admitted I was more handsome than her ex, in one of our more awkward, but kind of inspiring, moments.

It was awkward because it came with an element of doubt. Her grandmother had convinced her that good-looking men don't stick around, and while that may have been true of her ex, it sure as hell isn't true of me. Although, when I asked if that was what she thought of me, she didn't give me a straight answer.

And I guess that's another reason for my frustration.

I want to know how she feels… not just about handsome men and their ability to commit, but why she left me after we'd made love. I'd also like her to explain why she's so embarrassed about having willingly gone to bed with me in the first place.

Still, I guess I should be grateful for small mercies. At least she admitted to finding me attractive. That thought won't help me sleep tonight. I know it won't. Just like every other night since she ran out on me, I know I'll lie awake, thinking about her and trying desperately not to jerk off. The temptation is enormous – as is my hard-on – but I'm resisting the urge, because I know it won't be the same. Without her, it'll never be the same.

I sigh, shaking my head, and get on with changing out of my suit and into a pair of jeans. Once I've pulled them on, I rescue Peony's panties from my pants pocket, smiling down at them as I re-fold them and transfer them to my jeans pocket instead.

I'll admit, I was a little surprised when she asked about them this morning. I'd assumed she was too embarrassed to bring them up, being as she's so self-conscious about everything else relating to the night we spent together. It's been a while, too, so maybe her motive was to humiliate me. In her eyes, I probably came across as a little arrogant when I was talking about her farm, although that wasn't my intention. I was being realistic, and sensible, which is something she needs to be herself, rather than romanticizing history in the face of financial ruin.

If that was her plan, it backfired. It takes a lot more than that to embarrass me, especially as she was too shy to mention the word 'panties', and just referred to them as 'something' she'd lost. We both knew what she was talking about, though, and I found it amusing to see her reaction when I offered to check with housekeeping at the hotel, to see if they'd found what she was looking for. I think she regretted asking then, and I wondered how she'd react if she knew I had them in my pocket… that I'd been carrying them with me all along.

For a moment or two, I wondered about giving them back to her, even though I knew I couldn't.

What would I have said about having kept them for so long? And how would she have reacted to that? Badly, I assumed. Besides, I didn't want to give them back. I still don't. Especially now. Despite those moments of sexual tension, and the fact that, deep down, I think she wants me nearly as much as I want her, she's fighting it. I think she'll go on fighting it, too. She can't seem to reconcile her feelings for me with the fact that I want to buy her farm… and while her underwear is a poor substitute for the real thing, it's all I've got right now as a memento of the best night of my life.

I pull out a clean shirt, unbuttoning it before I shrug it on, and refasten the buttons, just as my phone rings. I left it on the coffee table, and I stroll over, wondering if it might be Peony… if she might have changed her mind… either about me or the offer.

My heart sinks when I see the name 'Gabe' on my screen, and even though it's Sunday, I connect the call, because he's more than my second in command; he's my best friend.

"Hi." I sit down, trying to get comfortable.

"Hello, stranger."

"It hasn't been that long."

He chuckles. "No, I guess not."

"But you're missing me?"

"Don't flatter yourself."

"I wasn't, but if you're coping so well in my absence, you won't mind me staying up here for a little longer, will you?"

"Why? Is it going that badly?"

"Let's just say I've hit some resistance."

"Are you sure it's worth pursuing? You know I had some reservations about this one. The drainage is gonna cause us a problem, and…"

"The drainage is only really poor in one of the lower fields. According to the initial plans we came up with, it's where we're thinking of locating the parking lot, so that shouldn't cause any difficulties."

"But the woman who owns the place doesn't want to sell?"

"No." I hear him tap on a keyboard. "What are you doing?"

"Looking up the report." There's a brief pause. "This is Peony Hart, right?"

"Yes."

"The woman who's on the verge of going bankrupt, unless I'm much mistaken."

"You researched the financials, Gabe, so you tell me."

"I checked everything thoroughly, because I couldn't believe how bad it looked for her. That's why I thought she'd jump at eighteen thousand an acre. It seemed to me she'd be crazy not to. And yet, you're saying she's turned it down?"

"She's turned down thirty thousand an acre."

"What the fuck?" I hear rapid clicking, like he's scrolling as fast as he can. "The report I've got says eighteen thousand."

"I know. I increased the offer."

"You let her talk you up?"

"Yes, and no. I increased the offer to thirty thousand an acre, which made it one point two million for the land, and then I let her talk me up to one point five to include the house and outbuildings."

"Excuse me, but why the fuck were you offering her anything at all for the buildings? We're gonna knock them down."

"I know."

"Then why on earth…" He falls silent for a moment, and then I hear him sigh. "Oh, shit… she's in her mid-twenties, isn't she?"

"She's twenty-six, according to the research."

"And I'm gonna guess she's beautiful… and single?"

"Yes."

"And you wanna get into her panties?"

"No."

There's another silence. It's slightly longer this time. "You mean you already have? You've fucked her? And now she's the one dictating the price? What's wrong with…"

"It's not like that." I cut across him, not wanting to listen to his criticism of me… or, more importantly, of Peony.

"Then what is it like? Are you saying you haven't fucked her?"

I sigh, switching the phone to my other hand, knowing I'm going to have to tell him. "I've slept with her." *Albeit far too briefly.*

"Slept with her. Fucked her. What's the difference?"

"There speaks a man who's never been in love."

The silence is palpable, but short. "D—Did you just mention the 'L' word?"

"Yes."

"Jesus… I knew it was a mistake to let you go out on the road again."

"It wasn't a mistake."

"You mean you're really in love?"

"Yes."

"With the woman whose land you're trying to buy?"

"Yes."

"But she doesn't want to sell it to you?"

"No, she doesn't."

"Because she doesn't feel the same way?"

"I have no idea how she feels. We haven't discussed feelings. We haven't talked about us at all, really. She sees me as the enemy."

"Then why did she sleep with you?"

"Because she didn't know who I was. We met in the hotel bar on my first night here, and we… um… we didn't bother to ask each other's names before we… um…"

I've never floundered over my words quite so much, but I guess that's because it's never mattered before.

"You mean you had sex with her, and neither of you knew the connection?"

"That's exactly what I mean." Although I still prefer to think of it as making love, not having sex. It feels more accurate.

"And you couldn't have found out the next morning?"

"I could have done, if she hadn't left in the middle of the night."

There's a brief pause, yet again, before he says, "So, you mean, the first time you both realized who you were was when you arrived at her farm?"

"Precisely."

"That must have been embarrassing."

"Not really. At least, I didn't think so. I was more interested in finding out why she'd left."

"And why was that?"

"I don't know. She didn't tell me. She just got mad at me for wanting to buy her farm."

"Hmm… not the greatest start to a relationship."

"No."

"I take it you've been back to see her since."

"Several times. But she's not interested."

"In you, or your offer?"

"She's definitely not interested in the offer."

"And you?"

"I'm not sure. Like I say, she sees us as being on opposing sides, and I think she always will, until I withdraw the offer."

Wait a second…

Is that the way forward? Is that what I'm going to have to do to win her over? Let her commit financial suicide?

It feels wrong… unless…

"So, you're gonna be up there for a while yet?" Gabe says, interrupting my train of thought.

"Yes. Is that a problem?"

"No."

"There isn't anything I need to know about at the office?"

"Other than Adrian sulking, no."

"Adrian can sulk. He needed to be told. I can't allow him to spend the company's money on something that might end up costing us a fortune, without consulting me."

"I got that, although I'm still not sure he has. He's murmuring about how unfair you were."

"Really? He thinks that was unfair? Can you reiterate the situation to him? Make sure he understands he won't get another chance. All his deals have gotta be authorized by you or me before he signs on the dotted line. Is that clear?"

"As crystal."

"While we're discussing Adrian's deals, can you make some initial inquiries about the kind of building permissions we're likely to be able to get on that plot he's just purchased in Vermont? Adrian said he bought it with a residential project in mind."

"Even though we're commercial developers?"

"Yeah. I pointed out that I didn't appreciate him unilaterally trying to change the direction of the company, but the land is ours now, so we might as well see what we can do with it."

"I'll look into it first thing tomorrow and email you when I've got some answers."

"Thanks."

"Keep me posted on how things go up there, won't you?"

"With the land, you mean?"

"With all of it."

I'm not surprised by that. Gabe cares, just like I care about him, and as we end our call, I sit back, my head spinning.

I'm not wrong, am I? The only way Peony is going to take us seriously, or even consider a relationship with me, is if I withdraw my offer. That feels so wrong to me, given her situation, but I guess there are alternatives to simply pulling out. I'd have to come at it from a different angle, but even then, it won't be easy.

It'll mean a complete change of plans… although quite what that will involve is beyond me.

Having fallen for Peony, I suppose I'd imagined that, if she'd accepted my offer, and sold me the farm, she'd have moved back to Boston with me. Maybe not 'with me' straight away… but as a woman of independent means, she could have bought her own place. We could have gotten used to being a couple, and eventually, when she was ready, we could have moved in together. Call me presumptuous – call me arrogant, if you like – but it never occurred to me that she'd be so wedded to this town… or to her forty acres.

She is, though. There's no getting away from it.

Leaving isn't an option.

And therein lies the problem. I'm tied to Boston, and I've had a taste of what happens when I turn my back for five minutes.

It doesn't end well.

So, does that mean I'll have to walk away?

And what would I be walking away from? My relationship with Peony, or my business?

I shake my head, because whatever angle I come at it from, I know I can't do either. Which I guess means I'm going to have to come up with an alternate solution…

Chapter Thirteen

Peony

I haven't had the best day so far.

I had every intention of putting last week, and Ryan's visit yesterday out of my mind, and starting afresh. I probably would have done, too, if I hadn't gone outside this morning, and discovered a patch of oil underneath my truck.

Obviously, that had nothing to do with Ryan, but it reminded me that if just the slightest thing goes wrong, it has the possibility of becoming catastrophic for me.

Something had clearly happened to my truck, and it was going to cost money to put it right. Did I have any options? No, of course I didn't. There's no way I can survive without transportation.

So, I called Levi at the auto repair shop and explained the problem.

"It sounds like a gasket. Bring it down this morning and I'll have a look at it."

"Do you think it'll take long to fix?"

I wasn't worried about the length of time he'd need to keep my truck, but I knew time meant money, and was trying to gage how much I might be looking at.

"An hour or so. That's if I'm right about it being the gasket, of course."

"Okay."

I called Laurel after that… not because I expected her to help me, but because I didn't relish sitting around at the auto shop for an hour. Levi's lovely, in an avuncular way, but I can think of nicer places to spend an hour than at his office.

"We could meet for coffee?" she said, once I'd explained my problem. "I could do with getting out of the house."

"Oh?"

Laurel's house is her pride and joy, so I was surprised by her obvious desire to leave it.

"Yeah… we're having some work done in the kitchen, and I'd rather be anywhere than here."

"Really? I didn't know you were having anything done."

"Neither did I until yesterday, but I've been saying to Mitch for ages that I wish the kitchen had an island unit, and he decided to surprise me by having one put in."

"Today?"

"I think it's gonna take more than one day, because we're having a new floor laid at the same time, but yeah."

She sounded pleased, but a little mind-blown. "Can I guess that some advance warning might have been nice?"

"It would. Not that I'm complaining about having such a fabulous husband, you understand?"

"Of course not."

Dropping off my truck takes almost no time at all. A quick look under the hood confirms Levi's diagnosis, and he gazes down at me, the smile on his lips making the corners of his eyes crinkle, as he tells me it'll take him an hour at most.

"Thanks, Levi."

"Anytime. Do you wanna wait in the office?"

I shake my head. "I've arranged to meet Laurel for coffee, so I'll come back when we're done."

He nods his head, his smile widening. "Say 'hi' from me."

Levi's in his late-fifties, probably around the same age as my father would have been if he'd lived, and he knows everyone in Hart's Creek. I guess that's partly because he's married to Angela, who works at the Hart's Creek Courier. She's the receptionist and seems to make it her business to know everything that's going on in town. She's not a malicious gossip, though, and if you ask her to keep something to herself, she will. It's also because Levi's auto repair shop is one of those places we all need to visit every once in a while… even if we'd rather not.

That's no reflection on Levi. Like I say, he's lovely… and very good at his job.

Going outside, I glance across the road at Dawson's bar. It's closed at the moment, which isn't a bad thing. There's less chance of me coming face-to-face with Dawson, and I cross over the road at a diagonal, stepping up on the sidewalk outside the dentist's office.

The windows are frosted, so no-one can see inside. The lettering etched on the window reads 'Cooper White' which I've always thought was an appropriate name for a dentist.

Like just about everyone else here, I've known Cooper all my life. He's nearly ten years older than me, so he's more of an acquaintance than a friend, and as I have an innate fear of dentists, I'm happy to keep it that way. As dentists go, he's fine… but he's still a dentist.

I can see Laurel's car parked outside the gym, but there's no-one inside it, so I hurry to the coffee shop to find her and Addy sitting at a table by the window. It's not the same one I sat at with Ryan the other day, but further in the corner.

She stands as soon as she sees me, and I smile, taking in her designer jeans that hug her figure, and the fitted pale pink blouse she's wearing on top. Her hair is a similar shade to mine, but where mine is wild and untamable most of the time, hers is smooth and silky, worn shoulder length and cut to crisp perfection. I make my way over, giving her a hug before I bend and kiss Addy on the forehead.

She smiles up at me, her blue eyes fluttering beneath her light blonde hair. "Hello Aunty Pee-nee." I smile. She's always struggled to say my name, and 'Pee-nee' has so far been the best she can manage. I don't mind in the slightest. She's only missing out one syllable, and in fact, it's grown on me so much that, even when she can say Peony properly, I think I'm gonna ask her to still call me 'Pee-nee'.

"Hello, baby girl."

Laurel has brought a coloring book and some crayons to keep Addy occupied while we talk, and as I sit beside her, she returns her attention to a drawing of a princess, which she's currently scribbling over.

"I was waiting for you to get here before I ordered any drinks," Laurel says with a smile. "So, what will you have?"

"I'll get them."

She shakes her head. "No, it's fine."

"In that case, a flat white, please."

"Can I have a cookie, Mommy?" Addison says, looking up from her coloring.

"As long as you promise to eat your lunch."

"I promise." She holds up her hand like she's swearing an oath, and I have to stifle a laugh.

Laurel goes to order our coffees, while I help Addy with her coloring, attempting to get her to shade the princess's dress in pink and purple, although she seems more interested in scribbling bright red all over the background. To be honest, she's happy, and she's quiet, so what does it matter?

Laurel returns, carrying a tray, which she sets down on the table and I help her offload our coffees, some milk for Addy and her chocolate chip cookie, although Laurel takes the plate, breaking the cookie into pieces before she passes it to her daughter.

"Not too much at once," she says, and Addy smiles, taking an enormous chunk and popping it into her mouth.

Laurel rolls her eyes and settles down opposite, so she can watch Addy and talk to me at the same time.

"I'm sorry I haven't been in touch about coming over to look at your accounts," she says, straightening Addy's crayons, although she's more focused on eating her cookie. "I haven't had a chance to speak with Mitch yet."

"Don't worry about it."

She smiles. "Have you heard anything more from your friendly property developer?"

"I don't know about friendly, but yes, I have."

She sits forward, picking up her cup. "Tell me more."

"I bumped into him on Saturday afternoon."

"Accidentally?"

"Of course. I'm not stalking him."

"Ahh… but is he stalking you?"

"He said he wasn't."

Her mouth drops open. "You didn't ask him that, did you?"

"I asked if he was spying on me." It felt appropriate at the time, although it sounds big-headed now I come to think about it.

"Okay, so having started your conversation so auspiciously, what happened next?"

"He asked me to have dinner with him."

She raises her eyebrows. "So, he's not all about the business, then?"

"Yes, he is… which is why I said 'no'."

"You turned him down?"

"I did."

"Why?"

"For the reason I just gave. He's all about the business."

"Hmm… sounds like it." She tilts her head, narrowing her eyes just slightly. "Admit it, you were scared, weren't you?"

"Scared of what?" I can feel myself blushing and I sip my coffee, trying to hide it.

"That he'd talk you back into B-E-D again."

I love how she spells out words when we're with Addy, like she'd know what we were talking about.

"So what if I was? It still didn't work."

"What didn't?"

"My refusal."

"What did he do then? Tie you up and force you to have dinner with him?"

I choke, even though I've swallowed my mouthful of coffee. The memories of being bound by Ryan are way too fresh in my mind to treat her remark as a joke.

"N—No." I stutter out my words once I've recovered. "He came over later on and brought dinner with him."

She sighs, her shoulders rising and falling. "I've forgotten what romance feels like, you know?"

"Says she, whose husband is having her kitchen remodeled for her."

"You think that's romantic?" She looks bemused.

"It's not hearts and flowers, but it's something you wanted, and Mitch has obviously paid attention and is getting it done, so yeah… I'd say that's romantic."

"You're setting the bar way too low, Peony."

She giggles and so do I.

"Besides, Ryan wasn't being romantic. He was being a businessman, trying to close a deal."

"Yeah… bringing you dinner sounds really businesslike." She's still smiling, and she watches me while I sip my coffee, and then leans a little closer, lowering her voice. "Why don't the two of you just get through the business, one way or the other, and then move onto enjoying the personal side of your relationship?"

"Because we don't have a relationship… and in any case, we kinda tried that."

"I know you've already done the deed, but…"

"That's not what I meant." And I don't need reminding. "What I meant was, he came round yesterday morning to make me a formal offer for the farm… and to flirt with me, I think."

"You only think?"

"It felt like he was flirting… at least when he wasn't making me feel worthless, anyway."

"Making you feel worthless? That doesn't sound very kind… or gentlemanly."

"I never said he was a gentleman. I don't recall saying he was kind, either."

"You also didn't say he was downright mean."

"He wasn't… not really. He just reminded me how close I am to losing the farm… not to him, but to the bank."

She frowns, all jokes forgotten. "Are things really that bad?"

I shrug my shoulders. "I'll admit to having had a few sleepless nights."

"Seriously?"

"I may not have done my accounts for months, but even I know I don't have enough money in the bank."

"Then take his offer."

"I can't. I'll never sell my farm… not to him, or anyone."

"But if you're in danger of losing it to the bank anyway…"

"You sound like him. And besides, even if I wanted to take his offer – which I don't – he probably thinks I'm crazy now."

"Why would he think that?"

"Because I made a stupid attempt at embarrassing him before he left."

"What on earth did you do?"

She's smiling again, her eyes alight with anticipation. "I asked if he'd found anything of mine in his hotel room."

"Like your P-A-N-T-I-E-S, you mean?"

"Yes, although I didn't mention them by name."

She leans closer, lowering her voice, although I don't know why she's bothering… not when she's just spelled out the word 'panties' loud enough for the entire coffee shop to hear. "What made you think bringing your lost property into the conversation was a good idea?"

"Like I say, I wanted to humiliate him, because he'd made me feel like such a failure. Except it didn't work."

"Why not?"

"Because he used it as an opportunity to remind me I'd run out on him."

"So it backfired?"

"And how."

"Had he found them, after all that?"

"No. God knows where they are. He offered to check with housekeeping for me, but I said 'no'. He'd have had to ask what it was I'd lost, and there was no way I was gonna explain. I already wished I hadn't started the conversation by then."

Laurel's lips twist up, and we both start laughing.

"I wonder who's got them now," she says. "And what they're doing with them?"

"Ew… don't."

It was bad enough when I thought Ryan might have my underwear, but the idea of a stranger pawing over my panties is so much worse.

Laurel's phone rings, interrupting her laughter, and she pulls it from her purse, frowning at the screen before she connects the call.

"Hello?" She nods her head, then rolls her eyes. "Didn't Mitch tell you?" She listens and then lets out a sigh. "Okay. I'll come back and check it out."

She hangs up, putting her phone away, and pushing her fingers back through her hair, although it still looks pristine when she's finished.

"Who was that?" I ask.

"The guys at the house. They want to know which end of the island unit to put the wine refrigerator."

"They're that far along already?"

"I don't think so. I think it's about deciding where to put the power outlets, or something." She shakes her head, gathering up Addy's crayons. "I'm sorry, but we're gonna have to go."

"That's okay. My truck will probably be ready by now, anyway."

I help her finish packing Addy's thing away into the bag she brought with her, and then lift Addy onto the floor, smiling at the pretty dress she's wearing. It's a lovely sunny day today, and it feels appropriate, even if it is only spring still. As I go to take her hand to make sure she doesn't run off, she holds her arms up.

"You wanna be carried?" I say, looking down at her, as I stand up myself.

"She's perfectly capable of walking." Laurel shakes her head at her daughter. "You're getting too heavy to carry now."

"I don't mind." I lift Addy into my arms and she nestles against me, tangling her fingers into my hair, which is something she's done since she was tiny, and was fascinated by my crazy curls.

I make my way to the door, with Laurel following, and once we're outside, I turn toward her car.

"I'll call you when I've spoken to Mitch about coming over," she says.

"Okay."

"And in the meantime, try not to lose any more underwear."

I turn, noting the smirk on her face, and then spin around again, walking straight into someone coming the other way.

"I'm sorry…"

"Excuse me."

My head darts up at the sound of the familiar voice, my cheeks pinking with embarrassment as my eyes land on the perfect face of Ryan Andrews.

Why him? Why now?

Please don't let him have heard Laurel's wisecrack about my underwear. I've already humiliated myself enough with this man.

He pulls off his sunglasses and stares right at me, although he screws up his eyes against the sunlight… not that I blame him. It's particularly bright this morning. After a second or two, he averts his gaze to Addy.

"Who's this?" he says, smiling, and she grins up at him. *Traitor.*

"This is Addy, and her mom Laurel… the friend I was telling you about."

He nods his head. "The one who's gonna help with your accounts?"

"That's it." I turn to Laurel. "This is Ryan Andrews… the man who wants to buy my farm."

Laurel holds out her hand, and he takes it, in the briefest of shakes, ignoring her smile, his eyes still focused on me.

"I'm sorry to cut and run, but there's somewhere I need to be."

"Oh… okay."

He turns to Laurel. "It was nice to meet you."

"You, too."

He nods and looks back at me. "I'll see you around." He doesn't wait for a reply but crosses the street, heading for the drugstore. I let out a sigh, which is more of a huff, feeling perversely disappointed. Why didn't he want to stop? And why does it bother me so much?

I glance at Laurel, who's studying me, her lips twitching upward as she reaches for Addy, and continues to her car, opening it and strapping Addy into her seat before she shuts the rear door and turns to face me.

"Are you crazy?"

Probably. "Why?" I ask.

"Because that man is utterly divine. Can you give me a reason why you wouldn't want to become a permanent fixture in his bed?"

"I can give you several, but I think you're forgetting, I've already been in Ryan's bed." I've even been fixed to it.

"I'm not forgetting anything, including the fact that you told me how earth-shattering it was. Why would you wanna give that up?"

It's not about wanting to. It's about having no choice. "Because he's trying to buy my farm from under me... remember?"

"You mean the farm that keeps you awake at night, worrying about how you're gonna make ends meet? The farm that even you admit you can't afford to keep going? That farm?"

"Yes."

She leans back against the car door, folding her arms. "How much is he offering?"

"One point five million."

Her eyes widen. "It's official. You're insane. You should take his money... and then take him. I'm pretty sure he's on offer, if you want him."

"What makes you say that?"

"The fact that he couldn't drag his eyes away from you."

"Hmm... because he's looking for the chink in my armor."

She sighs, shaking her head. "Why can't you just accept that he's trying to do the right thing here?"

"By buying my farm? You're kidding, right?"

"No. I seriously doubt your land is worth even half what he's offering you."

"It is to me," I say, tears welling in my eyes, and before she can reply, I turn and hurry down the street.

"Peony?"

I hear her calling after me, but I'm not in the mood for talking… or listening to how much of a failure I am.

I've already heard enough of that from Ryan.

The only good part of my day so far is that the repair to my truck wasn't as expensive as I thought, but now I'm back home, sitting at the kitchen table, I have to confess, I haven't felt this low in ages.

I never thought I'd say this, but why me?

What have I done to deserve a best friend who seems to think I should sell my family's heritage to the highest bidder? And why is it that the man who's gotten under my skin doesn't seem to want to spend time with me anymore? I know I shouldn't want him like I do, and I know I shouldn't let him get to me, but I can't help it. He's in my head and my heart the whole time, but judging from the way he scuttled off today, that's the last place he wants to be, regardless of what Laurel thinks.

And I know I'm being contrary, wanting the man who's trying to buy my farm, when I don't want to sell it, but that's how it is. That's how he makes me feel.

My phone rings, making me jump and I pull it from my back pocket, letting out a sigh when I see Laurel's name on the screen.

Do I feel like talking to her?

Not particularly.

Would it be childish to ignore her call?

Absolutely.

I press the green icon and switch it to speaker, feeling too tired to even hold up the phone, and I set it down on the table.

"Hello?" She sounds wary.

"Hi."

"I'm sorry I upset you. I wasn't being very sensitive, was I?"

"It's okay." It's not, but at least she's apologized, and we're talking again. I'm grateful for that.

"Will you do something for me?"

"That depends what it is."

"Please don't bite my head off, but will you think about Ryan's offer? I know this isn't what you wanna hear, Peony, but one and a half million is a lot of money to walk away from."

"I know it is. And you're right. It's way more than the land is worth. But the farm means more to me than money."

"I get that. But this is a way out. Can't you see?"

"I don't want a way out. I want a way to stay in… to stay here, where I belong."

She doesn't reply, but that's because I know she doesn't agree with me. She thinks I'm crazy for turning down Ryan's offer… and for not jumping straight back into bed with him, too.

What she doesn't know is how complicated it is… at least in my head.

And in my heart.

"Call me if you wanna talk… okay?"

I agree, even though I know I won't. What would be the point? She'd only tell me I'm wrong… again. We finish our call and I sit back in my seat, feeling lonelier than I have since my grandmother died. I know she'd agree with me. She'd want me to keep the farm, no matter the cost, and I fight back my tears, wishing she could be here with me, to tell me I'm doing the right thing.

I can hear her now...

"Why are you sitting there feeling sorry for yourself? Crying never solved anything, did it?"

It's not that she was unsympathetic, but she was a realist, and she had a point.

There's no point in crying, is there?

Not when there's work to be done...

Chapter Fourteen

Ryan

It was a surprise to see Peony in town this morning.

I'd made plans in my head to call on her this afternoon, and I'd only gone out this morning to pick up some painkillers from the drugstore, having woken up with the mother of all headaches. That's not like me, but I guess the lack of sleep is taking its toll.

All I could think about last night was Peony, and while that's nothing new, my thoughts are no longer just about her and all the things I want us to do together. Now, I'm worrying about the future. Not just hers, but ours too… oh, and how to get her out of the situation she's in without butting heads at every turn.

On top of that, I'm still hung up on the geography.

A hundred miles doesn't sound too far, when you say it. It's nothing. No distance at all. But it might as well be a million miles when you want to spend all your time with someone who lives a hundred miles away… especially when you both have good reasons for staying exactly where you are.

It's complicated, and right now, I'm struggling to find a solution. There has to be one. There has to be some way we can be where we need to be, and still be together – assuming, of course, she feels anything at all for me – but at the moment, it's evading me.

Having barely slept, in twenty minute fits and starts, and woken with a blinding pain behind my eyes, I struggled through the shower and initially sought solace in breakfast and coffee. Neither of those worked any kind of magic and after sitting in my darkened room for a while, absorbing the silence, I realized I'd have to brave the bright sunshine to buy some painkillers.

The last thing I expected was to bump into Peony as she walked along Main Street, or that she'd have a toddler cradled in her arms.

Seeing her like that did something weird to my chest… or to my heart, to be more precise. It wasn't just because she looked so cute, either. There was more to it than that. It was like the yearning I have for her suddenly became stronger… went deeper.

I'd have loved to stay and work that out, or just talk and spend some time with her, but the pain in my head was becoming too much, especially as I'd taken off my sunglasses, and was struggling against the glare of sunlight. So, I made my excuses and left. But I'll still go to see her this afternoon.

Why?

Because seeing her once a day isn't enough for me, and because I'm not giving up.

On Peony, that is…

I'm fairly sure in my own mind that I'm going to withdraw my offer for her farm. If that's what it takes for us to be together, then it's a small sacrifice to make.

Is that why I'm going to see her? To tell her the deal's off?

No, it's not. I feel like I need to solve the problem of how we're going to make this work before I tell her that.

So, why am I going?

Aside from the fact that I feel as though I belong with her, and I'm happier when I'm with her than when I'm not, I'm hoping that, if I spend some time with her, a solution might present itself. I'm not getting very far by myself, and I can't help wondering if maybe she'll say something, or I'll think of something while I'm there that will solve the problem.

Even if it doesn't, at least we'll be together. It's a chance to get to know her, and for her to get to know me, and hopefully see beyond the deal, past the business, to the man I want to be with her.

My headache takes ages to shift. I've spent that time lying in my room, my eyes shut, the drapes closed, and for a couple of hours, I've even managed to sleep.

It seems to have helped and by just after three in the afternoon, I'm feeling a lot better. I'm certainly feeling well enough to visit Peony, and as I quickly wash up in the bathroom, I wonder about going across the street to the florists to buy her some flowers.

Would that be too much?

Would she think I'm trying to sweeten her up, or bribe her into taking the deal?

I guess there's a chance she might, and with that in mind, I veto the idea. As much as I'd love to buy her flowers, I'm not ready to explain that I'm not in the market for her farm anymore, so I won't be able to contradict her… not with any conviction. And the last thing I want is for us to fall out again over something that doesn't matter.

I come out of the bathroom, feeling reasonably refreshed, and contemplate changing into my suit… or more precisely, my tie. I love the effect it has on Peony, and if today goes as well as I'm hoping it might, I guess it could be useful to have it with me.

I glance across at it, recalling how she held her hands out to be tied, gazing up into my eyes, all needy and expectant, and I feel a shiver run through my body, not at the memory, but at the thought that, for the first time in seventeen years, I don't want to use a restraint. I shake my head. No… it's more than that. I don't *need* to use a restraint.

I shudder at the thought of Peony's touch… of her gentle caress on my skin while I love her. But this isn't fear. It's longing.

"Oh, fuck…" The words leave my lips on a low groan, and I grab my keys and wallet, heading for the door.

There's no sign of Peony as I park my car beside the fence, and I switch off the engine, getting out, and wandering up to the house.

Her tractor isn't here, either, and I guess she must be out on it, doing something.

Not that I'm in a hurry. I can wait.

I'm about to sit down on the bottom step when I hear the throaty growl of an engine in the distance and I wander to the side of the house, glancing around it.

Sure enough, she's coming this way, along a track that divides one field from another. She's not looking in this direction, but is glancing at the trees on either side, and occasionally wiping at her eyes with her sleeved arm.

She's crying?

I step out, surprised by the pain in my chest, as I start toward her.

It takes a moment or two, but eventually, she looks up, steering the tractor, and notices me. I see the way her body stiffens, and how her shoulders seem to drop as she makes more of an effort to wipe away her tears. *There's no need, baby. I can do that for you.*

I move out of the way as she maneuvers the tractor into place beside the house, and then I hold out my hand to help her down. She stares straight ahead, like she hasn't seen me, even though I know she has, so I guess she's choosing to ignore me.

No chance.

I climb up so I'm standing right next to her, our legs touching, my hand resting on the steering wheel.

"What's wrong, Peony?"

She shakes her head and bites on her bottom lip, holding back her tears as she looks up at me and says, "I can't believe this, but I think I've got apple scab."

"You've got what?"

"Not me… the trees." She leans back and waves her arm around. "They've got apple scab. I need to go inside and check, just to be sure. I've never seen it before, but if I'm right…" Her voice fades and she looks up at me, tilting her head.

I guess that means she wants to get down, and that I'm in the way.

I turn and jump to the ground, but before I can hold up a hand to her again, she's already climbing off of the tractor by herself, making it clear she needs no help from me.

Without a word, she strides off toward the front of the house, and although I haven't been invited, I follow her. There's no way I'm going to leave… not when she's this upset.

Inside, she goes straight over to the kitchen table, pulling forward an ancient laptop as she sits down, sighing deeply. She opens it, and I wander around behind her, watching as she goes to a browser and searches for the term 'apple scab'. Ignoring all the articles, she clicks on the images and scrolls through them slowly before letting her head rest in her hands.

"Well?" I say and she startles, like she'd forgotten I was here.

"I was right," she whispers, and I move around, pulling out a chair and sitting beside her.

"What can you do? Is it treatable?" The images on her screen are telling me nothing, except that the leaves on her trees probably have brownish-colored spots on them.

"Yes. There are fungicides. I don't like using them, but with something like this, I don't have any choice."

"Okay."

She shakes her head. "It's not that simple. The fungicides are expensive… at least they are to me. It's gonna practically wipe me out, and as for the work involved…" Her voice cracks and I can't help myself… I move closer, letting my hand rest on her arm. She looks up at me, her eyes betraying her confusion.

"At the risk of repeating myself, you can't carry on like this."

I hadn't planned on telling her I was going to pull out of the deal, but I think I'm going to have to. While I'm about it, I may as well pay for the fungicide, and maybe offer to pay off her bank loan as well. I open my mouth to speak, but she gets there first, standing up and pushing her chair back, so it nearly falls over.

"You think I can't carry on? Just watch me."

Her eyes are on fire, and she pulls her phone from her back pocket, walking across to the kitchen sink and leaning against it as she scrolls up and down, presumably through her contacts list and finally stops, tapping on the screen and holding the phone to her ear.

"Hi. It's Peony Hart here." She pauses and then says, "I'm good, thanks. How are you?" She's polite, I'll say that for her… even in the face of adversity. I sit back, watching her as she stares up at the ceiling, waiting and then says, "I suppose you shouldn't complain about being busy," and then laughs, although it's a half-hearted effort. "I—I called to say my trees have got apple scab." She stops talking, swallowing hard, and then continues, "I know, but I'm not sure which one is best. What would you recommend?" Again, she waits and then nods her head. "Okay.

No, it's forty acres, and the leaves are still in tight clusters." She rubs her hand down her face. "No, no blossom at all yet." She sighs, her shoulders rising and falling with the effort. "Okay. I'll be over as soon as I can to collect it. Thanks, Joseph."

She hangs up, putting her phone back in her pocket, and although I can feel the hostility pouring off of her still, I get up and go over, standing a couple of feet away from her, as I look down into her upturned face.

"What was that about?" I ask.

"It was about me ordering the fungicide to spray my crops. I'm gonna drive over to Willmont Vale to collect it."

"Where's Willmont Vale?"

"About six miles away."

"Do you want me to take you?"

"In your nice shiny car? I don't think so. This stuff comes in enormous barrels, not dainty little bags."

I hold up my hands, surrendering to her mood. "Okay. I didn't realize." As I shake my head, turning away, she grabs my arm, pulling me back.

"What did that mean?"

"What?"

"You shook your head at me." She releases my arm but glares up at me. "Why?"

I move closer, towering over her. "If you want me to be honest, I think you're crazy."

"For turning down your offer, I suppose?"

"No. For not listening. I hadn't finished what I was saying."

"When?"

"Just now. When I said you can't carry on like this."

She huffs out a half-laugh. "Maybe not, but it's obvious what you were gonna say."

"Oh? Is it?"

She steps forward, so our bodies are almost touching. "Yeah. You were gonna tell me that staying here is gonna bankrupt me, that being stubborn about refusing your offer is the same as handing the farm to the bank." She sighs, shaking her head. "Maybe you're right, Ryan. But this is where I belong."

"I know. I get that… and for your information, I wasn't gonna say anything of the kind. There's more to this than my offer, and your farm."

"There is?"

"You know there is. This is about what happened between us the other night."

"For God's sake… do we have to talk about that the whole time?"

She steps aside, ducking around me, and darts to the other side of the table. I turn, facing her, regretting the space and the three feet of oak that's now separating us.

"We don't talk about it the whole time. That's the goddamn problem. We haven't talked about it at all. Not properly. We've teased around the edges of it, but we haven't really talked."

"And you wanna do this now? Can't you see I've got more important things to worry about?"

I can't describe how much that hurts. Her words are like knives, cutting through my flesh, stabbing at my heart. "More important?" I whisper and she blushes, biting on her lip. She doesn't retract her words, though, and for a moment or two, we just stare at each other. It's not a pleasant sensation, not like it has been before, and I turn away, glancing toward the door. "I'll leave you to get on." I take a couple of steps, but then turn back. "Can I ask you something?"

I half expect her to say 'no', or at best, 'if you must', but she just says, "Yes," and continues to gaze at me, like she never stopped, even when my back was turned.

"If we hadn't slept together first, would you have accepted my offer?"

She shakes her head. "I already told you, it's got nothing to do with that. And as you keep telling me, this is business, and that was…" She stops talking, like she can't find the words, and I step over, skirting around the table, so I'm right in front of her again.

"Something you'd rather forget, even if I can't?" I hear and see her swallow hard, but she doesn't say a word and just stares up at me until I can't take it anymore. "Fine. I get the message, Peony."

I turn again, striding to the door, which I throw open, stepping out onto the porch.

I'm at my car in no time at all, and I risk a glance back at the house, unsurprised to discover there's no sign of Peony. She hasn't followed me. She's not interested in me, or what we did together. That much is clear to me now.

And that being the case, there's nothing worth staying for, is there?

I turn my car, speeding down the track and onto the main road, getting back to the town in minutes.

There's no-one in the hotel lobby. Even the reception desk is deserted, and I make my way up the stairs to my room, slamming the door behind me and finally letting out the breath I think I've been holding on to since I left Peony's farm.

No matter how I feel, she regrets what happened between us, and even if the thought of never seeing her again makes me empty inside, I can't stay here.

I grab my laptop holder, throwing it onto the bed, and pull my laptop from its charger, zipping it into the bag, and rolling up the charger cable so it fits into the side pocket. With that done, I take my clothes from the closet and dump them on the bed before picking up my jacket and tie from the back of the chair.

The tie feels heavier than it should, and I run its silky length through my hand, sitting down on the mattress, and staring at it. I can't forget the way she looked up at me as I fastened her wrists, or the way her bottom lip trembled. It wasn't with fear. It was with anticipation. She yelled at me for more. She begged me to fuck her, and afterwards, she fell asleep, cradled in my arms, all soft and satisfied.

And now she wants to forget it?

How is that even possible?

How am I supposed to pack my bags, drive back to Boston and pretend I didn't leave my heart here... leave *myself* here?

It can't be done.

"Then don't do it," I murmur.

I picture her, as she was just now, staring at me, uncertain... lost... helpless... and I know, no matter how much she's hurt me, I can't walk away.

Chapter Fifteen

Peony

I glance up at the sky, taking the turn that leads back to Hart's Creek, and shake my head. It's still clear, the sun shining, with barely a cloud in sight, but I know it'll be getting dark in a couple of hours, and even though I've got lights on my tractor, they won't be enough.

If I could wait until tomorrow to treat the trees, then I would. But I can't.

There's a rainstorm due tomorrow evening, and although it'll blow through by the following morning, we're supposed to have showers until the middle of next week.

I'd already heard the forecast earlier today, but Joseph just confirmed it.

"You'll need to get this fungicide on today," he said, as he helped me load up the truck. "That'll give it a good twenty-four hours before the rain starts. Then you can do the second spraying at the end of next week."

"Will twenty-four hours be long enough between applying it and the rain coming in?"

"It'll be fine, but you'll have to get it done tonight. If you wait until morning, you'll be wasting your time… and your money."

I nodded my head and thanked him for his help, knowing even then how hard it was going to be.

The drive back hasn't helped.

The apple scab infestation might be quite mild at the moment, but Joseph also warned me it can take hold quickly, and if it does, my entire crop will be ruined.

I felt like crying when he said that, but I think I'm all cried out.

It was my initial reaction when I first noticed the brown spots on the leaves. I think I knew instinctively what was wrong, and even though I didn't want to believe it, my tears wouldn't stop. They coursed down my cheeks as I brushed them away, trying to focus on the blight that seemed to have overrun my orchard.

As if I didn't have enough to worry about already…

I mean, wasn't it bad enough that Ryan's trying to buy my ailing farm, and that my best friend thinks I should sell out, even though I don't want to?

Didn't I already have enough to think about, having slept with Ryan… and fallen for him?

Did I really need to risk losing all my crops as well?

Crying wasn't going to help. I knew that. The problem was, I couldn't help it. I was still crying as I drove the tractor back to the farmhouse. I needed to go online and check that I hadn't made a mistake… that the trees really were infected.

What I hadn't expected was that Ryan would be waiting for me.

Was that why I was so rude to him? Because I hadn't expected him to be there?

Was that even a valid excuse?

Of course it wasn't.

And even if it were, my behavior still wouldn't make sense.

Let's face it, it was only this morning that I was upset because he didn't hang around to talk. Why, in that case, did I practically throw him out of my house, just this afternoon?

What's wrong with me?

Is this what love does?

Does it make you behave like an idiot?

It certainly seems to make me ungracious… and rude.

I mean… why did I have to fly off the handle at him like that?

He was only stating the truth, after all. We haven't really talked about what happened between us, have we? I've ducked the subject at every chance, and I did the same thing again today, in the most hurtful of ways. He didn't deserve that, even if he does want to buy my farm from under me.

Not only that, but I lied to him, too.

Or at least, I didn't tell him the truth, which is practically the same thing.

Silence can sometimes be the same as lying, especially when you don't correct the misconception it creates. And I didn't.

All he did was to ask if I'd rather forget what we did together, and I couldn't answer. My lips wouldn't open. My voice wouldn't work. I was busy warring with my feelings. I was wondering what he was doing at the farm… why he'd come back after walking away so abruptly this morning. At the same time, I was debating whether to deal with the problem at hand, and leave to pick up the fungicide, or do what I really wanted, and rip his clothes off, to prove to him in actions, rather than words, that I didn't want to forget the other night, or anything he'd done to me.

How could I possibly forget when he haunts my dreams… when he's part of my every waking moment?

Would succumbing to him and my feelings have solved anything?

Of course not.

It certainly wouldn't have helped with the apple scab, and as for everything else, I imagine it would just have made me want him more… and more.

And he knew that.

Just like he probably knows that, given time and enough persuasion, I'll succumb to anything he wants… maybe even his offer for my farm.

"No!"

I say the word aloud, just to give it credence.

I'll never give in on that.

No matter what happens, I'll never give in on that.

I slow, turning into the farm entrance, and pull up sharply when I see Ryan's black Mercedes parked alongside the fence. He left. I know he did. So why is he back?

I drive slowly up the track, parking in front of the house, and turn off the engine, jumping down, just as he gets out of his car and looks over at me.

"Not now, Ryan. I'm really not in the mood," I call as I lower the tailgate of my truck, and he frowns, walking up to me.

"In the mood for what?"

"Another fight."

He shakes his head. "I'm not gonna fight with you. I'm here to help."

I look up at him, shielding my eyes from the lowering sun, which is directly behind him. "Help?"

"Yeah. You've got forty acres to spray. Unless I'm much mistaken, you're gonna need to get it done before it rains tomorrow, and you're running out of light."

"You worked that out?"

"Sure."

"And you wanna help me?"

He nods his head, although I can't help shaking mine. "What's wrong?"

"I—I don't get it. This morning, you didn't even wanna talk to me. This afternoon we had a fight, and you walked out, and now you're back, and you wanna help?"

His brow furrows. "Who says I didn't wanna talk to you this morning?"

"I do. When we met on Main Street, you couldn't get away from me fast enough."

He smiles, his brow clearing again. "Oh, I see. That wasn't personal, Peony. I had a lot on my mind at the time… and I also had the worst headache of my life. I needed to get to the drugstore for some painkillers as an alternative to ripping my head off. That was all. I'd have loved to stay and talk, if I'd been capable."

I feel guilty now for assuming the worst. It seems to be a common theme with me at the moment.

"Are you feeling better now?" I ask, and his smile widens.

"Yes, thank you. And, as for the fight, I'm sorry about that."

He's apologizing? "Why are you sorry? I'm the one who was ungracious… yet again."

"Maybe. But I was insensitive. You needed to concentrate on the farm, and getting out to collect the supplies. I was holding you up, talking about things that don't matter… at least, not to you."

I reach out, placing my hand on his arm, and I swear to God, he tenses, and gasps, loud enough for me to hear it.

"I didn't say they don't matter."

"You didn't need to, Peony." He steps back, breaking the connection between us, and looks at the fungicide in my truck. "Now… what do you need me to do?"

I gaze up at his perfect face… his generous lips and stubbled jawline, and I open my mouth to ask if he'll hold me. The thing I need more than anything else is for him to take me in his arms and tell me it'll be okay, but I can't say the words, because I'm scared he'll refuse. So, instead, I nod toward the barrels. "If you can help me offload the fungicide, we'll need to fill my sprayer with it, and then attach that to the tractor."

"Okay," he says, pulling forward the nearest canister. I reach out to help, but he lifts it up onto his shoulder, making it look easy, and carries it over to the sprayer. "Are we gonna need all this?" he asks as he returns for another one.

"We'll use half today, and I'll have to do a second spraying in about a week's time."

"Where do you want the ones for next week? Can they be stored outside, or…"

"In the barn," I say, and I go over to the barn, opening the door, so he can stack the spare barrels in there.

I realize now that doing this job my myself would have been impossible.

Sure, I could have just about lifted the canisters off of the truck and then rolled them along the ground to where I needed them, but how on earth did I think I was going to fill the sprayer? This brand of fungicide comes already prepared, in liquid form, unlike my usual sprays, which have to be diluted, so I can tip the concentrate into the sprayer and just add water from the hosepipe. Lifting a massive barrel and tipping its contents accurately into the sprayer would have been beyond me. Ryan, on the other hand, takes it in his stride. Anyone would have thought it was something he did all the time, from the way he handles himself, and I stand back and admire the way his muscles flex as he pours each of the canisters into the sprayer.

"Okay. What next?"

He turns, looking at me, and I suck in a breath. God… he's beautiful.

Still, there's a job to be done, and time is running out.

"I'll bring the tractor around, if you can attach the sprayer to it?"

"Sure."

He stands while I run around to the other side of the house, pulling my keys from my pocket and clambering onto the tractor.

It starts first time, and I drive it around the front, reversing it back into position.

Before I've even climbed down again, Ryan's already hooking the sprayer attachment to the rear, and I join him just as he straightens up and turns around to look down at me again.

"How long is this gonna take?"

"A few hours. Why? Do you have somewhere you need to be?"

"No. Not at all. I was just wondering about the light, that's all."

"We're gonna be doing it in the dark, that's for certain. I've never had to do a spraying like this, where it's so important to get to every single leaf. I'm gonna have to take it more slowly than I normally would."

"In which case, it'll be much better if you drive the tractor. You know your way around it… and the farm." He studies the tractor for a moment, and then turns back to me. "Do you have any portable lights?"

"I do, but there's nowhere to attach them to the tractor."

"That's okay. I'll hold them, if you don't mind me riding shotgun."

I smile up at him, unable to help myself. "Not at all."

I run back to the barn, relieved I tidied up in here the other day. It means the lights are easy to find, and I come back out, handing them to Ryan.

"At least now you'll be able to see where you're spraying."

"I know. That was worrying me on the way back here."

"Well… worry no more."

He smiles and I smile back, both of us staring at each other for a moment until a gust of wind catches my hair, and he coughs. I let my eyes drop, realizing he's only wearing a button-down shirt on top of his jeans.

"Have you got a sweater with you?" I ask.

"No."

"Then you're gonna freeze. Once the sun goes down, it's gonna get cold out there."

"Don't worry. I'll be fine."

I'm not sure he will and I wrack my brain, wondering what I can do about that, when a thought occurs. "Hold on…"

I rush into the house, going straight to my bedroom, where I rummage through the drawers and find my blue sweater… the one granny gave me. It's enormous on me, as Ryan pointed out the other day, and there's a chance it might be big enough for him.

I take it outside, closing the door behind me and trot down the steps, and back over to him, holding it out.

"Try this. It might fit you."

He puts down the lamps and takes the sweater, turning it around and pulling it on over his head. Once he's put his arms through, it's clear it's going to be a little tight, and I step forward and tug on the hem, pulling it down, so he's covered.

"It's better than nothing." I smile up at him. "It looks…"

"Don't say it," he says.

"Say what?"

"Don't tell me it looks better on me than it does on you, because I know damn well that's not true."

I feel something spark inside me, like a bolt of electricity, and even though we have things to do, and time is running out, I have to say something. I can't just leave it. He's bending to pick up the lights again, but I have to stop him and I place my hand on his shoulder. He startles and stands upright again, looking down at me, his eyebrows raised.

"Is something wrong?"

"Not wrong, no."

"In that case…"

"I just needed you to know… silence doesn't always mean what you think."

"It doesn't?"

"No." I pause, and then whisper, "What we did… it mattered, Ryan. It still matters."

He sucks in a breath and nods his head, although he doesn't say a word, and after a second or two, I turn and climb up onto the tractor. We have to get on, and if I stare at him for very much longer, I'm going to give in and kiss him.

Ryan picks up the lamps as I re-start the engine, and he climbs up behind me, wedging himself into the tiny space.

I turn in my seat, looking up at him, and even though I know we've got a job to do, his presence makes me feel safe. I certainly feel a lot better than I would have done if I'd been doing this on my own.

"If you can point one lamp onto each side," I yell above the sound of the engine, pointing at the same time, and he nods his head, getting himself steady as I turn back around and we set off…

Chapter Sixteen

Ryan

It's nearly nine by the time Peony parks the tractor back alongside the house, and despite the sweater she insisted on me wearing, I'm absolutely freezing.

She doesn't seem to have been so badly affected by the cold, but that's probably because she's been turning the wheel of the tractor, while I've been stationary, pointing the lights so she can see what she's doing.

She shuts off the engine, and I notice her shoulders sag. She must be exhausted. I know I am, and I haven't done anything like the amount of work Peony's put in. I've just been concentrating on the angle of the lamps, and not leaning in to kiss her... and that's taken every ounce of willpower I possess.

I wriggle out from behind her seat and climb down to the ground, extinguishing the lights before putting them by the back wheels. It takes a moment for my eyes to acclimatize to the darkness and then I hold up my right hand to her.

There's sufficient moonlight for me to see her clearly, and she's hunched over the steering wheel, completely spent.

"Peony?"

She turns her head and looks down at my hand, smiling as she takes it. Her skin feels icier than I'd expected, and she twists in her seat, giving me the chance to put my hands on her waist and lift her down to the ground.

"Thank you," she says in a soft voice as she gazes up into my eyes, my hands still resting on either side of her waist.

"That's okay."

She tilts her head, surprising me by not stepping away. My cock is aching for her, pressing hard against my zipper, but I keep enough space between us so she won't be aware of that. I don't think it would help. "The thing with working like that is it gives you time to think."

"It does, doesn't it?" I'm dying to tell her I've been thinking of little else but kissing her, but I'm intrigued by what's been occupying her mind. "What have you been thinking?"

"That I'm surprised you're still here."

I hadn't expected her to say that. Having stood so close behind her for the last few hours, I suppose I'd hoped for something a little more romantic, but maybe I'm aiming too high. "Why?"

"Because earlier on, when you left, I assumed I'd offended you once too often. I thought my rudeness had proved too much, and you must have left Hart's Creek for good."

She's talking about us. She's actually talking about us… willingly, and of her own volition, with no prompting from me. And even if she's not declaring her undying love, or inviting me to her bed, it feels like a start. "Was that wishful thinking?" *Really, Ryan? Is now the best time to tease?* She bites on her bottom lip, remaining silent, and I think about apologizing. Except I don't want to. I like teasing. I like flirting… and it would be good to get back to it. "Is that another of your silences that doesn't mean what I think it does?"

"Maybe."

I smile and the corners of her lips twist upwards, which is a relief. "To tell the truth, I was going to leave." Her smile fades and I move a little closer. "I went back to the hotel with every intention of driving home to Boston. I even started packing. But then I thought about you struggling to spray the trees all by yourself, and I couldn't do it. I couldn't abandon you to cope all by yourself."

"Why not?"

I open my mouth and then close it again, wondering if I should tell her the truth. She's admitted twice that she didn't mean to imply that what we did had meant nothing to her. The second time she did that, she touched my shoulder, and I almost jumped out of my skin. She'd touched me before, placing her hand on my arm, and even that fairly innocuous gesture made me tense, too. I guess that's because touching is still an unknown phenomenon for me. I've got to allow myself time to get used to it. Even so, I hadn't expected to respond quite like that. I'd been thinking about how much I wanted her touch, but I guess that would have been under different circumstances. I'd been contemplating the idea of making love with her, and in that situation, I'd have known what was coming. It would have been more predictable, and I'd have been prepared for it. What she did today was unexpected. Does that mean I can't be honest with her now, though? If I say 'I couldn't leave because I'm in love with you', what might she do? I guess there's always a chance she'll be so shocked, she'll pull away from me... that she'll reject my affections. Or, she could – just could – return my feelings. *God, I hope so.* But in that case, might she throw herself at me? I wouldn't mind, just as long as I was ready for it. The problem is, I don't know. If I could guarantee her reaction and know what was coming, I'd take the chance... but as it is...

"Coming back was the right thing to do."

That's the truth. It's also safe. It's a comment that's unlikely to provoke an extreme response, and given that we're both so tired, I think it's wise to avoid making rash statements. Not that saying 'I love you' would be rash. I'd just rather say it when I'm a little more awake and less likely to screw things up… especially as we seem to be getting along, for once.

I've still got my hands on her waist, so it can't be all bad.

She smiles, nodding her head. "I'd like to say I'd have managed, and usually I'd be too pig-headed to admit I need anyone's help, but there's no way I could have done all that by myself."

"You're not pig-headed."

"Oh?" She looks up at me, that smile returning, and I have to smile back. "Anyway, as you've done the right thing and stayed to help me, will you let me do the right thing and invite you to have dinner with me? We both need to warm up, and although I'm not offering three courses of fine dining, I'll be able to manage something hot."

"I don't doubt it, and I'd love to stay, thank you."

She doesn't need to make me anything hot. She's hot enough herself. In fact, just holding her like this is making me burn with need for her. My cock is positively screaming at me to do something about that, but unfortunately, the moment I've accepted her invitation, she steps out of my grip, and I'm forced to let her go, although I feel lost without her.

She moves toward the rear of the tractor, bending to pick up the lights.

"I'll just put these back," she says.

"Here… I'll do it."

I reach out and take them from her, surprised when she gives them up so easily. "Thanks. Just put them anywhere in the barn. I don't like leaving them out when it's so damp."

"Okay. I'll see you inside."

She nods her head and trudges toward the house while I make my way to the barn. The door's still open and I step through it, my nostrils immediately assailed my the smell of moldering apples and damp sackcloth. The moonlight won't allow me to see beyond a few feet inside, but that doesn't matter. All I need to do is put the lamps down on the floor, and once I've done that, I step back outside, pushing closed the tall double doors with a loud, aching creak.

I walk back to the house, climbing up the steps and pull open the door, letting myself in.

Peony is over by the fire, adding logs to warm the place, although it feels cozy enough in here to me. She turns, hearing the door close behind me, and smiles.

"Can I get you a coffee?"

"Sure."

She makes her way across the room, from one side to the other, and I notice the coffee is already brewing in the machine, and that there are some onions cooking on the stove, alongside a pan of water. By the time she's fetched cups from the cabinet, the coffee is ready and she pours it out, adding milk to hers before she brings the cups to the table.

"Please… sit."

"I will, once I've taken off this sweater."

I cross over my arms, lifting it at the hem, and pull upwards, hearing Peony's giggle as I get stuck. I'm sure I could extricate myself, but I'm worried about what I might do to her prized sweater.

"Bend over," she says.

"Which way?"

"Toward me."

I do as she says, feeling the touch of her hands on my back, my body stiffening. *Relax. She's only trying to help… and besides, you want this. You want her touch.* I take a breath and attempt to stay calm.

Peony grabs the hem of the sweater, pulling it up my back toward my neck.

"You need to let go," she says, and I release it at the front, letting her do the work as she tugs and tugs. I steady my feet, and with one last effort, she pulls it over my head.

"I hope I haven't stretched it too much," I say, standing up.

She's gazing at my chest and I look down, seeing that my shirt has almost been peeled off, too. My chest is exposed and Peony seems to be enjoying the view, if her expression is anything to go by.

"I—I'm sure it's fine," she stutters, and I smile, dragging my shirt back into place, although I leave it untucked, all of which seems to startle her back to reality. "I'll leave this here."

She folds the sweater over the back of the chair, and darts around the table to the stove, embarrassment getting the better of her, unfortunately.

I decide against making anything of that moment, and pick up my coffee, wandering over to join her.

"What are you cooking?" I ask as she quickly chops some garlic, adding it to the onions in the pan.

"Just some pasta."

"It smells divine."

She glances up at me. "It's onions and garlic… when doesn't that smell divine?"

Her eyes are sparkling, her cheeks rosy red from the chill air outside, and I'm so tempted to lean in and kiss her. I don't get the chance, though. The water splashes over, hissing as it does, and Peony returns her attention to the stove, adding some pasta to the pan.

"Would you like me to stir that?"

"Is that okay?"

"Sure."

She offers me a long-handled wooden spoon, and keeping hold of my coffee with one hand, I stir away, while she adds tomatoes and black olives to the onions and garlic. She drizzles in just a little balsamic vinegar and I turn to face her.

"Balsamic vinegar?"

"Yes." She smiles up at me. "It gives the sauce a kind of sweetness. Trust me."

"I do. Implicitly." Her eyes fix on mine for a moment, until I remember I'm supposed to be stirring the pasta, not just letting it boil. "I think this is nearly done."

"Hmm… so is the sauce." She ducks around me, grabbing the jug of silverware, which she hands to me. "Do you want to put this on the table and sit down? I'll be two minutes."

"Sure."

I do as I'm told, taking a seat that's facing her, and I watch as she drains the pasta, mixing it with the sauce, and serving it into bowls. Before she comes over, she fetches some parmesan from the refrigerator, and brings it to the table, along with a grater, and then she goes back for the bowls, setting one in front of each of us, as she sits opposite me.

"I don't have any wine, I'm afraid."

"That's no problem. The coffee is warming me up just fine."

"Hopefully the pasta will, too."

She takes a sip from her cup, offering me the cheese and grater, and I help myself before pushing them across the table to her. While she's grating, I grab a couple of forks from the jug, handing her one, and we start to eat.

The sauce is superb, and there is a hint of sweetness, just like she said there would be.

"What do you think?" she says, looking at me and sounding nervous.

"I think I'll be using balsamic vinegar in my pasta sauces from here on."

She giggles and my cock twitches against my zipper. I need something to distract me from wanting her.

An earthquake would do…

Maybe.

"Tell me about the farm."

She frowns and that has the same effect on me as something around a force six or seven on the Richter scale. Why did I say that? Why start with the one big bone of contention between us?

"What do you want to know?" she asks, a hint of suspicion in her voice. I can't blame her for that. She thinks I still want to buy the place.

"I get that it means everything to you, but give me some context. How long have you lived here?"

"All my life. I was born here."

"Under this roof?"

"Yes." Okay. Now I never want to leave, either. "This was my father's home, too, and he and my mom carried on living here after they were married. Mom loved it, and I think they had plans to raise a big family, and have lots of children playing in the orchard, and eventually helping to run the place."

"What happened?"

"Mom got sick not long after she found out she was pregnant with me. She had cancer, and she had to choose between having the treatment or keeping me. She chose me."

I can hear the heartbreak in her voice and I reach out my hand across the table. She doesn't take it, but I leave it there, anyway.

"Was it too late…?" I don't need to finish that question. Peony nods her head.

"They did what they could, but it wasn't enough. She died when I was three months old. I—I never even knew her, but I've always felt that she gave her life for me. She could have chosen to live herself, but…" She lets her voice fade and lowers her head.

I lean over, stretching my hand even closer. *Take it, please… take it. Touch me.*

"Hey…" She looks up, her eyes alighting on my hand before she raises them to my face. "You're here because of her. I'm grateful for her sacrifice… although I can't imagine what your father must have gone through."

She raises her hand, pushing her fingers back through her hair, and then lets it drop directly on to mine. The action seems unintentional, but I know it wasn't, and her touch is like an electric shock, charging through my body. I turn my hand and clasp hers, partly because I don't want to let her go, but also because I still need to be in control. I still need to know what's going to happen next.

We both continue to eat with our free hand, and after a couple of mouthfuls, she puts her fork down again and looks up at me. "He stayed on. Well, we both did… obviously. I don't think he knew what else to do. He always seemed kinda lost without her, and I think the farm gave him somewhere to ground himself."

"Was he a good father?" I ask, and she smiles.

"He was. There was always an underlying sadness, but he tried his best to hide it from me."

"And he never remarried?"

She shakes her head. "He never even looked at another woman."

I know how that feels. I can't imagine ever wanting anyone but Peony… not now.

"What happened to him?"

"He died when I was fifteen. He was involved in a really dreadful accident."

"A car accident?"

"Yes, although it wasn't just cars involved. There were trucks and… well… bigger vehicles." I can't imagine she wants to think about that, and I don't blame her. "He was taken to the hospital, and Granny and I got there in time to say goodbye, but…" Her voice fades again, and I squeeze her hand.

"I'm sorry, Peony."

"It's okay."

"No, it's not."

She pulls her hand away, picking up her cup and taking a long sip. I regret the disconnection, but there's not a lot I can do about it, and once she's put the cup down, she lays her hand in her lap and smiles over at me.

"You're right. It's not okay, but at least I still had my grandmother. I wasn't alone in the world." I half expect her to add, 'like I am now', but she doesn't. If she did, I'd be willing to contradict her. I'd tell her she's not alone, because I'm here, and I'm not going anywhere. As it is, she pops some more pasta in her mouth and once she's finished chewing, says, "We had each other, and we got along just fine, running this place… until Luca moved in."

"Luca?" I've got no idea who she's talking about, but she stares at me, her eyebrows raised, until the penny drops. "Would he be your ex-boyfriend?"

"He would."

"I see." I drink some coffee to steady my nerves, surprised by how jealous I feel of the fact that he lived with her, while I'm struggling to get through dinner. "Was he from here?" Maybe that's the answer. They'd known each other all their lives, so the trust came more easily.

"No." She shakes her head slowly. "He moved to the town about four years ago."

There goes that theory.

"What did he do?"

"He used to work at the gym."

Great. A bodybuilder. Just what I needed.

"Was that where you met?"

She smiles. "No. I've never set foot in a gym in my life."

"Then, if you don't mind me asking, how do you stay in shape?"

Her cheeks flush, and I wonder if I've gone too far… if my recollections of her perfect body tied to my bed have spoiled the moment.

"Working around here seems to do it for me," she says, and I nod my head.

"Hmm… I guess I can understand that." I watch her eat a little more pasta. "So… if you didn't meet him at the gym, where did you meet?"

"At the Fall Festival."

"What's that?"

"It's a fair we hold every year on Hart's Green, which is opposite the hotel."

"I see. Do you sell your cider there?"

"I do."

"And Luca came to buy some, did he?"

"No. It wasn't like that."

I lean forward. "Then how was it?"

She stares at me, and I half expect her to ask why I need to know. If she did, I'd tell her. I'd explain that I need to understand her. I might have always done my best to avoid anyone with baggage, but it's important to me to unravel her past. It's not one sided, either. If she asks about my life and what I've done, I'll tell her.

I don't want us to have any secrets from each other.

"He was working."

"At the fair?" I ask, finishing my pasta.

"Yes. The gym is owned by Laurel's husband, Mitch, although he wasn't Laurel's husband at the time. That came later. He'd only just opened the gym a few weeks before, and decided they should come to the fair and hand out leaflets offering memberships. I think he felt as though he'd have a captive audience. In any case, Luca and I got talking, and while I was packing up to come home, he asked me if I'd have dinner with him that night."

"And you said 'yes'?"

"I did. That dinner led to another, and then drinks, and then… a picnic, I think. And before I knew it, we were together."

I wonder if that's her way of saying they ended up in bed, after what sounds like four dates. I don't know why I'm surprised. She's irresistible, and it's four more than she and I had, I suppose…

"He moved into the farm then, did he?"

I feel like we may as well cut to the chase.

"Not straight away, no." She looks a little scandalized, which is adorable on her… especially as I can still remember the look on her face when she was begging me to fuck her. "He'd taken a six-month rental on a small house in Maple Street. When it came to an end, he had the option to take it for another six months, or to move in with me."

"And, not surprisingly, he chose the latter." She blushes again and nods her head. "How long did he stay?"

"I don't know… just under three years, I think."

"Don't bullshit me." She sits back, putting down her fork. She's left a little pasta on her plate, but I think she's done eating. "You don't think, Peony. You know. Women don't forget things like that."

She sighs, her shoulders dropping. "Okay. It was two years and ten months."

"And how many days?" I ask, although she doesn't answer. She just glares at me. "That's a long time."

"Yes, it is."

"Did you love him?"

She opens her mouth and then closes it again, clearly struggling with the answer to that question.

"I—I don't know. I thought I did." She lowers her head. "H—He was my first, and it seemed important to say the words before we…"

"Before you had sex?"

I don't want to think of them making love.

"Yes. Of course, that's just nonsense, really, isn't it?"

"Is it?"

"Yes. Saying the words is very different to meaning them… and he clearly didn't mean them, or he'd never have cheated on me."

"I told you before, the guy must have been crazy for doing that."

She raises her head, gazing up at me. "If you say so."

"I do… with even more certainty now I know."

"Know what?"

I lean across the table a little. "What he was risking. He was mad to give you up."

She stares at me. "He didn't think so."

"Then he didn't know you."

"No. He was too busy getting to know Stevie Pine."

"Who's Stevie Pine?"

"She's the wife of Dawson Pine. He owns the bar in town, and she's the woman Luca confessed to falling in love with."

"He confessed?"

"Yes. That's how I found out he was cheating. He admitted it, right before she came here to collect him, and they drove off into the sunset together." She shakes her head. "I can't even say he went off with a younger woman. She was at least five years older than me."

"So? What's age got to do with anything?"

"Nothing, I suppose, and even in my darkest moments, I knew it had to be a lot worse for Dawson than it was for me. Luca and I weren't married. We didn't run a business together…" Her voice fades and I stretch my hand across the table again, although she doesn't seem to notice.

"It still hurts, though, doesn't it?"

She tilts her head, staring at me, like she's thinking. "It doesn't hurt, no. Not any more. Other things have happened that have made it easier to forget."

"But not to forgive?"

"Hell, no." She smiles and so do I. I don't like the idea of her forgiving him for what he did. She sits forward, checking her cup and clearly finding it empty. "Can I get you some more coffee?"

"Sure." If it means I can stay a little longer.

She stands, taking the cups over to the countertop and pouring more coffee, while I stack up the dishes, pushing them to one side, so the table between us is clear. When Peony returns, she puts the cups down and sits again, facing me. Once she's comfortable, she looks up, a gentle smile touching at her lips.

"I feel like I've been talking about myself for far too long."

"I'm not complaining."

"Maybe not, but I'd like to hear something about you now."

Is she going to ask about my past? I'll tell her anything she wants to know…

I just hope it doesn't put her off, especially as this evening is going so well.

"What do you want to know?"

"Were you born in Boston?"

We're going that far back, are we? Okay…

"Yes, I was."

"How long ago?"

It occurs to me that she doesn't know my age and I smile at her.

"Thirty-five years."

She nods her head. "I'm gonna guess that your researchers have already told you how old I am?"

"They have." She sighs and takes a sip of coffee, wincing slightly because it's so hot. "Does that bother you?"

"What? That you know my age, that you had me investigated, or that there's a nine-year age gap between us?"

"All of the above."

She rests her hands on the table. "I don't mind that you know how old I am, although I'm not particularly keen on the idea that you had me investigated. That's mostly because it was for the purpose of buying my farm."

"And the age gap?"

"I couldn't care less about that."

I smile and lean forward. "Sorry about the research. It's part of the job, I'm afraid."

"That's okay," she says, with a shrug of her shoulders. "But we weren't supposed to be talking about me. We're meant to be talking about you. So… tell me about your childhood."

"There's not much to tell, really. My mom died when I was four. I guess that makes me luckier than you, in that I have memories of her, although they're very faded."

"What can you remember?" she asks, her voice softening.

"Snippets. The color of her hair, the sound of her voice. She used to sing. I can remember that."

"What happened to your father? Was he as lost as mine was?"

"I don't know. He was good at hiding his feelings, and we never really talked about Mom and how either of us felt about her. I'm not saying he wasn't a good father, because he was, but he was very… reserved."

"Was he like that even before she died?"

"I don't know. I can't remember him being any different, but like I say, I was only four."

"So, who looked after you?"

"I had a nanny." I let a smile touch my lips. "Trust me, that's very different to having a grandmother."

"I can imagine."

"Oh, I really don't think you can."

"What was she like then?"

"She was strict." And devoid of emotion. Not that I'm about to admit that. "I learned very quickly what to do, and what not to do. And in a way, she probably did me a favor."

"How do you work that out?"

"She taught me to be independent… to stand on my own two feet." She also left me with an aversion to physical intimacy and affection, but that's a whole other story… and to be fair, it's not entirely Nanny Ivy's fault that I can't bear the thought of being touched.

"It sounds lonely."

I tip my head from left to right, pretending to give that some thought… not that I need to. "Maybe, but if being alone was the alternative to being with Nanny Ivy, then it was preferable. And besides, being single-minded and focused has stood me in good stead for my career."

"Of ruthlessly taking over other people's properties, you mean?"

"Most people are quite happy to sell. My job is just to negotiate the best price… or at least it was."

"What does that mean?"

"It means this isn't really my job anymore. I came up here for a change, and to prove I could still do this… that I hadn't lost my touch."

She struggles not to smile, pursing her lips, and then biting on the bottom one. "Sorry. Has my stubbornness about selling my farm dented your ego?"

"Not in the slightest. I'm still the CEO, and that was what my father trained me for."

"Trained you?"

"Yes." There's no other way of putting it, really. "He wanted me to take over his company when he died, and he groomed me for that from an early age."

"So, your father's dead too?"

"Yes. He had a major stroke about a year ago, and I stepped into his shoes."

She looks down at the table, like she's thinking, and then she raises her head, her eyes meeting mine. "Can I ask you something?"

"Of course."

"Are you a millionaire?"

"I am, but does it matter?" She shrugs her shoulders, taking a sip of coffee, and I wonder if this is going to be a stumbling block. I hope not, because it feels like we've changed course this evening, and I'd like to think I'm not imagining that… or that we're going to fall at the last hurdle, just because I've got a few zeros at the end of my bank balance.

Chapter Seventeen

Peony

We finished eating ages ago, and my coffee is going cold, although I don't want him to leave… not yet.

Not ever?

I can't decide.

I know I want him.

But then, I think I also *want* him.

And yes, I know that doesn't make sense.

I guess that's what love does for you, though. And this is definitely love.

How do I know?

Because when he asked me if I'd loved Luca, I realized I hadn't. Not in the same way. Sure, it felt like love at the time, and I know I made a big deal out of saying 'I love you' before we first had sex, but that's not what love is about, is it? I know that now.

In any case, the feelings I had for Luca – whatever they were – were nothing compared to the way I feel about Ryan. I didn't say so in as many words, but it's being around him that's made it easier to forget what Luca did.

Obviously, that's all very muddling.

If it wasn't, I wouldn't be sitting here, staring at him, wondering whether I just want him, or whether I *want* him, too.

Without a doubt, I know I want him to make love with me again, just like he did before. I want to be held down… tied down… taken. Above all, I want to be his.

When he said just now that he knew what Luca was risking by sleeping with someone else, and that he was mad to give me up, I wanted to get on my knees and beg him to prove it… to prove that he wasn't mad, too. That he'd never give me up, not for anyone, or anything.

But I couldn't say or do anything.

I'd tried holding hands with him, and the physical contact of having my hand in his had driven me crazy, just like it had outside, when he'd put his hands on my waist to help me down from the tractor, and left them there. Being touched was too much.

I wanted more.

I wanted everything. And in the end, I couldn't handle it. Outside, I had to slip away from his grasp, and just now I had to pull my hand from his. I even had to put it in my lap, beneath the table, so he wouldn't see me shaking. My whole body feels like it's trembling with need for him… like if he doesn't do something to slake this thirst, I'm going to explode.

Maybe it's my need for him that's making me so confused. Or maybe it's just being so deeply in love. I don't know.

I just know that I want him.

And by that, I mean something more than the physical ache I have for him.

I want him to be with me, to stare into my eyes and tell me he feels the same… that it's not all one-sided, and that it's not just physical for him, either.

I don't think it is. At least, I hope it's not.

When he said he was grateful for my mother's sacrifice, I wanted to cry. I was close to tears anyway, but there was something about his words, and about the look on his face. I felt a change between us then. I don't know what it was, or where it might be leading us, but I knew I wanted him to hold me, and never let me go.

Never?

Do I really mean that? Can I really mean that?

Can I be so in love with the man who I've sworn is my enemy? The man who wants to buy my farm? I feel less inclined to say he's trying to take it from me, now I know how much he's willing to pay… but that's part of the problem, isn't it?

The man's a millionaire.

That's foreign territory for me, especially as I've almost emptied my bank account to pay for the fungicide to treat my trees. It had to be done to save the orchard… but a millionaire?

I wouldn't even know how to behave.

"Shall I help with the dishes?" he says, putting down his cup, his question breaking into my thoughts.

"You don't have to."

"I want to."

"Do you wash the dishes when you're at home, in your modern apartment?" I ask, hating the resentment in my voice, and wishing I could take back the words.

He frowns, like he doesn't understand why I've changed. I get that. I don't understand it either. "No. I have a dishwasher."

"So do I, but mine doesn't work anymore."

"Then let me buy you a new one."

"Certainly not."

I stand, picking up the plates, and carry them over to the sink, turning on the water before I feel him come up behind me. I'm aware of the heat from his body a fraction of a second before I feel his hands on my waist as he turns me around to face him, reaching behind me to shut off the water.

"Have I offended you?" he asks, his eyes boring into mine.

Yes. "No."

"If I bought you a dishwasher, there wouldn't be any strings attached. You know that, don't you? I wouldn't expect anything in return."

"Like my farm, you mean?"

"This has nothing to do with your farm. There wouldn't be very much point in me buying you a new dishwasher and then knocking down the house it's been fitted into, would there?"

"No. I guess not."

He steps a little closer, so we're almost touching. "Can you forget about the farm?"

"I thought we'd already established I can't. Even when I try, I'm not very good at it. But surely you can't be surprised by that. It's my home, Ryan. How can I pretend it doesn't matter?" I lean back slightly, putting some necessary space between us. "Just out of interest, though, if you'd bought it and knocked it down, what would you have built in its place?"

"A hotel."

I can feel my brow furrowing. "You mean like the one we already have in town?"

"No." He shakes his head. "It would have been nothing like that. It would have been a luxury resort and spa."

"But you're not a hotelier, are you?"

He smiles now. "No, I'm not. I've a got a client who is, though, and he's always looking for new locations. This would have been perfect for him. It would have brought employment to the town, too."

"Are you saying it's my fault?"

He steps back, pushing his fingers through his hair. "Am I saying what is your fault?" He sounds confused, as well as frustrated.

"The unemployment."

"What unemployment?"

"There were a lot of people who were laid off when two companies in the industrial area closed down last year. Are you saying it's my fault they won't be able to find work now, because I won't sell you my farm?"

"Not at all. The only thing I was saying was that, if I'd been able to go ahead with my plans, and build the hotel for my client, then as a natural progression, it would have created employment within the town. I didn't realize there had been lay-offs, and I'm certainly not blaming you for any of it."

I've over-reacted… allowed my confusion to get the better of me. "I'm sorry."

"It's okay." It feels like he understands, although I'm now sure how. I don't even understand it all myself. "The farm is yours and you were entitled to say no to my offer."

I frown up at him. "You're talking in the past tense. Does that mean you're giving up?"

He moves a little closer again, although he doesn't touch me. "I wasn't gonna tell you yet, but yeah, I am."

"You are? Why?"

"Because some things are more important than doing a deal. It's taken me far too long to work that out, but I'm there now. I know when I'm beaten, Peony, and when it comes to your farm, you win."

Why does that feel like such a hollow victory? I ought to be happy. I ought to be singing from the treetops. The farm is safe. He's going to leave me alone…

My heart lurches, its beat slowing to a stop.

How can I be happy knowing he's got no reason to stay now?

How can I sing, knowing he'll be leaving soon, and that he'll take my heart with him?

"I guess I'd better get going." He moves away, and although I'm tempted to beg him to stay, my mouth won't seem to work. He's at the door before I find my voice.

"Thanks for helping… with the spraying, I mean."

He turns, smiling. "Anytime."

Ask him to stay. Think of something… quickly… before he goes for good.

I wrack my brain, but can't think of a single reason for him not to leave, and after just a second's hesitation, he opens the door and steps through it, letting it close softly behind him. Within seconds, I hear his car starting, and the tires on the track as he drives away.

Should I have told him I love him?

No. That would hardly be playing fair, would it? And in any case, if he loved me, he'd never have gone. He'd have stayed, because he'd have wanted to. He'd have wanted me, like I want him.

So, I guess I imagined that change… that difference between us tonight.

I push myself off of the sink and turn out the lights. I can't be bothered to wash the dishes. They'll keep until the morning.

For now, I just need to sleep, so I don't have to think about what I've lost.

Or is that what I've thrown away…?

So much for sleeping.

I've been awake most of the night, haunted by what might have been, but the sun's up now, and even if I'm not sure what time it is yet, there's no point in lying here any longer.

I throw back the covers and wander through to the bathroom, getting straight into the shower. I'd like to say it feels cleansing, or cathartic, but it doesn't. The water jets almost hurt, and I can't help wondering why my skin feels so sensitive.

Is it because I want Ryan so much? Because I want to feel his hands on me?

Probably.

I shudder, thinking about all the things I know he'll never do to me again.

Because I let him go.

"Fool."

Saying the word out loud doesn't help. I am a fool. I should have found a way to ask him to stay, or at least to prolong his visit. As it is, he's probably back in Boston by now... although he might as well be on Mars.

I rinse off my hair, and tip back my head, letting the water wash over me before I shut it off and step out, wrapping myself in a towel and padding through to my bedroom.

It's a sunny morning and I'm already quite warm, so rather than reaching for a sweater, I grab a white blouse from my closet, laying it on the bed, alongside my jeans, and then I open the top drawer in my dresser, finding some white lace underwear. I try not to imagine Ryan peeling me out of this, although it's hard, and my skin tingles at the pointless thought.

"Dammit."

I slam the drawer shut and wander over to the bed, taking mere moments to get dressed.

My hair will dry naturally, and doubtless look as wild as usual, and once I've made the bed, I go out into the kitchen, letting out a sigh, when I see the mess I left last night.

My shoulders drop at the prospect of housework, but I suppose there isn't much to be done on the farm right now, so I roll up my sleeves and run some water into the sink...

I might hate housework, but once it's done, there's always a sense of satisfaction.

Not only did I do the dishes, but in my efforts to forget about Ryan, I gave the kitchen a thorough clean, including the floor and the stove. That alone is worthy of a medal, although once it was done, I also tidied the living room, did the laundry, and even cleaned my boots.

I seriously think sainthood is an appropriate reward for all my efforts.

Still, it's all finished now, and the place looks immaculate.

At least, it will for the next hour or so, and in the meantime, in the absence of a medal or a sainthood, I feel like I've earned a cup of coffee.

I could sit on the couch with it, but that would feel too much like relaxing in the middle of the day, so I pull out a chair at the kitchen table, taking a sip, and wondering why it is I still feel so out of sorts.

So Ryan left.

So what?

We only had one night together.

"What's the big deal?"

I shake my head. It looks like I've started talking to myself again.

Maybe because there's no-one else here to talk to.

God… that's sad.

I wish… I wish he'd felt able to stay. For me, not the farm.

I wish I'd meant something to him.

Some of the things he said made me wonder… as did the look in his eyes and the twitch of his smile.

Did I really mean nothing?

I can't have done… can I?

I get up, striding over to the pile of letters stacked neatly beside the refrigerator, and I rifle through it, until I find Ryan's card. I dumped it here the other day, when he gave it to me and I'm relieved now that I didn't throw it in the trash. Holding it in my hand, I glance down at his name, running my fingers over the lettering, as I suck in a sharp breath and pull my phone from my back pocket.

"There's no time like the present…"

Stop talking to yourself!

I dial the numbers carefully, double checking them before I press the green button, and I lean back against the countertop, wondering where he'll be. I imagine him in his office in Boston, or possibly on his way there still, if he decided against driving home last night. It's unlikely he'll still be here, but if he is, what will I say? Will I beg him to stay? And if he's in Boston, will I ask him to come back? What reason do I even have for calling?

I pull the phone from my ear, regretting my rash actions, just as his voicemail kicks in and I'm saved the embarrassment of finding an excuse for having called him.

Thank God.

I'm not about to leave a message… not when I can't think what to say, and I hang up, putting the card down on the pile, and my phone back into my pocket.

That was close…

And very silly.

Honestly, what would I have done if he'd answered? Made myself look a complete fool, that's what I'd have done. Thank God he was otherwise occupied.

It might be lunchtime, but I'm not hungry, and even though there's nothing much to do on the farm today, that's no reason to sit around moping. I can still take a look at the trees and see how they're progressing.

The tractor is just where we left it last night, with the sprayer still attached, and I can't be bothered to un-couple it now. Besides, my shoulders are aching from driving it for hours yesterday. The walk will do me good and give me the chance to inspect the leaves… not that I expect there will be much change from yesterday.

Still… it's something to do…

The sun might be shining, but in the lower fields, the grass is still laden with dew in places, and it licks at the leather of my boots as I study the leaves. As I expected, they're still coated with apple scab, and I let out a sigh, hoping that the work Ryan and I did yesterday will be enough to save my crop. Because it is my crop. At least, it is now that Ryan isn't trying to buy my farm anymore.

I take a long, slow wander through each of the fields, my hands buried deep in my pockets, no longer bothering to examine the trees, but just enjoying the moment… knowing that even if there are problems, they're my problems. The farm is mine, the threat of being ousted from my home has gone, and I'm safe.

I stop walking and shake my head, tipping it back and staring up at the light blue sky.

Who am I kidding?

I may have bluffed my way around Ryan's arguments, but I know as well as he did that I'm anything but safe.

Having spent so much money on the fungicide, I don't know how I'm going to survive until harvest time, and with the next loan payment due to be made at the end of the month, telling myself I'm safe is foolhardy, to put it mildly.

I guess all I can do is hope that Laurel can come over fairly soon, and that we can go through my accounts. Once I've done that, I'll probably have a better picture, and at least I'll have something to go to the bank with… because I'm going to have to go to the bank. There's no doubt about that.

Whether they'll be sympathetic is another matter…

I let myself back into the house, feeling even less inspired than I was earlier. I feel like I've swapped one battle for another, and no matter how much I might try to deny it, I miss Ryan.

Although I'm not sure there's any point. He's gone, and I'm here, and missing him won't achieve anything.

The problem is, I don't know what will.

My stomach rumbles, hunger finally getting the better of me, and I wander to the refrigerator, pulling it open, just as I hear a car coming down the track. I'm not expecting anyone, and I close the fridge door and move to the front window, glancing out and gasping when I see Ryan's black Mercedes pulling to a stop by the fence.

He hasn't gone?

My heart beats loud in my chest, my hands shaking and my skin tingling with excitement.

What does it mean?

Why is he here?

He turns off the engine, opens the door and climbs from the car, my heart lurching when I see he's wearing his suit and that tie.

Memories flood back… straining against the restraint as he made me come on his tongue… begging him to fuck me… the look in his eyes and the way his breath hitched as he untied me and watched me…

"Oh, God…" I whisper the words, staring at him as he walks slowly toward the house, admiring his perfect body and handsome face. He's smiling, just slightly, and while I don't know what that's about, I can't just stand here and watch.

I go to the door, opening it, and step outside onto the porch. His eyes meet mine, and I struggle to breathe as he climbs up the steps and stands in front of me.

He doesn't say a word, and neither do I. For a full ten seconds, we just stare at each other, and then, with a low growl, he clasps his hands on either side of my face and bends his head, kissing me. His tongue demands entrance and I grant it willingly, responding to his claim. I need more. I want more, and my hands creep up his arms, my fingers dusting over his muscles, until they come to rest on his shoulders. He tenses slightly, although he quickly relaxes again, and he lowers his right hand, brushing it down the side of my body, making me whimper as he lingers for a moment over the curve of my breast. Then he continues downward to my hip and around to my ass, pulling me closer as he flexes his hips into me and lets me feel his arousal.

I moan into his mouth, breathing hard, my breasts crushed against his chest, as he deepens the kiss, his tongue exploring, seeking… and hopefully, finding whatever it is he needs.

He's giving me everything I could ever want, and it's with regret that I feel him slow the kiss. He nibbles at my bottom lip, then lets his forehead rest against mine for a second, before he leans back, staring into my eyes.

"I—I thought you'd given up," I whisper, my voice refusing to work properly yet.

"No. I was just regrouping." He shifts his feet slightly, moving his left hand down to join his right, so they're both just above my ass, holding me still and tight against him.

"What does that mean?"

"It means I had some business to attend to this morning."

That's news. "Oh? Have you decided to buy somewhere else in town, then?"

"In a manner of speaking."

He's being very enigmatic, his eyes sparkling with mischief, and a smile playing at his perfect lips. It doesn't look like he's going to elaborate, though, and a part of me doesn't want to give him the satisfaction of asking.

"I noticed you called earlier," he says, and I feel myself blush. He must have saved my number into his phone… dammit.

"Yes."

"I'm sorry I didn't take your call. I was in meetings for most of the morning. Was it something important?"

I shake my head and although he waits, I decide it's my turn to be mysterious… mainly because I can't think what to say. Eventually he nods his head and steps back, letting me go, which is a shame. I liked being held. I liked feeling his arousal pressing into me, too. But it seems he's got other ideas, and he lets out a long sigh, pushing his fingers back through his hair and then delving into his pants pocket.

"Before we take this further, there's something I need to give you."

We're taking this further? Thank God for that. I was starting to wonder if that kiss was just an enormous tease… but it seems not, and I nod my head, looking down into his hand. He's pulled it from his pocket and is holding it out to me, something white and lacy sitting in his palm. I take a moment to recognize my panties, and I raise my head, looking into his eyes.

"You found them?"

"Kind of."

"Oh, God… you didn't ask housekeeping about them, did you?"

He shakes his head. "No, I didn't." He frowns, looking a little bashful. "If I'm being honest – and I feel like I need to be honest with you – I've had them all along."

I step away, almost stumbling backward, and although he reaches out a hand, I swipe at it.

"Don't you dare touch me."

"Peony?" He's confused now… although heaven knows why.

"How could you? I asked you about my… my underwear. I specifically asked if you'd found my panties, and you said you hadn't."

He steps closer. "You didn't specifically ask about anything. You didn't mention the word panties, if I remember rightly."

"That doesn't alter the fact that you must have known what I was talking about, and you didn't give them back to me."

"No. I didn't want to."

"Why? What have you been doing with them?"

"Carrying them around with me, if you must know… and I'm aware of how weird that sounds, before you say anything."

"Oh? You think it's more weird than getting your kicks from tying women to your bed?"

He winces, physically flinching at my words. "Maybe," he whispers. "Maybe not. But there's a reason I do that."

"I don't wanna know, Ryan. I want you to leave."

"Are you serious?"

"Damn right, I'm serious."

"You don't wanna talk?"

"No, I don't. We've established this is my farm, and I want you to remove yourself from it. Now."

He stares at me, his eyes darkening, and I feel the intensity of his glare right down to my core.

"Fine," he murmurs, and turns, sliding my panties back into his pocket as he strides over to his car.

The slam of the door makes me jump, and I shrink back toward the house, watching while he turns the vehicle, kicking up dust from the track, his tires spinning as he drives away.

My body slumps, sliding down the wall, and although I'm still a little mad at him, my overriding feeling is one of regret.

Not just because he's gone – and for good this time, I think – but also because of what I said.

Okay, so it's a little weird that he's been walking around with my panties in his pocket for the last few days, but I can remember thinking I'd rather he'd found them than a stranger. And if all he's been doing is carrying them around, then what's the harm? It could have been a lot worse… even I know that.

As for the tying up thing… he really didn't deserve that.

He asked my permission, and I agreed.

And I enjoyed every second of it.

I've fantasized about re-living that moment ever since it happened. So, how can I criticize him for doing something that felt so good, and that I'd happily do again, if only I hadn't overreacted and pushed him away… again?

Chapter Eighteen

Ryan

It's only when I get into the town itself that I take my foot off the gas. I've been driving way too fast, and I need to slow down.

Luckily, there isn't much traffic anyway, and I make it along Main Street and park at the side of the hotel as usual. I slam my car door closed, just like I did outside the farm, although I don't know why.

I don't think that could have gone any worse, but it's not the car's fault.

Is it Peony's?

Not really.

It's mine.

I got it wrong. So spectacularly wrong.

When we were talking last night, I thought there was something between us… something different. It was one of the reasons I changed my mind and told her I was giving up on buying the farm. The other one was that I'd finally worked out what to do. That came to me during our conversation, when she mentioned the lay-offs there had been in the town. I knew then what to do, and how I could make it all work… not just for me and Peony, but for everyone. I'd figured it out, and even though it took me all night to refine the idea, I knew it was the way to go.

That's why I spent the entire morning and part of the afternoon making plans.

Plans I'm now going to have to scrap.

Because I got it wrong…

I wander into the hotel, going straight up to my room.

It's a mess, but that's because I was in such a hurry this morning. Having made my decision, I wanted to put it into action.

I showered and dressed quickly, and then spent about twenty minutes on the phone before I had a video call with Gabe. He wasn't even remotely surprised when I told him the deal was dead.

"I'm gonna put my relationship with Peony first," I said, and he just nodded his head. "You always said you had doubts about this one."

"I'm not arguing with you."

"Good."

"Does this mean you're coming home or staying up there?"

I took a deep breath, knowing his reaction to what I was about to say might be explosive… but I was wrong. He understood – or claimed to – and once I'd explained my plans in full, he even seemed pleased.

Now, of course, I'm going to have to call him back and explain that I made a mistake. A big one.

Peony doesn't care about me, no matter what I feel about her. She might have kissed me like her life depended on it, but I guess that means it's just a physical thing for her. I haven't touched her in the way she's touched me.

I sit down on the bed, resting my elbows on my knees, and I let my head fall into my upturned hands. I'm not sure I can face calling Gabe right now, and I guess I don't have to. It can wait until I get back to the city. We can talk face-to-face then… although I think that might be even harder than saying it all over the phone.

As for the people I've spent the rest of my day with?

Well… I guess they can wait a few more hours, too.

Or maybe until tomorrow.

I won't have to tell any of them why I'm backing out of everything I've spent my morning discussing, but that won't make it any easier to say, and I'd rather give myself some time to come to terms with it all first.

Come to terms with it?

Who am I kidding?

Like I'm ever going to come to terms with what I've lost…

I can't… even though I know I have to. And I guess the best way to start is to get the hell out of here.

It takes me no time at all to pack, and once I'm done, I check the bathroom to make sure I haven't left anything behind, and then come back into the bedroom, zipping up my bag.

It's raining quite hard, and I let out a sigh. I don't relish the journey back to Boston in this kind of downpour, but I'm relieved. At least we got Peony's trees sprayed before the deluge.

After one last glance around the room, I pick up my bags, just as I hear someone knock at my door. I didn't order any help. No-one here even knows I'm leaving yet, so I put the bags down again and stroll over, pulling the door open and biting back the gasp that escapes my lips when I see Peony standing before me.

She's a little out of breath and her hair is damp… as is her blouse, which is wet enough that I can see her lacy bra and the outline of her pert nipples quite clearly through it.

"Didn't you think to put a coat on?" I say, surprised by the depth of my voice.

"No." She frowns. "It's not that cold."

"Maybe not, but it's raining, in case you haven't noticed."

"Of course I noticed."

"Along with just about every man in town."

I let my eyes wander downwards and she follows the direction of my gaze, her cheeks flushing red when she notices how transparent her blouse has become in the rainstorm.

"Oh… I didn't realize."

"Did you rush out of the house with no coat on for a reason?"

"Yes." She raises her eyes to mine again, biting on her bottom lip. "I—I wanted to say sorry. I didn't mean everything I said just now."

My heart flips over in my chest, although I try not to react… not to hope. I've been here before, too many times. "Okay. Which parts did you mean?" That feels like a more positive way to go than asking which ones she didn't, and I feel like focusing on the positive.

She leans against the doorframe, folding her arms across her chest. I imagine she's trying to hide her exposed breasts, but all she really does is to push them upward and distract the fuck out of me.

It seems some things never change.

"I'm still kinda mad that you kept my panties… or at least that you didn't admit to having them when I asked," she says, and I nod my head.

"That's understandable."

"I've been worried sick that some pervert had gotten hold of them, and I can't begin to tell you what I thought they might be doing with them."

I edge closer to her and she gazes up into my eyes. I can't be reading this wrong, can I? She came here. She didn't have to do that. Any more than she had to make light of the subject. But she just did, and the look on her face is…

Oh, dammit. There's only one way to find out what this means.

"Yeah, you can," I murmur, my voice a low growl. Her eyes widen and she licks her lips, my cock responding painfully. "You can tell me anything you want."

She shakes her head, but it's not like a negative. This is a slow, sexy move… more like a tease. "You've got a far more vivid imagination than I have," she whispers. "I'm sure you can work it out."

I place my hand on the doorframe, right beside her head. "I can. And trust me, I haven't been doing anything like that with your panties, even if I have been carrying them around with me… which I guess makes me the pervert."

She shakes her head more vehemently this time. "No, Ryan. That's what I came to say. I didn't want you to think that's what I thought of you, because I don't."

"Okay."

She looks down at the narrow space between us. "And as for what I said about tying women to your bed…"

At that moment, a couple come out of the room opposite mine, and the woman turns, raising her eyebrows, her mouth falling open. She must have heard what Peony just said and before she can call the cops, I grab hold of Peony's arm and pull her inside the room, kicking the door closed behind us.

"I think we'll talk in here, if that's okay with you?"

She nods her head, and I let her go. She's not looking at me, but beyond me to the bed, which I guess must remind her of the night we spent together. Her reaction isn't what I might have hoped for and I let out a sigh as she says, "Y—You're leaving? Already?"

I turn, realizing she's staring at my bags, not the bed, and then I spin back around, gazing down at her. "Yeah. After our conversation just now out at the farm, I thought it was for the best."

She looks up at me again, tilting her head slightly to the right. "I overreacted. I didn't mean to offend you. What I said about being tied up… that came out wrong." The words pour out of her in a desperate rush.

"Are you saying you enjoyed it?" I'm teasing, trying to lighten the mood.

"I think you already know the answer to that."

"And you haven't changed your mind?"

She shakes her head. "No, I haven't. But I'd like to understand why you do it. You said there was a reason."

"Yes, I did. Although I thought you didn't wanna know."

"I didn't mean that either." She moves just slightly closer. "I'm sorry. I said some—"

"Hey… it's okay."

She swallows hard, blinking, and gazes up at me. "I really don't think it is, but I don't want to waste time fighting. I'd like you to tell me the reason."

I take a half step back, pushing my fingers through my hair. Where do I start? How to I explain? "This isn't something I've spoken about before," I confess and she nods her head, like she understands, which she can't. "I've never even given it that much thought… not really. I've just accepted that I don't like to be touched."

"And that's why you tie women up? So they can't?"

"Yes. I guess a shrink would probably say I have abandonment issues from when my mom died, and maybe I do. I don't know."

"You said you don't really remember very much about her."

"I don't."

"And you said your dad was reserved. Was that your way of saying he wasn't very affectionate with you?"

I stifle a half-laugh. "That would be one way of putting it. I guess you could say he did what he could, within the confines of his personality."

"Which means…?"

"He was a very closed off man. He spent time with me, when his work would allow… took me to football games, and taught me everything I needed to know about the business I'd one day inherit, but he wasn't physically affectionate."

"He never hugged you?"

"He never touched me. No-one did."

"Never?"

"No. I grew up in isolation, and I got used to it. The first time a girl kissed me and put her arms around me, I completely freaked out."

"You did?"

"Yeah. I was seventeen and I think my reaction scared her. It sure as hell scared me."

"So you decided to tie women up in future?"

"Eventually, yes."

"What do you mean 'eventually'?"

"It took me a while to work out what to do, and how to do it. I had the same thoughts and urges as every other seventeen year old male. I just didn't know how to go about making them work, given the problem that I couldn't afford to freak out every time someone touched me."

She shakes her head. "I can't believe you went through your childhood without being hugged, or told you were special, or loved. I mean… what about the nanny who looked after you?"

I shake my head, struggling against a shudder… or at least hoping Peony doesn't notice it. "She wasn't the kindest of people."

Peony moves closer, her eyes filled with concern. "You mean she was cruel to you?"

"That's a strong word. All I'll say is that she certainly wouldn't have been anyone's first choice if they were looking for any kind of human warmth. In fact, she was probably the coldest person I've ever known… except for myself, of course."

"You're not cold, Ryan."

"Really?"

"Yes. Really. And before you try contradicting me, I know you're not. You've said some beautiful things to me… and not only that, on the night I stayed here, I woke up in your arms. I don't think it was subconsciously done. It felt as though we'd fallen asleep like that."

"We had. I wanted to hold you… to feel you."

She frowns. "But that doesn't make sense. You just said…"

"I know what I said, but none of it applies to you. You're different."

"I am?"

"Yes. I knew, right from the moment you first walked into the bar, that there was something different about you… which was why I wanted to hold you while you slept. It was why I wanted you to stay."

Her frown deepens. "You mean that's not something you do all the time?"

"Holding someone? No." I thought I'd made that obvious.

"No. I mean, sleeping with them… spending the night with them."

"Oh, I see. No. I've never done that before, either. You're more vulnerable when you're asleep, and I've never been willing to let my guard down that far."

"But you were with me?"

"Yes."

"Why? You didn't know me. You didn't even know my name."

I smile, unable to help myself. "I know. Like I say, there was something different about you. That was why I untied you."

Her lips twitch upward, just at the corners, and two dots of pink appear on her cheeks. "You mean that wasn't because you wanted to watch me?"

My cock presses hard against my zipper as I recall the sight of her fingers playing over her clit, and I know I can't lie. "Yeah, it was… but I've been in that position before and resisted the temptation. My fear of being touched has always won over everything else. With you, I wanted more." Her lips part, a gentle sigh escaping them, and having come this far, I decide I may as well continue. Having shown her the bleakest side of me, I've got nothing left to lose. "I wanted to wake up and see you there." I nod toward the bed.

"You did?"

"Yes. I had plans."

"Plans?"

"Yes. The first thing I wanted to do was to ask your name."

"And then?"

"Then I wanted to make love with you again."

"Only I wasn't here anymore…"

"No. Why was that, Peony? Why did you leave me?"

"Because I was embarrassed," she says, surprising me with an explanation, at last. "I meant what I said. I've never had a one-night stand before. It was difficult for me to know how to react."

"Is that why you've been so self-conscious about it ever since?"

"In a way."

"So it wasn't because I tied you to the bed?"

"No." She looks down at the space between us. "We already established I enjoyed that. It wasn't what we did. It was the fact that we'd done it all without knowing each other's names." I reach out and place a finger beneath her chin, raising her face until our eyes lock. "I—I still shouldn't have said all those things about you. It was wrong of me. I was so rude… not just today, but every other day since it happened."

I inch closer, so we're almost touching. "Not every other day, and you weren't wrong about everything." I remember some of her accusations, especially the one that affected me most at the time, and I let a smile touch my lips. "You may not have had one-night stands before, but I have."

"And that's an excuse for me being rude, is it?"

"You weren't rude. You were embarrassed about what had happened between us, and you were scared about the farm. I should have made more allowances. I should have been kinder."

"You were kind. This isn't your fault, Ryan. It's mine."

I shake my head and let my hand drop, grabbing her arms just above the elbows and pulling her close, her body crushed against mine. I gaze down at her face, studying her glistening eyes, her perfect lips, her wild, crazy hair… like I'm seeing her for the first time, and I know I have to come clean.

"I might have packed my bags, but I don't want to leave, Peony."

"Sorry?"

"I don't want to go. All I need from you is a reason to stay."

My lips are barely an inch from hers, but I'm not going to kiss her… not until I've said what needs saying.

"I'm not gonna change my mind about the farm, if that's what you're asking."

"It's not. I've told you, I don't wanna buy your farm anymore. I'm talking about us now."

"Us?"

"Yes. Us. You and me. Can you give me a reason to stay?" I pause as she stares up into my eyes. "Please?"

I dip my head slightly, my nose touching hers, and she raises hers, so our lips meet. Have I said what needed saying? I don't think so. But I need this more than words, and I tilt my head, deepening the kiss.

"Don't make me go," I whisper into her mouth, our tongues dancing. "Don't make me leave my heart behind."

She pulls back. I'm still gripping her arms, but she leans away from me, staring up into my face, examining me, her brow furrowing as she shakes her head slowly from side to side.

"Your heart?"

"Yes. My heart. Can't you see? I'm in love with you."

Silence descends, which isn't the reaction I'd hoped for, and she breathes in and out twice, then swallows hard. "Y—You don't even know me."

I raise my right hand, releasing her arm, and caress her cheek with my fingertips. "You keep saying that, but it's not true. I know you better than you can possibly imagine."

"How?"

"Because I haven't stopped thinking about you since the moment I first saw you. I know that when the sun catches your hair, you look like an angel… and when you speak, it's like your voice kisses my skin." She stutters in a breath, and I pull her closer again. "I've never wanted anyone to kiss my skin, but you can do it with just a word… just a whisper. When you smile, you light up my world, and when I hold you, I feel alive. I'm a man who's spent his entire adult life in fear of being touched, but when you're in my arms, nothing else matters. Nothing else but you. That's what you do to me. You make me forget my fears… make me lose myself, and I don't want to give that up. I don't want to give you up. I—I can't."

I lean in, brushing my lips over hers, hoping she'll respond in actions, even if she can't in words. *Please… kiss me back. Show me you feel this too.*

There's a second's pause and then she comes alive, standing up on tiptoes, her lips locked with mine. I capture her face with both my hands, my fingers drifting back into her hair, and she moans softly into my mouth. I could kiss her forever, but there are things I need to know… questions that need answering, and I pull back, both of us breathing hard already.

"You don't have to love me back, Peony… not if you're not ready. But can you at least tell me there's a hope for us?"

She nods her head and, with a heart as light as air, I lead her over to the bed, lifting my bags onto the floor before I turn back and kiss her again. I can hear the stuttering of her breath, and the only question I have now is how quickly can I get us out of our clothes and into bed?

Without breaking the kiss, I reach between us, undoing her damp blouse, and letting my fingers wander inside, touching her bare, soft skin. She sighs, kissing me with everything she's got, although she keeps her arms by her sides, her body still and tense… and that feels wrong.

"Take my jacket off," I whisper, biting on her bottom lip.

She shakes her head, pulling back from me. "I can't. I'd have to touch you."

"I know. I want you to."

Her eyes widen. "You're sure?"

"I'm positive."

"You don't want to tie me up this time, then?"

"I don't need to. Not now." Something that looks like disappointment flashes across her eyes, but I can deal with that later. For now, I've got other things on my mind, and I place my feet either side of hers, so we're as close as we can be. "I'm not scared of being intimate with you. I crave it." She gasps and looks up at me. "Take my jacket off."

She reaches up, pushing it from my shoulders and lets it fall to the floor. "What next?"

"Whatever you want."

"You don't want to give me instructions, so you know what's going to happen?"

She's worked it out, all by herself, and that makes me smile, even as I'm shaking my head. "No. I want to you do whatever feels right."

"But I don't want to make you uncomfortable."

I cup her face in my hands. "You couldn't."

"Really? Because that's not how it felt before."

"When?" I frown down at her and she lets out a soft sigh.

"When you kissed me at the farm earlier, I touched your shoulders and I felt you tense against me. I didn't understand why then, but I do now, and I don't want to make you feel like that again."

"You won't, baby."

Her eyes widen, and she bites on her bottom lip. I free it with my thumb and she looks up at me. "You just called me 'baby'."

"I know I did. It's not a word I've ever said before… not in this context."

"It's not something anyone's ever called me before."

"Not your crazy ex?"

"No."

"Good. Now… do you wanna take my tie off, or shall I?"

She lowers her eyes, studying it for a second or two, and then steps back just slightly, raising her hands, as she unfastens the knot and pulls it from around my neck. Once she's holding onto it, she plays it between her fingers for a minute, and then drops it to the floor, gazing up at me again. She doesn't wait to be asked before she undoes my shirt buttons, starting at the neck and working down. I'm struggling to breathe by the time she's finished, but as she pushes it from my shoulders and lets it fall to the floor, she gives me a moment and then places her hand flat on my bare chest.

I can't help the gasp that escapes my lips, and she quickly withdraws her hand.

"No." I grab it back, replacing it, and holding it hard against me, her fingers flexing against my skin. "It's okay."

She stares up at me. "You're sure?"

"Yes." I release her hand. "Feel free to go anywhere you want."

Her eyes sparkle as a smile touches her lips. "Anywhere?"

"Anywhere."

Her smile widens, and she drops to her knees, my breath hitching in my throat as she reaches up and unfastens my pants, letting them fall to my ankles. She rubs her fingers along the length of my cock, through the thin fabric of my trunks, and I stagger backwards.

"Are you okay?" She looks up through her eyelashes.

"Yeah. Sorry about that. It was a first. I wasn't expecting it to feel like that."

"You mean, no-one's ever touched you there before?" I nod my head and she takes a breath, lowering her eyes again. "I'll just take your trunks off," she says, giving me fair warning and I smile as she lowers them, my cock springing forth, grateful for the release.

She takes her time, pulling off my shoes and socks, along with my clothes, before she looks up at me again, waiting. I give her a nod of my head as she reaches up and places her fingers around me. They don't quite meet her thumb and for a second or two, she just studies the connection between us before she moves her hand slowly up and down my length.

"Oh… fuck…"

She's gentle, but firm and I let my head rock back, groaning softly as she builds a steady rhythm.

"You have a beautiful cock," she whispers, and as I'm about to lower my head, I feel her lips surround me, her tongue swirling over the tip. I watch her take me and flex my hips as she moans, shifting a little closer. She wants more and even if she can't say so in as many words, I'm not about to hold back. I gather up her hair, clamping it around the back of her head and take her mouth. Hard. She moves her hand away, giving me control, her eyes never leaving mine.

"You like that? You like me fucking your mouth?"

I feel the nod of her head, her eyes saying 'yes', even if her lips can't, and she takes me deeper, my cock hitting the back of her throat with every stroke. It's more than I can handle, and with great reluctance, I release her head and pull out of her mouth.

She gets her breath back, wiping her lips with her fingers, and gazes up at me.

"Thank you," I whisper.

"Don't thank me. I enjoyed it."

"I noticed." She smiles and I place my hands beneath her elbows, raising her to her feet.

Without another word, I remove her bra, before I kneel and untie her boots, pulling them off, along with her socks. Next come her jeans, and finally her panties, all of which I leave in a pile on the floor before I lift her onto the mattress, kneeling between her parted legs.

"I wanna touch you, and taste you, but I'm so desperate to be inside you, I'm not sure I can wait."

"Then don't."

I smile down at her, letting my forefinger trace a line from between her breasts, down across her flat stomach, through her slick, swollen folds, finding her drenched entrance with ease.

"You want me here?"

"Yes. Now stop talking and fuck me."

I chuckle. "I think that's one of the things I love most about you."

"What?" She tilts her head to one side.

"The fact that you know what you want and you're not afraid to ask."

"No, I'm not." She parts her legs a little wider, making her desires obvious, and I shift toward the edge of the bed. "Hey… where are you going?" She leans up, grabbing my arm, and I surprise myself by not reacting at all, other than to stop and look down at her.

"To get a condom. They're in my wallet… which is in my pants pocket."

"You don't need one."

I freeze. Her touch may not have exacted a response, but her words certainly have.

"I don't?"

"No. I'm on birth control."

This is news. "You are?"

"Hmm… I didn't mention it before, because… well, we didn't know each other." She blushes as she's speaking and I lean over her, my hands on either side of her head as I dip my own and kiss her.

"It's okay. There's nothing to feel embarrassed about, and I'm not suggesting you should have told me before. The only reason I'm a little lost for words is because I—I've never done this before… not without a condom."

"You don't have to now, if it's too much. If it's too intimate, I mean."

I kiss her again, just briefly. "Nothing's too intimate with you." She smiles and I reach between us, palming my cock and finding her entrance. She gasps as I push inside and I pause, giving her a second to acclimatize before I edge in, further and further. "Okay?" I whisper, once we're joined, and I'm buried deep inside her.

"Oh, God… yes."

Her words make me smile and I bring my hand up again, resting it alongside her head as I start to move. I take it slow, and she matches me pulse for pulse, while I savor the feeling of her tight, wet walls surrounding my shaft, gripping me from tip to base. This is like nothing I've ever experienced… like nothing I've ever imagined.

"This is even more like making love than the first time," I whisper, as she brings her arms up, caressing my biceps with the tips of her fingers. I shudder, but it's with pleasure, not fear, and I think she knows that, because she doesn't stop.

"What does that mean?"

"It means that our first time wasn't just sex for me, even though it was for you."

"Who says?"

"You said. That's what you called it."

She nods her head, and then closes her eyes, like she's lost… just for a moment. When she opens them again, she smiles up at me. "Was that why you reacted the way you did, when I said we'd had sex?"

"What do you think?"

"Was it love for you, even then?"

"Yeah, I think so. I might not have known it at the time, but it was."

She nods her head, her fingers drifting upwards onto my shoulders. "It took me a little longer, I'm afraid."

I stop, half inside her and half out, my body frozen. "I'm sorry?"

"I said…"

"I heard what you said. My only question is, does what you said mean what I think it means?"

"It means I'm in love with you, too."

I drop to my elbows, my lips almost touching hers. "I—I thought you weren't ready."

"I didn't actually say that, did I?"

"No, but…"

"I didn't want to tell you before, Ryan, because I did that with Luca, to prove a point, and I didn't want it to be like that with us."

I realize the error of my ways. "You know that's not how it was for me, don't you? I love you, Peony. Those weren't just words that needed to be said, as a means to an end."

She clutches at my shoulders. "I know. If you'd been as insincere as he was, you'd have said it before our first time."

"When I didn't even know your name, you mean?"

She tips her head and shrugs her shoulders. "Okay, maybe not then, but you understand what I mean, don't you? You understand why I've waited? I didn't want to make the same mistakes all over again. Not like I did with him."

"It wouldn't have been a mistake, but it doesn't matter… as long as you mean it."

"I mean it. I'm in love with you."

She couldn't say the words any more clearly, or mean them any more sincerely. I can see that in her eyes and as I close the gap between us and kiss her, I thrust deep inside, giving her my entire length and making her gasp into my mouth.

She drags her head to one side, sucking in a lungful of air.

"Fuck me, Ryan… please, fuck me."

"With pleasure, baby."

I kneel up, grabbing her ankles and hold them wide apart as I lift her ass off of the mattress and pound into her.

"God, you look good." She lets her eyes wander over my chest and my arms before they roam downwards and she raises her head off of the bed, studying the place where we're joined. "I love your cock."

"I love you. Now, rub your clit. I wanna watch you."

She giggles, lowering her right hand and letting her fingers play across her swollen nub. Her head rocks back as she shudders and I feel her orgasm build already.

"More," she grunts. "Harder."

I give her what she wants. I give her everything I've got, struggling to hold back as I watch her raise her left hand from the mattress, twisting her nipple between her fingers and thumb.

"Tell me you're close, baby. I need this."

I can't hold back, and as she screams my name, writhing against me, I slam into her, coming so hard I can't focus. I'm vaguely aware of her name on my lips, and the word 'love' drifting around the room. Although it's not just me saying that. It's Peony, too. There's a ringing in my ears, and a certainty in my heart that nothing will ever be the same again... at least I hope it won't, because I've found my new home and I want to stay here.

Forever.

Chapter Nineteen

Peony

I slowly resurface, aware that Ryan has lowered my legs to the mattress and is lying on top of me. I can't feel his weight, though, and I crack my eyes open to find he's supporting himself on his elbows and is gazing down at me, his lips almost touching mine and a smile tweaking at the corners. He looks satisfied, but I get that. I feel satisfied, too, and I smile back at him.

"Are you okay?" he says, brushing a stray hair from my face.

"Don't I look okay?"

"You look amazing."

I lean up, closing the gap, and kiss him. He tilts his head to the left, changing the angle, and deepens the kiss, our tongues clashing as his cock twitches inside me. He's still bone hard and I let out a soft moan of pleasure as he moves back and forth, just an inch or two at a time. It's gentle, like a soft caress, and I wonder if we could just lie here and do this all day… and all night.

For the rest of our lives.

Is that too much?

Love is one thing, and it's a joyous thing, when it's returned… but forever?

I mean… how can we even make this work, when he lives in Boston and I live here? The distance might not be that great, but now we're together, I can't bear the thought of being apart.

What are we to do?

He asked me for a reason to stay, but I couldn't give him one, could I?

I can't expect him to give up his life and move here, but there's no way I can leave my home. It's the thing I've fought so hard for, the thing my ancestors…

"Hey…" He breaks the kiss, raising himself above me, his eyes filled with concern. "What's wrong?"

"Nothing."

"Then why did you just go all tense on me?"

Am I that transparent?

"I wasn't aware I had."

"Well… I was. So, what's wrong? You haven't changed your mind about me, have you?"

"Of course not… although I won't say I don't have my misgivings."

I plant a smile on my face, hoping to ease his fears, but as soon as the words leave my lips, his frown deepens, and I realize my plan backfired.

He drops to his elbows again. "Misgivings? Are you saying you don't love me, after all?"

"No. I'm just saying it's not as easy as all that."

"What isn't? Loving me?"

"No. Loving you is easy… at least it is now we've told each other. Before, it was kinda tortuous, when I thought you didn't care."

He kisses me, his lips dusting over mine before he pulls back again. "I always cared."

"I know that now. But before…"

"Forget about before. Tell me about your misgivings."

He seems more insecure than I'd expected, and I don't like that. So, I bring my arms up from the mattress, folding them around him. He flinches, just briefly, and I pull back, dropping my arms to my sides again.

"Sorry. I forgot." God knows how. That moment when he told me of his fear is etched in my brain, and always will be. Seeing him open up to me like that was a shock… but it's made me realize how much this means to him.

He shakes his head. "It's okay. Put your arms back." I do as he says, and he smiles. "That's better. It feels good to be held."

"Yes, it does. But if you ever find it uncomfortable, you only have to say."

"I won't. And I'm sorry about my reaction."

"Don't be."

"It's just that I wasn't expecting it, that's all."

I nod my head. "I understand. Would you rather I warned you when I'm going to touch you?"

"No. I'd rather you just touched me and let me get used to the idea."

I smile up at him. "As long as you're sure."

"I'm absolutely positive."

He kisses me, our tongues flicking against each other, even when our lips aren't touching, and he moves in and out of me again in that same slow, steady sway.

It's easy to lose myself, to forget about time… and life. But after a while, he pulls back, his eyes darkening, and he leans up.

"About these misgivings…"

"Yes?"

"Tell me about them, baby."

I love it when he calls me that, and I hug him just a little tighter. "I guess I'm scared."

"You're scared?" He frowns, looking worried.

"Yes. Of how we're gonna make this work. As if it wasn't bad enough that we started off as enemies…"

"No, we didn't. I was never your enemy, no matter what you thought. And in case you've forgotten, we started off as lovers… then we kinda fell out over your farm, and now we're lovers again. Why is that a problem?"

"It isn't… especially not when you put it like that. But we're so different. Can't you see that? You live in a modern apartment in the city. I live on a farm, on the edge of a small town. You're a millionaire. I don't have a dime to my name."

"You think any of that matters? Seriously? This has nothing to do with money, Peony."

I feel like he's missed the point… or at least part of it. That's not his fault. I didn't put it very well. But while we're discussing money, and his millions, I guess we might as well get it over with…

"Maybe. But I'm sure you're used to women who are a lot more sophisticated than me. My closet contains jeans and sweaters, a few blouses and maybe one or two dresses, buried somewhere near the back. I'm not feminine, Ryan."

"Yes, you are. That's the whole point." He shifts upwards slightly, his cock going a little deeper inside me, and I gasp, parting my legs instinctively. He settles against me, rolling his hips as he talks, like this is the most natural thing in the world. "You take jeans and sweaters, and dirty old boots, and you make them look so damn sexy. That's far more feminine and enticing than a woman who's wearing a revealing ball gown that cost a month's salary."

"I don't feel very feminine most of the time."

"Then you should. You look incredible. Besides, it can't have escaped your notice that I don't care what you're wearing."

"You don't?"

"No. On the whole, I prefer you to be wearing nothing at all, so clothes aren't my priority when I think about you. As for being with sophisticated women…" He leans a little closer, his lips just touching mine, although he doesn't kiss me. "I think I made it fairly clear already that I never felt comfortable with any of the women I was with before I met you."

"Were they sophisticated, though?"

"Some of them… I guess." He raises himself up again. "But what does it matter? This isn't about who we are, Peony. It's not about having money, or not having money. It's about two people falling in love and wanting each other."

"So, you want me, do you?" I tease, raising my hips to his.

"What do you think?" He slams into me and I cry out in pleasure, letting my arms fall to my sides. He grabs my hands, raising them above my head and holding them there as he moves harder and faster, taking me to the brink. "I think I might have given you the wrong impression," he says, slowing the pace at last, my body aching with need now, silently begging for more.

"Y—You do?"

"Yes. I said I love you. I told you I want you… but what I neglected to say was that hell will have to freeze over before I let you go."

I wriggle beneath him, in a very vain and half-hearted attempt to escape, because that's the last thing I want to do. "Oh? Really?"

"Yeah. Really. There's no way I'm giving up on us… even if I have to tie you down to prove it." I tremble, unable to hold in the slightly nervous giggle that leaves my lips, or keep my breath from hitching in my throat. "I thought so," he whispers.

"You thought what?"

"That you were disappointed earlier, when I said I wasn't gonna tie you up."

I can feel myself blush, although he's smiling down at me, his eyes sparkling with mischief. "Was it that obvious?"

"Yeah, it was. But don't worry. It's easily rectified."

He pulls his cock from me, and I sigh out my disappointment. "Come back."

"I will. This won't take long."

"It's too long already. I need you to make me come."

He smiles. "I love it when you say things like that."

"I love what you do to me with your amazing cock, and if you…"

"Oh?" he says, interrupting me and leaning over, so his lips are brushing against mine. "It's amazing now, is it?"

"It always was."

He tilts his head. "I thought it wasn't *that* amazing."

"I made that up." He nods, closing the gap so our lips meet in a deep kiss.

"Good to know," he says, pulling back, and he reaches over the side of the bed, retrieving his tie, which he holds up, with a broad smile on his face. "Now… hold out your hands."

I do as he says, breathing hard, and watching his face while he binds my wrists together and then ties them above my head to the iron bedstead. He's concentrating, although he looks different this time, to when he did this to me before. There's something more relaxed about him… about the way he studies me, and once he's done, he shifts down the bed, holding my hips as he pulls me lower, stretching my body, my back arching.

He kneels up, shaking his head.

"What's wrong?"

"Nothing. Absolutely nothing."

"Then why did you shake your head?"

"Because I'm in awe of you."

"That's lovely, Ryan… but when you've finished being in awe, do you think you could fuck me? I've waited long enough."

He grins. "You think?"

"I know."

He edges closer. "Okay. Where do you want me?"

"Everywhere."

"Be careful what you wish for, baby," he growls, and turns around, his back to me, as he straddles me and shimmies backwards up my body until he's kneeling above my head, his cock too tempting for words. I lean up, licking him, and he chuckles. "God… you're impatient."

"I know. Now… give me your cock."

He bends forward, and as I open my mouth, he gives me what I want. He's too big for me to take more than a couple of inches, but it's enough… for both of us, it seems. I swirl my tongue around the tip of his cock, which makes him groan, and then he starts to move, just gently, back and forth. I love this. He's done it to me before – twice now – and it's perfect. It's so uninhibited.

He shifts downward, and then I feel the heat of his breath between my legs. I part them as wide as I can, and let out a moan of satisfaction as his tongue glides across my clit. I wish I could touch him… could brush my fingers over his ass and up his back. But then, I like being bound and at his mercy.

He inserts a finger inside me… and then another, his tongue working its magic, while his cock goes a little deeper, just touching the back of my throat. It's not enough to make me gag, but it's enough to make me want more, and because I can't say so, I raise my hips, hoping he'll understand. He does… or it feels that way, because he ups the pace of everything… all at the same time.

It's too much.

My body can't take it, and I shatter, tumbling… falling… hoping he'll catch me. I squeal, then scream, pleasure overwhelming me, but he keeps going… relentless, until I can take no more and I move my head aside, gasping for air.

"Stop… please. I can't…"

"Yes, you can."

As he's speaking, he flips around, lying down next to me, and then he turns me onto my side, my back to his front. My hands are still tied above my head, but they twist, remaining comfortable enough, and he puts one arm beneath me, pulling me close to him as he raises my leg, holding it up, his cock finding my entrance with ease.

I sigh as he edges inside me and then starts to move again.

"See? I said you could."

I turn my head, looking up at the smile on his lips. "Prove it then. Make me come."

"Again?"

"Yes… again."

He raises my leg a little higher, slamming into me, over and over, as he clamps his other hand around my breast, squeezing it, and then tweaking at my nipple. I feel like I'm on fire… my body burning with need and I arch my back, wanting more of him.

He must sense the urgency inside me, and without breaking his rhythm, he lowers my leg and turns us over slightly, so I'm on my front. His legs are either side of mine and he's still pounding into me, his hands on my waist now, holding me down.

I turn my head to one side. "More…" I breathe. "Fuck me harder."

He moves his hands down, so they're just above my ass and leans up slightly, changing the angle enough that with the very next stroke, he pushes me over the edge.

I scream out his name… struggling to think… to breathe… to be. My body is an agony of pleasure, tearing at every sinew, and I thrash against it, vaguely aware of him swelling inside me, of a wild moment, when we're both lost, the room filled with his howls of love and my cries for more.

It takes a long time for it to be over, and for us to find ourselves again, but when we do, I'm on my side once more and he's lying in front of me, gazing at my face. We're both breathing hard still, but he reaches up, untying my hands… first from the bed and then from each other.

"Are you okay?" He studies my wrists, kissing them, one at a time.

I nod my head as he looks up at me again. "I'm fine."

"It wasn't too much? I didn't hurt you?"

"No. It was perfect."

"So, can I take it you wanna do that again?"

I lean back slightly, although he puts his arms around me, so I can't go too far. "Right now?" I ask, a little shocked by his suggestion. "Because I don't know about you, but I'm exhausted."

"That's a shame." He pouts, his eyes twinkling.

"Are you serious? You wanna go again? Now?"

"I'm not dismissing the idea, but that wasn't really what I meant."

"It wasn't?" Now he's got me confused.

"No. What I meant was, do you like being tied up? You came a lot harder – both times – so, I was wondering, if this is the way you wanna go… in the future?"

"Not exclusively. I'll admit it was more intense, and I like what you do to me."

"You don't feel like I'm using you?"

I lean back a little further, frowning at him. "Of course not. How could I, when you make me feel the way I do? You don't make it about you, Ryan. You make it about us. When I'm bound like that, I feel like I'm yours…"

He edges closer. "You are mine."

I smile. "I know. And I like the feeling of being yours… knowing you'll take me to places I've never been before, but that you'll always bring me back again." I tilt my head slightly. "It's about trust, I suppose."

"And you trust me?"

"Completely."

His lips twitch upwards. "So, you wanna carry on?"

"Yes. But not all the time, if that's okay? I meant everything I've just said, but I don't want you to tie me up every time we make love. I want to touch you sometimes."

"I want you to touch me, too."

"That's good, because I want to feel every inch of you, just like I can feel your love while you're doing wild and crazy things to me."

He reaches between us, clasping my chin in his hand and holding me still. "Hey… there's nothing crazy about loving you."

"But there is something wild?"

"Yeah… and I like that." He claims my lips with his in a frenzied kiss that's filled with moans and sighs, and heat and need. Our hands are everywhere, his on my cheek and ass, pulling me onto his erection; mine on his back and neck. We're so swallowed up in the oblivion of each other that he doesn't even notice my touch… and that makes me smile. "What's wrong?" he says, breaking the kiss and leaning back, although we're still locked in each other's arms.

"Nothing's wrong. I'm only smiling because you didn't react to my touch, that's all."

"No." He nestles a little closer. "I guess I'm getting used to you already."

I feel the shadow of doubt shrouding me, my earlier insecurities returning in an instant. "I—Is that a good idea?"

"Of course it is. I want to get used to you… and your touch."

I bring my hand around between us, resting it on his chest, and although I want to smile that he doesn't flinch as I curl my fingers through the fine hairs dappled across his smooth skin, I can't feel anything but miserable.

"Is that wise, though?"

"Wisest thing I've ever done." He leans back a little. "Why?"

"Because you're gonna have to leave soon, aren't you?"

"Am I?"

"Yes. You live in Boston, remember?"

"I know. But I asked you for a reason to stay, and…"

"And I couldn't give you one." I lower my head, trying to hide my tears.

He's holding my cheek, but moves his hand downward, resting his finger beneath my chin and nudging it upward, so I have to raise my head, our eyes meeting. "You told me you love me. That's all the reason I need, Peony."

"That's very romantic, but I can't see how we're gonna do this… not when your life is in Boston and mine is here."

"My life isn't in Boston." He lowers his hand, putting both arms around me and pulling me even closer, wrapping a leg around me, too, so I'm enveloped in him. "My life is wherever you are."

"But you have an apartment there. It's where you work."

"Apartments can be sold."

I'm struggling to breathe… not just because he's holding me so tight, but because I can't believe I'm hearing this.

"You're gonna sell your apartment?"

"Yes."

"And you're gonna stay here?"

"Not here exactly. I like this hotel, but I was kinda hoping you'd let me move in with you at the farm." He blushes, looking a little sheepish. "If that isn't too much of an imposition?"

"It isn't." I lean forward and kiss him… and he kisses me back. Before things can get too heated again, I break the kiss, gazing up at him. "Boston's still a hundred miles away, Ryan. You're surely not gonna drive there every day."

"No. I'm gonna move my office here."

I choke, unable to help myself. "Y—You're gonna what?"

He chuckles. "That's what I was doing all morning. I've been looking into buying some office space up here and talking things through with my deputy back in Boston."

"You're really serious about this?"

"Absolutely I am. I decided a couple of days ago that I wasn't going ahead with the deal to buy your farm…"

"You did?"

"Yeah. I knew it was the only way we could be together. I had to stop you from seeing me as your enemy, so we could be lovers again." He smiles and I have to smile back. "The problem was, just like you, I couldn't work out how we could be together when we live so far apart."

"But you've solved that?"

"Yes. It's gonna take a little time, but I've found a place on the edge of town. I think I'll fit everything in there… even once I've expanded the organization."

"You want to expand?"

He tilts his head to the right and then the left. "It's not so much about wanting, as about being required to."

"What does that mean?"

"It means that one of my negotiators has bought a plot of land in Vermont that I think we'll only be able to use for residential construction. It's not something we've ever done before, and while I didn't appreciate having my hand forced, I'm gonna look into what's involved, which means we'll almost certainly have to expand and start a new branch of the organization, separate from the commercial division. Fortunately, there are two units available in the industrial area, so I'm gonna take them both, and run each outfit independently. If it works as I'm hoping it will, it'll mean employing a lot more people."

"People who live in Hart's Creek?"

He nods his head. "Some of them, yes. That was how I got the idea of moving up here. When you said about the lay-offs, it occurred to me that moving my operation to Hart's Creek might solve two problems at once. It'll create employment, and we can be together."

"You'd really do all that… for me?"

"Of course I would. I love you." He's absolutely serious, not a trace of a tease in his voice, or his eyes. He means this. Every. Single. Word.

"I don't know what to say."

"You don't have to say anything… other than yes to letting me move in with you."

"I thought I already had."

"I'm just making sure." That mischievous twinkle is back in his eyes, and I smile up at him as he rolls me onto my back, resting in the space I create when I part my legs. We're still wrapped up in each other, but I like it that way. "I know things haven't been easy for you lately, and I know how worried you are about losing the farm."

"I was. Until you withdrew your offer."

He shakes his head. "Don't bullshit me. We both know how much you owe the bank, and you told me yourself you'd practically emptied your bank account to pay for the fungicide. Times are hard for you… I know they are."

"And?" I snap.

"And you don't need to be so defensive. Not with me. I wanna help you, if you'll let me."

I lean back, as far as the pillow behind my head will allow. "Is this a business proposition?"

He shakes his head. "No."

"So, you're not saying you still want to buy my farm?"

"Not buy it. Invest in it. I'll give you whatever money you need to make it work."

"No, Ryan. I can't let you do that. It wouldn't be…"

He dips his head, kissing me into silence, taking his time before he raises himself up again. "I knew you'd be like this."

"Like what?"

"Stubborn."

"I'm not being stubborn. It just doesn't feel right to take your money."

"Why not? There are no strings… other than my love for you. I'm not looking for a share in your business, and you won't have to account to me for what you spend, or what you do. Just let me know how much you need, and it's yours. The investment will come from me, Peony. That's what's different about it. This isn't business. It's personal."

Tears gather, pricking behind my eyes and, no matter how hard I blink, there's nothing I can do to stop them falling.

"Hey… hey, baby." He drops to his elbows. "Why are you crying?"

"Because I've been so scared…"

"I know you have. But you don't have to be scared anymore." He kisses my eyes, the right and then the left, and then lingers for a second, gazing down at me before he brushes his lips over mine, groaning deeply as our tongues meet. He parts my legs a little wider with his own and I feel his erection nudging at my entrance, raising my hips to complete the connection.

We're joined, and we let out a sigh of mutual satisfaction.

"Don't cry," he says, leaning back and breaking our kiss, even though he's moving so gently inside me. "Just let me help you."

I nod my head, although the tears keep falling. There's nothing I can do to stop them. "Can we go?"

"To the farm, you mean?" I nod my head and he smiles. "You wanna go there now?"

"I do."

"You don't wanna finish this first?" He swivels his hips, burying himself a little deeper inside me.

"We can finish it later, can't we?"

"Sure. If that's what you want."

He smiles down at me as he gently disconnects us and rolls us onto our sides, facing each other.

"I love you," I whisper.

"I love you."

"And thank you."

He shakes his head. "You don't have to thank me."

"Oh… I think I do."

He chuckles. "In that case, when we get back to the farm…"

"Back home," I say, and his eyes widen. "Call it home, Ryan. It's where I belong, and you belong with me, so…"

"It's home?"

"Yes."

He smiles. "Okay. As I was saying, when we get home, I'll let you thank me properly."

"Oh, you will, will you?"

"Yeah."

"And how am I gonna do that?"

"Wait and see…"

He kisses the tip of my nose, and releases me, rolling to the edge of the bed, and getting to his feet. I watch him, a smile etched on my lips, wondering how I got to be so lucky…

That's not just because he wants to help me with my farm, or because he's willing to move his life up here to be with me, or because he has a truly amazing cock.

It's because he loves me… and I know how rare and precious a gift that is.

Chapter Twenty

Ryan

She smiles up at me, and I stand for a moment, gazing down at her.

She looks so beautiful; her legs still parted, her pussy glistening and swollen, her nipples hard, and her hair spread wildly across the pillow.

"Do you know something?"

"Hmm? What's that?" She tilts her head lazily to one side.

"You wear the just fucked look to perfection."

"That's because you've just fucked me… several times."

I chuckle, reaching for her hand and pulling her to the edge of the bed. My cock is close to her head, and she stares at it, licking her lips.

"Don't get any ideas, or we'll never make it home tonight."

Home… I hadn't expected her to say that. Not yet, anyway. I knew it was an audacious move, asking if I could move in with her, but for her to call it 'home' already? That was beyond my wildest dreams.

She looks up into my eyes, letting out a sigh of disappointment. "I guess you're right."

I lean down and kiss her forehead, knowing I daren't go anywhere near her lips. "Hold the thought?"

She smiles. "Gladly."

She sits up and I help her to her feet, letting go of her hand and raising mine so they both rest on her hips. I daren't kiss her, but I hold her close, my cock still hard between us.

"Do you know how tempting you are?" I whisper and she leans up, trying to kiss me, although I pull back, making her frown.

"What's wrong?"

"If I kiss you, I'm gonna have to make love to you… which means we won't be going anywhere for quite a while."

"Hmm… I see. The problem is, I wanna be kissed." She pouts, although it's a tease, not for real, and I smile, unable to help myself. "What's funny?"

"Aside from the fact that you're adorable, I was just thinking about the irony of all this."

"Why is it ironic?"

"Because I've never really kissed anyone before."

She pulls away, although I don't let her go too far. "You've never…?"

I shake my head. "I told you about the first girl who kissed me, and how I reacted. I decided then that I wouldn't put myself through that again. Kissing is too intimate."

"Y—You mean you've had sex with women, but haven't kissed them?"

"Yes."

"And yet, you kissed me. It was the very first thing you did."

"I know. I already told you… you're different. You always were. It's what makes me lose control around you… makes me wanna throw you down on the bed, hold you there, and take you, so damn hard."

I pull her close again and she sucks in a breath, her breasts crushed to my chest as she gazes up at me. "That's a very tempting suggestion."

"I know. But you said you want to go home."

"Hmm… I do." She pauses, like she's thinking. "Would it help if we put some clothes on?"

"No. It'll only make me wanna rip them off again."

She giggles, and it takes every ounce of my strength not to put my words into actions. It seems she likes to be taken. That was what she said, anyway. She said she liked being mine. And that's good… because I like being hers, too.

"Why don't we get dressed, and then you can take me home and show me all the things you wanna do?"

"That's an offer I can't refuse."

I let her go, although my arms feel empty without her, and she bends down, picking up our clothes from the floor. My suit is crumpled, but I'm not gonna wear it now anyway, and I grab my bag, dumping it onto the bed.

I pull out some jeans and a freshly laundered shirt, followed by a second one, which I hand to Peony, who's just untangling her bra.

"What's this for?" she says, taking the shirt and gazing at me.

"Your blouse is still damp, and there's no way I'm letting you go outside wearing something that's practically transparent."

She smiles, moving closer. "I didn't realize it was… you know that, don't you?" I nod my head and she tilts hers. "You're not mad at me, are you?"

I grab her, pulling her close. "No, of course not. I'd just prefer you to wear my shirt for now. You're mine."

She nods her head. "Yes, I am."

She turns, grabbing her bra and fastening it behind her back, taking a moment to adjust the straps, and then sits and pulls on her panties. I'm mesmerized, and she looks up at me, smiling.

"Are you just gonna stand there, or are you gonna get dressed, too?"

"I guess I'll get dressed… although the view is spectacular."

She shakes her head, smiling, and while I'd love to stand and watch her finish dressing, I've just remembered something. I make quick work of pulling on my underwear, jeans and shirt, and while Peony is putting on her boots, tying up the laces, I surreptitiously rescue her panties from my pants pocket, and transfer them into my jeans. I've got my back to her, so she can't see what I'm doing… which is just as well.

"Ready?" she says, as I fold up my suit and zip it into my bag.

"Sure." I turn to find she's fully dressed, my shirt left outside of her torn jeans, undone enough to reveal the tops of her breasts, and coming almost down to her knees. "You see? This is what I mean. You take ordinary clothes and make them look so damn sexy."

"I don't look sexy," she says, shaking her head.

"Yeah, you do." I step closer, then reach out, placing my fingers in the top of the shirt, right between her breasts, pulling her forward, until her body hits mine, and then I hold her in my arms, my hands resting on her ass. "I wanna bury my cock inside you." My voice is low, demanding, and her bottom lip trembles, not with fear, but with need.

"Oh, God… yes."

I roll my hips, making sure she can feel how hard I am for her. "You wanna stay? Or you wanna go?"

She pauses long enough for me to know the decision isn't an easy one, and then she whispers, "Go."

I nod my head, giving her a smile and I release her, smiling when I notice her eyes drop to the bulge in the front of my jeans. She licks her lips, and I lean in, lowering my voice.

"Later, baby."

She nods, swallowing hard and I take her hand, picking up my bags, as I cast a last glance around the room to make sure I haven't left anything behind.

"Are we set?"

"Yes."

"Okay. Let's go."

I lead her from the room, letting the door close behind us, and we walk together down the hall to the top of the stairs. There's a man coming up the other way, and he almost trips over his tongue when he sees Peony, his eyes roaming over her, in barely disguised lust. I'm torn between wanting to punch him, and needing to protect her... and protecting her wins out. I step closer, releasing her hand and putting my arm around her. She nestles against me, looking up into my eyes, seemingly oblivious of the effect she has on the people around her, and once the man has gone, she starts down the stairs, a couple of paces ahead of me.

I've never felt this possessive or out of control in my life, and I have to admit, it's not a comfortable feeling.

When we reach the lobby, I'm relieved to take her hand again, but the moment I do, I turn to face her, looking down into her upturned face.

"Will you do something for me?" She nods her head without a second's hesitation.

"Anything."

"Will you fasten one more button on that shirt?"

She looks down, closing up the button so her breasts are concealed. "Like that?"

"Yeah."

"Was it too tempting for you?" she says with a smile.

"It's tempting, yeah... but I didn't like the way that guy was looking at you."

"What guy?" She looks around.

"The guy at the top of the stairs."

She frowns. "I didn't notice him."

"Because you were so busy looking at me?" I say, teasing her, relieved that my moment of possessive jealousy seems to have passed.

"Yes." She leans up on tiptoes and whispers, "And because I was preoccupied, thinking about all the things I want you to do to me when we get home."

"In that case, would you hate me if I asked if we could make a quick detour?"

"A detour?" Her brow furrows and I smile. She looks so damn cute, it's impossible not to.

"Yeah. I want to show you the offices I'm gonna buy."

"You do?"

"I do. I know they're not very exciting, but I'd like you to see them… to see where I'm gonna be working."

"In that case, I'd love to. I've got my truck here, so…"

"That's okay. You can follow me, can't you?"

She smiles. "I think I know the way, Ryan. But I'll follow you."

I step closer, putting my arm around her waist and holding her against me. "You will?"

"Yeah. Wherever you wanna take me."

I almost choke. I mean… how's a guy supposed to respond to that?

It takes all my willpower to check out of the hotel, rather than run straight back upstairs with her, but once I have, I go outside by myself, sprinting to my car in the rain, and grabbing my umbrella from the trunk as I throw my bags inside. I put it up and return to Peony, who's sheltering by the door of the hotel.

"Come on." I hold out my hand and she takes it, nestling against me as I help her to her truck.

She hasn't locked it and just opens the driver's door.

"I know this sounds pathetic," I say just before she climbs in, and she turns, looking up at me. "But I wish we weren't going in separate cars."

"Why?"

"Because I want you with me."

She smiles. "It's a five-minute drive, Ryan."

"I know. And that's five minutes too long."

She chuckles, and I silence her with a bruising kiss, pulling her body close to mine. I'd told myself I wouldn't do this. I'd even told Peony I wouldn't do it… that it would only delay us getting home. But I can't help it. She's irresistible, and she whimpers into my mouth, her arms coming around behind me, her hands resting on my ass, pulling me closer, even as the rain pours down around us.

"Stop…" I whisper into her mouth. "I can't fuck you up against your truck in a hotel parking lot, in a storm."

"Oh, God…" she breathes, heaving air into her lungs. "I wish you could."

"Do you wanna go straight home? We can visit the offices later… or tomorrow?"

She thinks for just a second. "No, it's fine."

"You're sure?"

She chuckles and gently slaps my ass. "I'm positive. Now, Mr. Andrews… are you gonna lead the way?"

"What do you think?"

She throws her head back, laughing, and I have to laugh, too… mostly with relief that an afternoon which started so badly is turning into an evening full of promise.

Before I can be tempted to kiss her again, I take a step back and then help her into the driver's seat of her truck, waiting while she puts on her seat belt, and then I close the door, blowing her a kiss before I turn and stride back to my car.

Once I'm inside, the umbrella dripping into the passenger footwell, I take a moment, just to catch my breath.

That really happened, didn't it?

The deep-seated sense of satisfaction in my body tells me it did… as does the need for more.

I glance through the windshield, seeing Peony's truck, and I start the engine, unable to stop the smile from forming on my lips.

She's going to follow me home.

Does it get any better than that?

I drive out of the hotel parking lot, and Peony follows me. I watch her in the rear-view mirror, unable to stop smiling as we make our way through the town. Sure, I wish she was sitting here beside me, but at least we're going in the same direction now… for the first time since we met.

And that feels good.

It only takes a few minutes to get to the industrial area, and I turn in, making sure she's still with me. It's early evening now, and most of the people who work here have gone home for the day, although there are a few cars still parked outside some of the offices.

I drive on past them, coming to a stop outside one of the vacant lots. Peony parks beside me and I reach over for the umbrella, getting out, putting it up, and running around to open her door.

She takes my offered hand, and we stand together, huddled close as she looks up at the two-story building.

"I'm taking this one, and the one opposite," I say, turning her and pointing to an almost identical office on the other side of the road.

"Can we go inside?"

"Not today. I haven't bought it yet, and I don't have the keys." She nods her head, looking up at the structure. "It needs work," I say, my eyes landing on the chipped paintwork around the window. "But I'll get it all fixed before we move in."

"How long will that take?"

"I don't know. A month… maybe two."

"Does that mean you're not here for good yet?"

I turn, facing her, and pull her into my arms. "Not quite. I've got my apartment to pack up and sell, and even though my deputy, Gabe, is gonna handle a lot of the planning for the relocation, I've still got a business to run."

She blinks up at me, her eyes glistening. "So… will I see you for the next month or two, or however long all that takes?"

I hold her closer. "Of course you will. I can stay until Sunday evening, and then I'll come back every weekend until I'm ready to make the move permanent. I'll do my best to limit that to as short a time as possible." She attempts a smile, but doesn't get there, her eyes giving away her sadness. "Look on the bright side, baby… it'll give us time to get used to living together."

She tilts her head. "Do we need time?"

"No, but I don't want you to think I'm pushing you into anything you're not ready for."

She rests her hands on my chest, and I don't flinch in the slightest. In fact, I welcome the contact. "You're not pushing me at all. I want this, Ryan. Please don't doubt that."

"I don't. But just think how good it'll be every time I come back."

She flexes her fingers and inches closer, looking up into my eyes. "Will you miss me, then?"

I let my lips hover over hers. "Yeah, I will. Will you miss me?"

She shrugs. "I might. A little."

Rain or no rain, I push her back against the side of her truck, kissing her hard. Our tongues collide, my body holding hers in place, and she writhes against me.

"We're not in the hotel parking lot now, baby." I flex my hips into hers and she gasps.

"There are still too many people here," she whispers, glancing around… although I can tell she's struggling to resist.

I pull back, just slightly. "Tell me you're gonna miss me when I'm gone."

"I'm gonna miss you."

"How much?"

"More than I can say."

I nod my head and step back. "Home?"

"Yes," she sighs. "Home."

I help her back into her truck, chuckling when she sets off before I've even closed the umbrella.

I guess she must be keen.

But so am I, and I catch up with her before she's even halfway back to the farm.

I park closer to the house than I normally do, grabbing my bags from the trunk, and running to the porch, where Peony is already standing, waiting for me. As I mount the steps, she holds out her arms, and I drop my bags, lifting her and twirling her around, before lowering her to the wooden decking again.

We stand together, arm in arm, gazing out across the orchard, the trees disappearing into the fading light.

"You're sure this is what you want?" she says and I turn to face her, surprised by the doubt in her eyes. "Don't say it is, just because you think it's what I want to hear. You're a millionaire. You said your apartment is modern, whereas my house is practically falling down, the roof leaks, the—"

I raise my hand, placing my fingers over her lips, and she stops talking, staring up at me. "I don't care about any of that. It's nothing that can't be fixed. And in answer to your question, I'm positive this is what I want. I asked to move in, remember?"

She pulls my hand away, keeping a hold of it. "I know. It's just, this is a very different way of life."

"And? That doesn't mean it's not for me."

"You're sure?" *Where has all this doubt come from?*

"Absolutely."

"You're not gonna change your mind?"

"No. Why would I?"

"Because you did before. You were gonna leave, remember?"
Ahh… I get it now.

I pull my hand from hers, putting my arms around her and I pull her close, our bodies molded together. "That was because I thought you didn't want me."

"You were wrong."

"I know that now, and believe me, leaving isn't a mistake I'm gonna be making again."

I hadn't planned on doing this now, but I think it just became a necessity, and without taking my eyes from hers, I let go of her and drop to one knee.

She gasps. "What are you doing?"

"What do you think?"

"Y—You don't think this is all going a little fast? You were the one who just said we needed time to get used to each other."

"No, I didn't. I said we'd have the opportunity to get used to living together… not that we needed to."

"Maybe… but it was just a few hours ago that you walked out of here and packed your bags."

"I know, but that wasn't what I wanted, or what I'd planned. This is what I'd planned. And in any case, we don't have to get married straight away. Not if you don't want to."

I put my hand into my pocket and pull out her panties, holding them up to her. She frowns, looking confused. "What on earth are you doing now? I thought you were proposing."

"I am. I was gonna do this when I was here earlier today… only you got mad and didn't let me finish."

"Oh. I'm sorry."

"Don't be. I think it's worked out okay. Hasn't it?"

She nods her head. "I think so."

"Good. To be honest, I wasn't going to try proposing to you again just yet. I thought I'd wait until I'd moved up here for good."

"Then why are you down on one knee?"

"Because you just went all doubtful on me, and I need you to know how committed I am to this, and to us."

"So, you're giving me my panties?"

"I'm asking you to be my wife, and to let me be your husband."

"Don't people usually buy a ring?"

"I think they do, yes." I reach up and unwrap her panties, revealing the white gold solitaire diamond ring that's buried in their folds. "Kinda like this one."

She gasps, her eyes widening. "Was that there the whole time?"

"Not the whole time, no. I put it there this morning, straight after I went out and bought it."

"This morning? How? There isn't a jewelry store in Hart's Creek."

"I know. I discovered that all by myself. So, I drove to Willmont Vale. You told me it was only six miles away, and I figured it was worth taking a look to see if there was a jewelry store there. Luckily there was, but I'd have gone on to Concord if I'd had to. Hell… I'd have gone to Mars, if it was really required." She nods her head, blinking and taking in that I haven't done this lightly. "My plan was that I'd come over here and confess to having kept your panties, then give them back to you, let you find the ring, and propose. When I played it out in my head on the drive back from Willmont Vale, it sounded romantic."

"Until I called you a pervert."

"You didn't. Not in so many words, and I had been walking around with your panties in my pocket, so I kinda deserved it." She gazes at the ring and then glances back at me. "And now I'd like to be your pervert, baby. If you'll have me."

She nods her head, my heart stopping for a second or two, while I take that in, and then I stand and take the ring, putting it onto her finger before I put her panties back into my pocket. She reaches out, grabbing my wrist.

"Hey… what are you doing? They're mine."

"No. They're mine. If we have to spend some time apart for a few weeks, I'm keeping them."

"Why?"

I lean in, moving her hair aside, and I place my lips right by her ear. "Use your imagination," I whisper, and I feel her shudder.

"C—Can we go inside?"

I smile down at her and pick up my bags, putting my arm around her and steering us toward the door. Peony opens it and I let her pass through ahead of me. It feels a little damp, and she shivers, turning to look up at me.

"I'll show you to the bedroom, shall I?"

It's strange that I'm about to move in, that we're engaged as of thirty seconds ago, and yet I've never even seen her bedroom, but I nod my head and follow her to the back of the living area, down a narrow hall that leads to the other wing of the house. There are four doors, and she opens the first one on the right, pointing it out as the bathroom, before we move on to the last one on the left.

She hesitates on the threshold, like she's nervous, but then goes inside, switching on the lights.

"My bed isn't as big as the one at the hotel," she whispers, turning to face me.

"No, but it's very pretty."

I'm not lying. Her bed is pretty. In fact, the whole room is. It's not too floral, or feminine, but I can feel Peony's presence here. The bed itself has a large oak frame, with sturdy posts on the four corners. It's covered with white bedding, and there's a quilted, patchwork throw across the end. Over by the window, there's a wicker chair, with a pale blue blanket folded over the back, and in the corner, a large oak closet, alongside a dresser. There are three rugs, shielding the original floorboards, one on either side of the bed, and one at the end. None of them match, but it doesn't seem to matter, and I turn to Peony, putting my arm around her.

"Is it okay?" she says, biting on her bottom lip.

"It's lovely. Honestly. Don't look so worried."

"I'll make some space, and you can unpack." I want to tell her it can wait, but she seems a little uneasy and I get the feeling she needs to be doing something, so I watch while she pushes her clothes to one side in the closet, and empties a drawer, piling her things onto the chair.

"Do you think we might need to look at getting some more furniture?" I say and she smiles.

"Maybe." She glances around, scratching her head.

"There's enough space in here for at least one more dresser and a larger closet."

"Probably. Can you make do with this for now?"

"It's fine." I don't have that much with me, and even if I did, I'd manage.

"Okay. If you wanna unpack, I'll go make some coffee."

I sense she feels awkward having me here, and although that's not ideal, trying to force the situation won't help, so I nod my head, and let her leave, making quick work of putting my clothes away. My suit is a mess, but I won't be needing it, so I leave it folded up in the bottom of my bag, which I put on the floor alongside the dresser.

Once I'm done, I flick off the lights and go back into the living area. It's much warmer in here now, but that's because Peony has lit the fire in my absence. She's also made coffee, and she brings over two cups, nodding to the couch.

"Shall we sit?"

"Sure."

I take the cup she offers and wait for her to sit in the corner of the couch before joining her. We're close enough that our thighs are touching, and I turn, looking down at her.

"Is everything okay?"

"Are you all right?"

We both speak at the same time, and then laugh, which seems to break the ice.

"I'm being silly, aren't I?" she says.

"No. It's bound to feel strange having me here."

She shakes her head. "It's not that. I've dreamed of having you here for ages."

That's news, but it's news that makes me smile and I take her cup, putting it and mine on the end table beyond her, and then pulling her into my arms. "In that case…"

She sighs. "It's just that I've realized there are a few impracticalities."

"There are?"

"Yes."

"Like what?"

"Like my bed."

"What's wrong with your bed? It might be a little smaller than the one at the hotel, but I'm sure we'll manage." I smile at her and she smiles back, her eyes twinkling.

"It's not the size that's worrying me, it's the frame."

"Why? Is there something wrong with it?"

"Not as such. It's just not very… practical." She blushes slightly and I frown down at her.

"Practical for what?"

She shakes her head, her brow furrowing. "What do you think?"

I twist in my seat, leaning in to her, bringing my hand up and cupping her cheek. "Are you talking about it being impractical for me to tie you to?" She nods, and I chuckle. "Don't worry about it, baby. I'm sure I'll be able to improvise."

"You will?"

"Hmm…" I bend my head and brush my lips over hers. "Relax, Peony. Everything will be fine. If we need a new bed, I'll buy us a new bed. Just like I'll get the roof fixed and have someone come and paint the outside of the house. I'll buy a dishwasher, too… and get anything else we need."

She shakes her head, even though I'm still kissing her, my lips touching hers between every few words.

"Y—You can't," she breathes, her breasts heaving. "You can't just spend money like that."

"Why not? The roof needs fixing, the house needs painting. I'd rather spend time with you than wash dishes, and as for the bed… let's just wait and see, shall we?"

"Wait and see?" She looks horrified by that suggestion and I struggle not to laugh.

"It'll be just fine, baby. There are other ways for me to tie you up that don't involve a bed, or its frame."

"There are?"

She's torn between confusion and excitement. Judging from the way her breathing just changed, I'd say excitement is winning.

"Yeah. Let's just say, a tie isn't my usual method of restraint."

"What would you normally use then?"

"Ropes… a hogtie, cuffs, a harness…" I let my voice fade as her eyes widen and she breathes even harder. "Do you like the sound of that?"

"Y—Yes, I think I do. I'm just a little sad you don't have any of those things here with you now."

I chuckle and hold her close. "Don't worry. I'm good at improvising, and the posts on the corners of your bed looked kinda… useful."

She shudders against me. "Do you wanna go try them out?"

"Not right now."

She pulls back, surprise written all over her face. "Y—You don't?"

"No. We said at the hotel that when we got back here, you could thank me properly…"

She narrows her eyes, although her lips are twisting upward at the same time. "I believe we also said you'd show me what you wanted to do with me."

"We did."

"So, which is it gonna be?"

"Both. You see… ever since I first came here, I've dreamed of making love to you, right here."

"On the couch?"

"No… in front of the fire." I don't say another word, but I grab her and roll us onto the floor, making sure I'm the one who takes the brunt of the impact.

She gasps, giggling at the same time, and I push her onto her back on the soft rug.

"You've dreamed of this, have you?"

"Yes. I've dreamed of doing all kinds of things with you, and I fully intend to… but if you really wanna thank me, this is one dream we can make come true. Right now."

She sighs and raises her legs, wrapping them around me, holding me close, her hands gliding up and down my back.

"The first of many," she whispers, and I nod my head and kiss her, while the wind whistles down the chimney and rustles through the leaves of the apple orchard we both call home.

The End

Thank you for reading *Resisting Ryan*. I hope you enjoyed it, and if you did, I hope you'll take the time to leave a short review.

The characters of Hart's Creek will return soon in *Wanting Walker*. This story is all about Walker Holt, whose life is turned upside down by the arrival in town of Imogen McNeil. She's hiding from her past, that much is obvious. The problem is, what will they do when it catches up with her?

Printed in Great Britain
by Amazon

26689546R00155